Joline

By

Jim Sano

(Father Tom #6)

Full Quiver Publishing
Pakenham, ON

Joline
copyright 2025
by James G. Sano
ISBN 978-1-987970-72-2

Published by Full Quiver Publishing
PO Box 244
Pakenham, Ontario K0A 2X0

Printed and bound in the USA

NATIONAL LIBRARY OF CANADA
CATALOGUING IN PUBLICATION
ALL RIGHTS RESERVED

Copyright 2025 James G. Sano
Published by FQ Publishing
A Division of Innate Productions

To Harper Elizabeth, the precious joy of the next
generation who will come to love and enjoy the coast of
Down East Maine.

Books by Jim Sano

The Father's Son

Gus Busbi

Stolen Blessing

Van Horn

Self-Portrait

Fallen Graces

The Journey

Prologue

She slowly opened the floral-covered journal and stared down at the clean, blank page before momentarily flipping back to an earlier page. She artistically drew a *J* at the top. She loved how easily she could create the beautifully curved lines and light curls at the ends. Would this natural talent ever offer more than satisfying her own amusement?

She gazed around the familiar surroundings of the room in which she had lived and daydreamed her whole life, from the shabby teddy bear, as old as she was, who had lost the fuzz off his ears years ago, to the tickets from a local concert she attended with her friends last year. She peered out the open window at the darkened street, tapping her pen nervously before getting her words on the page.

Who am I? Am I at the start of my journey, or would it be easier if it were the end? The crazier I get, or the more I achieve my objective, the more bored and frustrated I feel!

Do we ever get to know who we really are, or is it all a lie? A big fat lie wrapped in artificial love?? Can we achieve anything we want? But what do I really ~~want~~ need?

She stopped and started tapping again before writing:

I want to know, but maybe I'm just too scared to find out.

"I was the more deceived."

She added an embellished *O* after the quote, stared at it for several moments, then tore the page from the book, crumpled it in her clenched fist, and stuffed it in the pocket of her worn jeans. After making her way down the stairs and out the front door, she breathed in the summer air and lay on the front lawn to study the stars above. *I'm just one of so many,* she thought as she closed her eyes and felt the cool grass blades on her back. *Which way shall I go? Who can give me the answers I so desperately need to know?*

Chapter 1

Belfast, Maine, 2009

It was close to noon on Saturday morning when Father Paul O'Connell and Father Tom Fitzpatrick entered the local diner and stepped into the aroma of sizzling bacon and the buzz of multiple conversations.

The owner, Traci, leaning against the counter, pulled a pencil from a gray bun at the top of her hair where she had stashed a cigarette. "You boys, or should I say, you *Fathers,* look like ya had a rough mornin'."

Tom gave a half-smile and a slight nod. "And I came to town for a relaxing vacation of fishing and golf with a trusted friend."

Paul laughed, shrugging at Traci. "Hey, I thought Father Tom would enjoy a morning of real Maine lobstering."

Traci stared at him with a raised brow. "Solly's boat?"

Paul nodded, took his cap off, revealing thinning hair, and made the Sign of the Cross.

"Eighty years old and still leaving the dock at three-thirty in the mornin', haulin' all those traps to catch large bugs off the bottom of the ocean. I hope the smell of a hundred pounds of day-old herring bait made you hungry." Laughing, she pointed to an open booth with her pencil. "Coffees?"

Tom nodded, giving an exaggerated moan as he slid his tired bones into the booth.

A teenage busboy with dark-wavy hair approached with a pot of coffee.

Holding out his mug, Tom said, "Thank you, sir." Tom noticed a bruise on the young man's hand as the boy poured the coffee. "That looks sore."

The busboy glanced down at his hand and nervously smiled as he filled Paul's cup.

Paul raised his eyebrows when the coffee reached the brim. "Thank you, Rudy."

Before they could even raise their mugs, a dark-haired, stocky man with bronze-colored skin approached the booth, wearing a dark short-sleeved shirt sporting a gold badge on his chest and a Belfast police patch on his sleeve.

"Are you boys incognito today?"

"Good morning, Sheriff," quipped Paul. "We're just back from a morning on *Miss Lizzie*. We didn't want to wear our collars and tip off the lobsters that we were there to give them their last rites."

Tom reached out his hand. "Sheriff Coombs, right?"

The sheriff shook Tom's hand. "J.C. And you're Father Tom Fitzpatrick, if I remember correctly. It looked a little rough on the water today. Of course, that never slows down old Solly or his gift for gab."

"Yep. Solly needed our nautical expertise." Paul chuckled. "And Danny Haskell helped to give Father Tom extra lessons in the pleasures of seasick—"

"Sheriff!" The yell rose from a fit woman clothed in a light-pink blouse tied at her waist and tight jeans as she rushed through the front door, her long honey-blond hair swaying across her shoulders as she crossed the threshold. Tears welled in her red-rimmed eyes.

A man following close behind her tried in vain to grab her shoulder. "Laurie, we don't know anythin'!"

She glared at him and quickly turned. "Sheriff, I don't know what to do. Joline didn't come home last night. I just know somethin' ain't right. You have to help us!" Her eyes begged with desperation.

Sheriff Coombs squinted and tilted his head. "Hold on, Mrs. Chase."

The sheriff turned to the man. "Colby, what's going on? When did you see your daughter last?"

Customers sitting at the counter and booths turned and leaned in to hear the commotion.

Laurie didn't wait for her husband's input. "I told you.

Joline is gone. Something's happened to her. We need to find her!"

Colby Chase pulled off his worn Red Sox baseball cap and scratched his head. "I don't know, J.C. Yesterday was school graduation, and she went out to celebrate. She wasn't in her bed this mornin', so we've been to each of her friends' houses to see if she slept over, but none of them saw her after the movie."

Paul had mentioned to Tom that the sheriff was native Penobscot and served more than one tour in Afghanistan before joining the police force. His experience had given him a measured way about his calm, methodical, and focused mannerisms and speech. "Let's not get ahead of ourselves until we have more information. Joline's eighteen now, right? There could be a lot of explanations for why she's not home yet."

Laurie continued to shake her head as Colby held her. "My baby girl."

At the jangling of the bell over the door, all heads turned to see two lobstermen in their thirties, unshaven, soil-brimmed baseball hats, tee shirts, and still in their orange-colored Grunden oil pants and wet rubber boots, quickly entered, scanning the room. "J.C.! You gotta come down to the docks."

J.C. turned and narrowed his eyes at them. "What are you boys talkin' about?"

The men returned panicked stares and waved him to follow.

J.C. held out his hand to Laurie, gesturing to hold on as he quickly stepped out of the diner, followed by the priests and most of the patrons, and onto the sun-filled street sloping steeply down toward the picturesque harbor. The crowd made their way down the main street lined with historic brick buildings and storefronts from the 1800s, inspiring others inside the shops to follow. When the crowd reached the docks, the young lobstermen stopped in front of their red lobster boat, which sported the worn name *Emily*

Lauren on the transom of the stern. Then they turned to face the crowd.

Colby Chase stepped toward the boat, but one of the lobstermen held him back. "Colby, I think you should let the sheriff handle this."

Colby's brow furrowed as fear and anger flooded his face. "What are you talkin' about? What are you sayin'?"

Laurie Chase's wide eyes seemed to turn to terror as she squeezed them tight and clutched Colby's sleeve.

Tom edged closer as the sheriff pulled himself on board. The deck was crowded with heavy plastic lobster crates from their catch, a large bait bag, metal lobster traps, and a half-dozen brightly colored yellow and red buoys, but it was the shape under the blue plastic tarp that held his attention.

Squatting down, J.C. examined the situation.

Tom prayed but then spotted the grimace on J.C.'s face as he gently lifted the tarp so that only he could see what lay underneath. J.C. stared for several moments before a bystander broke the silence.

"What is it, Sheriff?"

J.C. stood up, the coarse skin on his face ghostly pale with shock as he stepped back out of the boat. Tom's eyes were fixed on Laurie and Colby Chase as J.C. slowly approached them and softly said, "Laurie. Colby. I'm very sorry."

Laurie broke down, her knees buckling as tears flowed, and she wailed, burying her face into Colby's shoulder as he pulled her closer. His face appeared paralyzed as he shook his head at the reality of a parent's worst fear.

Chapter 2

Father Tom watched Colby and Laurie enter the van and accompany Joline's body to the Chief Medical Examiner in Augusta, where an autopsy would be performed.

A short while later, Tom and Paul entered the police station to see the two lobstermen who had found Joline's body waiting outside J.C.'s office.

On the wooden bench by the door sat a teenage girl wearing denim shorts, a white shirt with a lace overlay, and a black band holding back her reddish hair. She stared at the wall across from her while tapping her shoes on the worn wooden floorboards.

She glanced up. "Father Paul, what are you doing here?"

"Ahh, I was going to ask you the same thing. Do you know—" Paul stopped short when he noticed one of the lobstermen giving a slight shake to his head.

Tom stepped forward. "I'm Father Tom. Were you one of the graduates this year?"

She stood much taller than he'd expected but with a smile in her eyes. "Yes, I'm Lizzie. You're not going to tell me you're a priest, too, are you? You're way too handsome." Then she turned to Paul. "No offense, Father Paul."

"None taken. Father Tom is a good priest, Elizabeth. Finding out God's plan is good for all of us."

A hundred questions for Lizzie filled Tom's mind, but if she didn't know about Joline's death yet, he didn't want to be the one to break it to her. "And, in case you were wondering, I'm a very happy priest."

The conversation was broken when J.C. opened his office door, accompanied by a female officer who approached Lizzie. "I'm Officer Nancy Rohde. Are you Elizabeth?"

She nodded. "Lizzie's better. Since I was born, they've been calling me that, and I'm kind of fond of it. Can someone tell me why I'm here?"

"Don't worry. You aren't in any trouble at all. I just had a few questions that you might be able to help us with. Maybe we can sit in the room over there, where it would be easier to talk. Would you like water or anything?"

Lizzie shook her head and followed the officer to the small conference room, staring back at Paul. Not long afterward, they heard a shocked, "What?" and then sobbing, "Oh, God, no!" from Lizzie. Tom stared at the closed door, wishing he could do something for her.

J.C. pursed his lips, then turned his attention to the two lobstermen and nodded. "Jay. Rich. I know it must have been hard, but I wanted to thank you, boys, for bringin' in Joline's body. Such a shame. I'm still in shock myself, but I have a few questions, if you don't mind?"

Jay, the sturdier of the two, ran his fingers through his light brown hair and shrugged as he shook his head. "I couldn't believe it. We were just dropping the last of our trawl when Rich saw something floating just ahead. With the fog, I don't think I woulda caught it except for the shine on that metal clasp in her hair."

Tom asked, "She, Joline, was floating when you saw her?"

J.C. raised his hand. "Padre, can I ask the questions here? And why are you here, anyway?"

Paul stepped aside with J.C. and Tom. "J.C., we don't want to be in the way. We were out there lobstering close to that area where Jay and Rich were hauling and just wanted to see if we could help." He lowered his voice. "Father Tom, here, has been very helpful with several crime cases back in Boston. If there was any foul play, he might be a good person to have around."

J.C. leaned in. "Just what I need, two Father Browns snoopin' around what might be an accidental drownin'."

Tom placed his hand on J.C.'s shoulder. "I understand. Do you mind if I just ask them one question?"

J.C. rolled his eyes and motioned his head toward the lobstermen.

Tom smiled. "Jay. Rich. I had the pleasure of being out on *Miss Lizzie* with Solly and Danny this morning. You're right; the fog was pretty thick out there, which didn't help my sea legs."

They glanced at each other with a knowing look.

"You said that you saw Joline floating and the shiny clasp in her hair. Was that in the back of her head?"

Jay glanced at Rich and nodded. "Yeah. It was in the back of her hair." He clenched his hand to the back of his head.

"So she was face down, then?"

Jay continued glancing over at Rich. "Yeah. Facedown. We pulled alongside and could tell it was a woman. We were careful pullin' her onto the boat. The water is pretty cold, so I don't know. Her skin was a bluish-white, and her eyes—her eyes were wide open. It was spooky. I didn't even realize who it was until we brought her in and saw Chase."

J.C. nodded. "Thanks, boys. If you can just spend a few minutes fillin' out those forms with times and any details you can think of, I'd appreciate it. And I'll need you to take me out to where you found her. How far out do you think it was?"

Scratching the back of his head, Jay checked with Rich. "Ah, maybe about a quarter-mile or so from the harbor, would you say?"

Rich nodded. "Yeah, that's about right."

"Did you see anythin' or anyone else out there?" asked J.C.

They shook their heads and then moved to a table to work on filling out the forms J.C. had handed them.

Tom and Paul stepped into J.C.'s office and closed the door as he sat down at his well-worn desk. J.C. placed his palms on the wooden top, clearly hesitating to tell them what he was thinking.

"She didn't drown," said Tom, breaking the silence.

J.C. shook his head with a smile. "A city boy priest who can't hold his breakfast on the water is an expert on drownin'—or not drownin', should I say?"

Tom stared at the whiteboard behind J.C., all blank except for the name Joline at the center with a big question mark after it. "Live bodies only stay afloat because of the air in our lungs. If we drown, they fill with water, and we sink pretty fast."

J.C. interrupted. "And dead bodies sink and then float, too."

"They sink unless they land in the water face down, then the air can't get out, and they stay afloat because the body is the same density as water. I'll admit the sea was choppy, but she definitely could have floated for several hours after dying. You're right that dead bodies tend to sink until the gut and chest cavity bacteria produce enough gas to float it to the surface like a balloon."

J.C. shook his head. "I know. The torso fills with the most gas, so bodies tend to float face down, as she was when they found her."

Tom nodded and stayed silent.

"*Right*?" asked J.C.

"Right, but that decaying process usually takes days or weeks before there's enough gas to cause a body to rise to the surface. Joline was only in the water for a few hours. Unfortunately, I think she must have died or been killed before she was in the water."

"Killed?" quipped J.C. "Now you're saying she was murdered?"

Paul ran his hand across his thinning hair. "Wow. I don't think there's been a murder in Belfast since the '80s. Isn't that right, J.C.? Wasn't that one a drug-related hit job or something like that?"

"Uh-huh. In '83. A forty-six-year-old Navy chief petty officer named Mervin 'Sonny' Grotton was gunned down with three shots from a rifle as he walked from his pickup truck to his front door. Now, let's not get ahead of ourselves and start panickin' the town," replied J.C.. He scowled and shook his head. "What am I sayin' '*us*' for?"

"Seriously, J.C., what if this *was* a murder? I don't think you guys have dealt with that before. I still can't believe it was Joline. So sad."

They sat in silence for several moments until Paul gave a deep sigh. "Look, all I'm saying is that Tom would be a good sounding board. Pride won't help anyone solve this."

J.C. stepped toward Tom, staring directly into his eyes. "Are you an expert detective?"

Tom shook his head.

"Then you do your job, and let me do mine, Father. Please."

Chapter 3

The white wooden-steepled church of St. Francis of Assisi was situated a short walk from the town center. Next to the church was a white Victorian-style house, the rectory, where Father Paul O'Connell lived and served the small town's Catholic parishioners. Tom relaxed in a comfortable white wicker chair on the front porch as Paul handed him a tall glass of iced tea.

"It's a nice spot, isn't it?" said Paul, sitting in the cushioned chair next to Tom, listening to the light breeze stir the umbrella of trees shading the rectory.

"That it is."

"I've got to say, Tom, I just feel numb about this tragedy. I called Laurie and Colby Chase's house to see if I could drop by, but no one answered. You know, I just can't imagine what they're going through. I can still picture Joline receiving her Confirmation just a few years ago. She was so full of life and had a good heart." A half-smile crossed Paul's face. "Full of mischievousness, too. I just don't know why anyone would kill a young girl who was just starting out in life."

Tom nodded. "I'm so sorry for you and the town. Evil is the opposite of everything we teach, and it's so hard to wrap your thoughts around it when it happens." He paused and took a sip of the cold tea. *The evil that men do lives after them; the good is oft interred with their bones.*"

"That sounds like Shakespeare. Is it?"

Tom nodded. "*Julius Caesar.*"

"Right. I never got whether that tale was about the betrayal of Caesar by Brutus or really a veiled story about the betrayal of the Catholic Church by King Henry VIII."

Tom laughed. "You know your Bard, then. In his time, Billy-boy would have certainly been charged with treason and jailed if he had made it too easy to figure *that* out. I think he was a great teacher of truth, challenging us to live either by the standard of Christ or face the consequences of the devil, nothing in between. He also wrote in a way that only the oppressed would see the message in his stories."

Paul stared at his iced tea. "But why does he say that only evil lives on?"

Holding out his drink, Tom stood up. "*Friends, Romans, countrymen, lend me your ears; I come to bury Caesar, not to praise him. The evil that men do lives after them; The good is oft interred with their bones; So let it be with Caesar.* It seems as if the evil things people do can affect others for a long time afterward and get more press than the good. Maybe it's a positive sign that people expect other people to do good, so it doesn't leave the same lasting memory. Brutus thought he was doing a good thing getting rid of the ambitious Caesar, but he's considered one of the greatest traitors of all time."

Paul said, "I didn't know there was a list."

"Remember Dante's *Inferno*? How the types of sin got worse as he traveled deeper down into the rings of hell. Do you remember what was considered the worst of all sins?"

"Murder?" asked Paul.

"No. Betrayal, because it's not your enemy who can betray you. Only a friend you love and trust can do that. Brutus, Cassius, and Judas are Dante's three men in that bottom ring of hell alongside an indifferent Satan. Caesar certainly did some good things, but they thought only the bad things would be remembered and, therefore, exonerating Brutus's betrayal for the good of Rome."

"Huh. But we're in Belfast, and the Joline I knew was a good kid, a young woman with a promising future snuffed out for no good reason," replied Paul as he gazed beyond the porch. "I just can't believe this is true. I really can't."

Tom reached out and patted Paul's back. "That's because you have a good heart. That's what stood out about you when we met that first day in seminary."

"Ahh. So that's why you put that salt in my sugar bowl for morning coffee the next day, is it?"

They both chuckled at the memory.

Tom and Paul co-officiated the 4:00 p.m. Mass at St. Francis on Saturday. The procession of people coming to Mass was overwhelming. The church pews were packed, with some standing along the sides.

Tom felt a lump in his throat as he and Paul proceeded down the center aisle of the small church, seeing silent, grief-stricken faces. He prayed that the words and presence of Christ in the Mass would provide strength and grace for each of them to move forward.

When they reached the front, three girls sobbed together in the first pew. One, Tom recognized as Lizzie from the police station. Their eyes were full of tears and red as summer roses. Tom stopped in front of them and reached out his hand to each girl.

Before the start of Mass, Paul wanted to say a few words to break the painful quiet that filled this sacred space. He gazed around the room; the shock on their faces was apparent. Before he could begin, a murmur rose as Laurie and Colby Chase appeared at the back of the church, slowly proceeding down the aisle to find an open seat. Paul motioned for them to come to the front, where the three girls slid over to make room for them to squeeze in. Paul shook Colby's hand and gave Laurie a long hug before she sat down clutching a handkerchief already soaked with tears.

Tom watched Paul let out a big sigh as he struggled to begin. "I, uh, I want to thank all of you for being here. It means a lot that we come together in times of deep pain and loss for Laurie and Colby—and this entire community. In many ways, that is what we are—a larger family that shares both joys and tragedies."

Paul paused as Laurie leaned in closer to Colby.

"We often say that young people graduating from high school are just beginning their lives, but Joline lived her life every day from the beginning. The all-too-soon loss of her life that took her from her family and us isn't fair and doesn't make sense, but she lives on in each of us in the life she shared and the memories she left. May this Mass be said for her soul and for the grace each of us needs to struggle through this time, knowing God will take the most loving care of her."

Tom managed a slight smile and nodded at Paul, appreciating the spontaneous invocation before they began the Mass celebration, bringing Christ's true presence to all those who continued to believe in Him—even in pain and tragedy. A movement at the back of the church caught Tom's eye when he saw a man in his mid-thirties with a closely cut beard abruptly exit; Colby Chase furrowed his brow as he watched him leave.

After the Mass ended, Paul and Tom stood outside the main doors chatting with departing parishioners until all had gone, or so they thought. One person remained when the priests stepped back into the church.

Paul put out his hands. "J.C., is this the first time in a while we've had the pleasure of your company at Mass?"

J.C.'s eyes rolled upward. "Yes. And I'm not coming back if you give me a hard time, Father." He paused. "That was a nice service for the town."

Paul smiled. "I hope so."

Tom said, "I don't envy you. I imagine you'll be interviewing many of the people who came today?"

"We'll see."

Tom nodded. "Did you notice the man who left in a hurry at the beginning?"

J.C. sighed. "Jordy. That was Ray Jordy. He was close friends with Colby Chase until a few years ago."

"Did something happen?"

J.C. ran his hand along the back of the pew. "Not sure. Never been one for Belfast gossip."

Tom said, "I understand. When will you know about Joline's autopsy result?"

J.C. cleared his voice. "The prelim autopsy report should be ready tomorrow afternoon, and we'll know what we are dealing with. Too bad it's a Sunday, and you'll be busy with your priest stuff."

"Hey, good news," Paul interjected, patting J.C.'s shoulder. "If you came to church more often, you'd know morning Mass is over by 9:15 a.m., so Father Tom and I are more than available!"

J.C. made his way toward the back door, shaking his head. "Comforting to know I'll have two priests in town snooping around on police business." He turned and eyed Tom. "Oh, and I called that Detective Brooks in Boston. He warned me about a Father Tom and his sidekick, An—"

"It's Angelo. He's a good man and smarter than any criminal out there," said Tom.

J.C. laughed as he proceeded out the door. "Is that because he is one?"

Chapter 4

Around seven p.m., Tom stepped into the kitchen to check out what might be on the menu for dinner. When he opened the refrigerator to see the barren shelves, he yelled, "I'm guessing we're going out for supper?"

Paul entered the kitchen, face flushed. "Yeah. I should be better prepared as a host. How about a burger and a beer?"

"Or a burger and two beers. Sure. It's on me."

"Tom, you're the guest."

"And your guest will expect a nice two-pound lobster and some steamers tomorrow—on you!" He laughed as they headed out the door, down the side street, and onto the steep grade of Main Street lined with diagonally parked cars until they reached Rollie's Tavern. Tom liked the small-town pub feel, the long wooden bar. Patrons of all ages perched on stools, relaxed in old booths, and sat at small wooden tables. The noisy chatter added to the pleasant atmosphere.

Paul shook hands with the owner at the door. "Ryan, this is Father Tom from Boston."

A loud cheer erupted as the Red Sox scored a run during the ballgame on the large screen over the bar.

Tom leaned in to be heard. "I like your place already, but I'm concerned about eating anywhere that would let someone like Father Paul in."

Ryan nodded. "Only when he behaves himself; otherwise, he's out on the curb like last time." He pointed to a table opening up for Tom and Paul. "First time in the pub gets you a drink on the house."

"That's awfully generous of you, Ryan," said Paul.

Ryan smiled broadly. "On the house for him. PFA squatters don't qualify."

Tom and Paul sat down, and Tom glanced at the score of the Sox game. Red Sox 3, Orioles 2 in the second inning, and two men were on base. "What's a PFA, if I dare to ask?"

Paul laughed. "PFA? Oh, 'People From Away.' I'll always be a 'People From Away.'"

"Even if you've been living here for forty years?"

"Even if I was born here!"

Tom scratched his head. "You'd have to be native if you were born here."

"As a wise man once said, 'Just because a cat has kittens in the oven, that don't make 'em biscuits.'"

"Very funny," said Tom as the waitress approached and asked what they'd like to drink.

"Hi, Katie. This is Father Tom."

She eyed him up and down, tapping her pencil against her ordering pad as her lip curled in apparent approval. "I don't know if I believe you, but who knows what people will do these days. What'll you padres have?"

Tom held up two fingers. "Two Guinness drafts should do it." The patrons cheered again. He turned toward the bar to see what that was about as two more runs crossed the plate. He stared through the standing crowd. "Paul, is that Danny Haskell sitting at the bar talking with a couple of guys?"

Paul glanced up. "Yep."

"It seems like they are having a serious conversation about something."

Paul nodded. "It was a tough day, and tomorrow is their only day off. Who knows?"

Katie returned with two tall pints of dark brown Irish brew and placed them on the table. "I guess these are on the house to get you started. Let me know when you need a refill."

Paul took a sip and wiped his lips. "Katie, who is Danny talking with at the bar?"

She tilted her head. "It's, um, Jay McMahon and Rich Lowe, those two poor boys who found that girl's body this morning. I don't know what I'd have done if I saw her out there. So sad, just graduating and all. Did they say what happened yet?"

Tom shook his head. "Not yet."

As Katie made her way to another table, Tom noticed three young women entering the pub. They headed toward the booth that had just opened up next to Tom and Paul's table, but Danny Haskell turned and reached out to grab one by the arm. It was Lizzie from the police station with the two other girls who'd sat in the front pew at Mass earlier that afternoon. Lizzie argued with Danny for a few minutes, then joined her friends in the booth, putting her close enough for Tom to hear their conversation.

"What did he want?" asked one of the girls.

Lizzie shook her head. "He wanted to know if I was drinking again tonight. After what happened to Joline, I can't believe he would be on my back about something like that."

"Everyone's on edge, Liz," said the other girl. "I don't think I want to even try to fall asleep tonight because I know I'll only have nightmares."

Tom could see the girl wiping away tears with her napkin.

Lizzie squeezed her eyes tight and stood, appearing shaken. "I'm goin' to use the bathroom. Order me a raspberry iced tea or something?"

As she headed to the back of the pub, Tom turned in his chair to face the two girls. "I'm assuming you were good friends of Joline Chase? My name's Father Tom, and I think you know Father Paul here."

The girls nodded, wiping the tears from their cheeks.

"I'm so sorry to hear about your loss. I lost a very close friend at about your age, and I was devastated," said Tom empathetically, his eyes misty with the pain of the memory.

The girl with brown hair tied in a ponytail replied, "I just feel numb, like I can't believe it. I'm Sue, by the way. Sue Jenkins and this is Megan Connors."

Megan nodded, her blond curls bobbing around her heart-shaped face. "Lizzie is the other girl with us. We were all close friends with—Joline, but Lizzie was the closest. They've been friends since before preschool. She's kinda in pieces right now, and we thought it might be good to take her out, but I'm not sure it's turning out to be a good idea."

Tom pushed the conversation a bit while making mental notes about their demeanor and apparel. Both of them wore colored wristbands. "You are good friends. Were you with Joline on Friday?"

"Yeah," Sue replied. "Pretty much all day. We met for breakfast at Traci's before graduation. Joline was wired and psyched about being done with school. She didn't want to go to college, but she was super smart and so pretty. I kinda felt jealous at times, but she was a good friend, too."

Megan added, "After graduation, we went to parties at each other's houses."

"They were pretty lame," said Sue, "so we were looking forward to spendin' time together that evening—you know, reminiscin' and talkin' about what we might do. That movie *The Hangover* was playin' at the Colonial, so the four of us planned to go."

Megan glanced at Paul and raised her brow. "We got in for free 'cause Lizzie's boyfriend works the ticket window. I think that's okay if someone gives us free tickets, isn't it, Father Paul?"

Paul rolled his eyes and bobbed his head.

Tom asked, "Was the movie as funny as they say?"

Sue nodded with a smile.

"So, you went from your parties right to the movies?"

Sue shook her head. "We were goin' to meet there at just before seven. The three of us were there on time, but Jo was late."

"I think she said she wanted to drop by the school for something. Weird since she was so happy to be done with it," added Megan.

"I hope you didn't miss too much of the beginning," said Tom.

Sue shook her head. "We would have, but we decided to wait until the nine o'clock show and hung around town a bit, nothing too excitin', just girl talk."

"Except when those Norsemen biker guys almost ran us over," said Megan as her eyes widened. "Remember, we were walking down Bridge Street, and there was this loud rumble coming up behind us. I really thought they were going to hit one of us."

"Yeah, yeah," said Sue. "They circled us with their engines revvin' to get us worked up, but then one started harassin' Jo."

Father Tom furrowed his brow. "Did they touch her?"

"No. They asked her if she wanted a ride, and when she said, 'No,' the guy with the blond goatee said she was nothin' but tease and could get herself in trouble gettin' guys all worked up like that," replied Sue. "I was shakin', but Jo didn't seem intimidated at all, just givin' him a smile before they peeled out. One of the neighbors came out on the porch to see if we were all right. My heart was poundin' a mile a minute, but Jo just said that we were fine, and we turned back into town. Lizzie yelled at Jo about it all the way back."

Lizzie returned from the bathroom, appeared to have collected herself, and slid into the booth. "You said, Father Tom, right?" She glanced toward Sue and Megan and then back at Tom. "I didn't know you guys went out for food."

Father Tom quipped. "Priests are allowed to eat food once a month, so who wouldn't pick Rollie's Tavern?" His eyes softened as he gazed at Lizzie, taking in the pain that might lie inside her at that moment. "Lizzie, my heart goes out to you. I'm so sorry about Joline. Sue and Megan said you've been best friends for a long time."

"I don't remember not knowing her. She was like my sister," stuttered Lizzie. "I still don't understand what happened. I can't believe she's not here with us right now."

"I can't imagine. The girls said you went to the movies together last night," said Tom.

Lizzie paused. "Yeah. Nothing to laugh about now. Joline left early, and we never saw her again."

Tom furrowed his brow. "She disappeared without telling you?"

Sue paused. "No, she got up halfway through the movie and said she didn't want to stay. She told us to watch the rest, and she'd see us on Saturday."

"We should have gone with her," said Megan. "We should have stayed together."

Suddenly, the jukebox blared Dolly Parton's song, "Jolene." The rhythmic lyrics repeat the song's name, begging Jolene not to take her man just because she could.

Tom spotted Ryan approaching the small gang of bikers at the jukebox, then he abruptly yanked the plug on the music. They had some words, and then the fuming bikers, dressed in grungy pants, leather jackets with "Norsemen" across the back, and one with a red-white-and-blue bandana on his head, staggered out of the tavern.

Lizzie shook her head. "Sorry. I shouldn't be out tonight. I think I want to go home." Leaving her iced tea untouched, Lizzie stood and headed toward the door, with Megan and Sue close behind. A flood of questions filled Tom's mind as he and Paul sat silently for several moments.

Paul tilted his head. "You're doing it, aren't you?"

"What?"

"I can see those wheels spinning. You're trying to figure out what happened, and we don't even have any results from the autopsy yet."

Katie came back, and they ordered two Rollie's Ultimate burgers. Tom turned back to Paul. "I guess. I don't know; I guess Joline is making me think of someone I used to know. Someone who died that I loved very deeply." He didn't say the name *Corlie*, but he could picture her name written on the last note she wrote to him.

"Sorry to hear that." Paul paused. "Joline had so much going for her. Like the girls said, she was smart, a good friend, a stunningly attractive girl, and had a good family. I keep wondering about how the Chases are holding up. I want to check in with them."

When the burgers arrived, Tom said, "Wow. Katie, I think we could have ordered one and split it. These are huge." Katie smirked and left as Tom took a bite of his burger. "Paul, why do you think Danny Haskell stopped Lizzie on her way in?"

"Well, he's her father, and she's coming into a pub at eighteen."

"Ah. Lizzie Haskell. Makes sense. He seems to be tying one on tonight."

Paul glanced over as Danny finished another beer, still animated in his conversation with Jay and Rich. "It wouldn't be the first time. His wife died from cancer more than ten years ago. Raising Lizzie on his own has been tough. He's been lobstering with Solly forever. Even named Lizzie after Solly's boat, thinking he would own it someday, but Solly is a tough old salt." Paul laughed. "And so's his wife, Dotty. She doesn't want him going out alone, so he took on Danny almost twenty years ago."

Tom glanced at Danny, mulling over the man's past. "You never know all the things going on in a person's life from the outside, do you?"

Paul laughed and handed a napkin to Tom. "I think that burger juice dripping down your chin tells us all we need to know about you, though."

On their way out of the tavern, Tom paused beside Danny, sitting alone at the bar and staring into his half-empty beer. "Captain Haskell, how are you doing?"

Danny slowly turned his head and stared up with red-rimmed eyes. "I have no boat to be captain of and no Haskell to carry on my name."

"Well, you are a dad of a wonderful daughter. I didn't even know you had a child."

He turned back to his drink. "It's hard to tell, sometimes."

Tom put his hand on Danny's shoulder. "You take care of yourself, now. Okay?"

There was no acknowledging nod.

Tom stepped out of the busy pub into the peaceful quiet of the small coastal town, lit by a scattering of vintage black street lamps, the lights in windows, and a million stars—until the loud rumbling of three Harley motorcycles raced by, accompanied by a few obscenities hurled by their riders.

Paul turned to Tom. "Do you want to head back to the peace and safety of city life?"

Tom cocked his head and smiled. "Only after I mercilessly trounce you at chess tonight. I never have a chance with Angelo, so I'll have to build my confidence back at your expense."

Paul laughed as they headed back to the rectory for the evening.

Chapter 5

After morning Mass, Tom leaned into the empty refrigerator. "I was hoping maybe it grew some bacon and eggs while we slept."

He stood up and glanced at Paul. In unison, they both said, "Traci's."

Sunday morning breakfast out can be an act of patience, but the line outside Traci's Diner was short. The family in front of them was understandably talking about Joline's tragic death. The large, heavy-set mother turned. "Father Paul. I wanted to thank you for what you said at Mass. The whole thing is so sad." She touched the tops of her children's heads, leaned in, and softly added, "And scary. No one knows what even happened to the poor girl. Thank you, too, Father Tom—I have that right, don't I?"

Tom nodded.

"I had a sister who went to live in Boston years ago, but she came back. Everyone does." She paused. "To think that Joline was at this diner Friday morning. Who would have ever imagined it would be her last day?"

Tom said, "So, you were here on Friday morning?"

"Yup. I meet with a group of girlfriends every Friday for an early breakfast. Joline came in with some of her friends and sat in a booth in the back. They were having so much fun, laughing, and just being young girls. I can't believe it," she said, staring into Tom's eyes for some kind of answer.

"A tragedy can make us stop to think of our lives, our family, and what we value. Did you know her or the family well?"

The woman pursed her lips. "Just as neighbors down the street. They seemed like a happy family, well, until a couple of years ago; then, there were some arguments. They could get so loud you could hear them from my house at times.

One time, Joline came down the street all upset and with a dark bruise under her eye. I asked if she was okay, and she said she just hit it against the door. I don't know. I don't like to gossip."

"I understand." Tom smiled as Traci opened the door to seat the woman and her family and then offered Tom and Paul two seats at the counter, where the non-stop bustle of cooking and serving was on full display.

"Coffees?" asked a lean, wiry-built man wearing a grease-stained tee shirt under a much cleaner apron. He stood five inches shorter than Tom and cast him a stare that had an edgy intensity that matched his rough, pockmarked face.

Paul nodded, holding up two fingers. He leaned over to Tom. "That's Ralph. He normally works the counter here during the night shift but helps out on Sundays with the breakfast rush."

Ralph brought back two cups of black coffee and pushed over a dish of creamers and the sugar dispenser.

Tom said, "Thank you, Ralph."

His black eyes moved from the counter up to meet Tom's. His squint and awkward half-smile seemed to ask if they knew each other.

"Father Paul, here, said you work the night shift."

Ralph gave a slight nod, glancing at Paul and back to Tom. He nervously wiped his hands on his apron and then scratched his head of dark, greasy hair. "Yeah. Ten to eight, except Sundays, then it's ten to ten. Sunday mornin's get extra busy, so they need the counter help."

Tom sighed. "It must keep you in good shape. A good diner is important to a town. So, you weren't working Friday morning, then?"

Ralph's deep-set eyes narrowed. "Not after eight, like I said. Why?"

"No reason. A woman said Joline was here for breakfast that morning. I didn't know if anyone remembered seeing her."

Shooting a wary glance at Tom, Ralph shook his head, pressing his lips together. "It was busy. I don't remember seein' her in the mornin'."

"Sure. Sounds like she may have dropped by that evening?" queried Tom.

Ralph ran his hand across his forehead. "I don't know. I've got customers waiting. Let me know when you're ready to order."

As Ralph disappeared into the kitchen, the man sitting on the next stool set down his coffee after a sip. "I saw Joline here that morning and then again at night."

Tom turned. "You saw her both times?"

The man scratched the scruff of his week-old beard and then tipped back his baseball cap. "This is pretty much where I eat, so I'm here a lot and hear a lot. Ned Parker, by the way."

As Tom reached out to shake his hand, Paul leaned over. "Hey, Ned. Anything unusual when you saw her?"

Ned slowly exhaled, the air filling his cheeks and blowing off cigarette smoke. "Ah. Not really. She was in a pretty good mood, here with her friends."

Tom asked, "Did she talk with anyone else?"

"Um. I don't think so—wait." He squinted to think for a second. "She did get up from the counter at one point and went outside. She talked with someone loud enough to be an argument."

"Do you remember who it was?"

"Yeah, Yeah. It was Ray. Ray Jordy. They didn't talk that long, but she seemed kinda agitated when she came back in. Later that night, the more interesting conversation was after she came into the diner as if searching for someone."

"What time was that?"

Ned paused. "Maybe sometime around midnight. I remember Ralph saying, 'Hey, Joline' or something like that. She was a pretty girl, and Ralph always has his eyes on the pretty ones, don't you, Ralph?"

Ralph had come back to take their orders and didn't respond outside of a glare that could have pierced Ned through his stare alone.

When Ralph had disappeared into the kitchen, Ned shook his head. "Usually, you can't shut him up." He paused. "Let's see. Joline stepped into the back area and must have found who she was searching for because I remember her sitting at a booth talking with someone. I couldn't see the other side of the booth from here, and I was more focused on finishing up my pie. I don't think it was a kid, though."

A few moments later, one of the waitresses approached, served Tom and Paul's breakfasts, and freshened their coffees.

Tom asked, "Is Ralph still on?"

She peered at her watch and shook her head. "Ten-o-five. Ralph's probably long gone unless he's having a smoke out the backdoor first. To tell you the truth, I try not to think about him too much. He gives me the creeps." She turned abruptly and scurried off.

Tom glanced at Paul and shrugged.

Paul picked up a crispy piece of bacon and took a bite. "So, what exactly are you up to, Sherlock?"

"I guess it's a force of habit. I thought if we pieced together the timeline of Joline's movements that day, it might help lead to some kind of answer."

"Your idea of a vacation?"

"More than turning my stomach upside down on a smelly boat at three-thirty in the morning." Tom laughed as he dipped the corner of his toast into the soft yolk of his egg and then noticed a figure looming in the doorway. Sheriff Coombs waited, then approached them with a look of apprehension.

"Good mornin', J.C.," said Paul.

He frowned. "It is morning, but there is nothing good about it."

"What is it, Sheriff? Did you get the results early?" asked Tom.

J.C. rolled his eyes upward and sighed. "Yes, I did. You were right." He lowered his voice. "Joline died before she ended up in the water."

Tom sighed and peered up at J.C. "Did they say how she died?"

J.C. bit his lip and hesitated. "Look, this is not for blabbin' around. I just thought I owed you that much. There were marks of manual strangulation around her neck and a gash to the back of her head. They are still tryin' to determine which caused her death. They need more time to finalize the actual cause, but I couldn't wait until they finished."

"So, we are talking about a murder?"

"Or an accident that someone tried to cover up," said J.C. as he broke off a piece of Tom's bacon and took a bite before leaving the diner.

Chapter 6

Outside the diner, Tom gazed up at the blue sky. Puffy white clouds drifted lazily with the gentle sea breeze. He followed the sky downward until it met the gray water of the ocean dotted with sailboats and lobster buoys. He thought of Joline's body drifting for hours in the cold waters. He knew almost nothing about her, but deep down, he felt a strong desire for the truth and justice for her.

"Tom. Tom. Are you still with us?" asked Paul as he tried to get Tom's attention. "What are you thinking about?"

Tom continued to stare out at the harbor. "Belfast is such a beautiful small town." He scanned one end of the harbor to the other and then settled his sights on a small boat motoring out across the water, early morning waves tipping it this way and that, like the ripples of life.

"Too many things are just not right about Joline's death. No accident includes marks of strangulation. Someone got pretty angry with her and went to great lengths to ensure there was no evidence."

Paul nodded. "I know. I would assume our golf game is off for today. What do you want to do?"

"Well, I don't think the sheriff is too keen on us snooping around, but it would be great to retrace Joline's steps that Friday. Do you think the Chases would be willing to talk with us, and maybe we can offer some consolation, too?"

Paul stared downward, pausing before he answered. "Maybe. They must be in a state of shock, but they may need to talk to someone as well. Since you're licensed in psychiatry and do a lot of counseling, we can approach them from that perspective."

Laurie Chase answered the phone after several rings. She hesitated for several moments before agreeing to see Paul and Tom. Tom understood it was a time for trusted people, and neither she nor Colby knew him.

When they arrived at the modest colonial house on a quiet street, Laurie opened the door wearing a soft denim blouse and black yoga pants and showed them to the back porch, where she had iced tea and scones set up. Laurie shared with them that she worked at Reny's department store in town, and Colby had been at the Front Street Boat Repair since they got married at nineteen.

"Mrs. Chase—"

"Father Tom, please call me Laurie. I appreciate your visit." Her eyes and cheeks were noticeably red from crying. "I can get you something else if iced tea isn't all right."

"It's perfect."

Laurie closed her eyes tight. "Perfect was what she was when they first handed her to me in the hospital." Tears rolled down each cheek. "I feel like I'm going insane. I feel numb, and I don't know what to do other than cry. I'm powerless."

Tom squatted down next to her chair and held her hand.

"Why?" she asked as she stared directly into Tom's eyes. "Why?"

"That is what I would ask, too. Why her? Why did she have to leave so soon?" asked Tom.

She squeezed Tom's hand. "I need to know why. We need to know what happened." She stood up and took a photo off of the wall. "This is Joline. My baby girl."

Tom held the frame and gazed at what must have been her senior photo. She was as stunning as people had said. Her fine auburn hair, ivory skin, and piercing emerald-green eyes were features a man could fall for in an instant without even knowing what happened to him. "Such a beautiful girl. Laurie, can I ask if you believe in God?"

"Sometimes, yes. Right now, I'm struggling. I'm really struggling. I feel so angry."

"I can understand that. She was a gift from God to you and Colby. When couples have a baby, they don't always ask why they were so blessed or why they deserved so much unconditional love. Parents are asked to do everything they can to keep their children safe and help them get to heaven. Whatever the 'why' is today, please know that she is in God's loving arms, and I promise to try to help find the truth and bring her the justice she deserves."

Laurie continued to stare at the photo, nodding and wiping tears. "I'd appreciate that."

Father Tom sat down. "I would like to help. Do you feel comfortable telling me about her day on Friday?"

She sighed. "I keep running it through my mind over and over. The things I could have said. The hug I could have given her. The things I wished I hadn't said. It was an emotional day for all of us. We were scrambling to get things ready for the graduation party before she headed out the door."

"Was that to meet the girls for breakfast?"

Laurie nodded, wiping her tears.

"What time?"

She shook her head. "Ah, let's see. It was early. I was surprised she was up that early. Maybe six-thirty or so. I think it was because she wanted time for me to do her hair before graduation at ten." Her eyes closed, and tears streamed down her cheeks. "Her hair was always so beautiful. I loved just being with her and brushing it. I felt close even when—"

Tom set a tissue box in front of her. "Anything unusual?"

"No. She was off, and Colby and I scrambled to get things ready, pick up some food we had ordered from the co-op, and get dressed for the graduation at the high school. Joline came back later than I expected and rushed to get herself ready and for me to do her hair. Nothing unusual at the graduation. We took a lot of pictures of her and her friends and with us. You know, the usual graduation pictures."

Tom nodded. "You're doing well. Are the photos—"

"They were just on my phone." She got up, retrieved her phone, and scrolled through her photos before handing it to Tom. The first one made him smile as Joline gave the typical teenage expression when being forced to be in a picture with her parents before leaving for graduation. A few distanced shots of her receiving her diploma. And then several photos of her with Laurie and Colby, with friends from school.

Tom said, "I met Lizzie, Sue, and Megan. Who are the other friends in the photos?"

Laurie responded, "Let's see. That's, um, Rudy, Melissa, and Nick."

Tom noticed that, in the picture, Joline was eyeing one of the boys. "Which boy is this?"

"That's Nick Campbell. He's a handsome boy, isn't he?"

Tom flipped through the photos. "Are these friends of the family?" Tom asked as he stopped at a few photos of Joline standing by a man with a close-cropped beard and reddish-brown hair.

"Yeah." She paused. "This is Ray Jordy, a friend of Colby's, and these are the next-door neighbors."

"Would you be okay if I sent a few of these to my phone? Only if you're comfortable."

Laurie nodded as she retrieved another tissue to wipe her cheeks. "Afterward, we had her party an hour later, but she left with her girlfriends, hopping from one party to another. We were supposed to have dinner together as a family that evening, but she only popped back in to change her clothes, and she went back out again. That—" She paused and squeezed her eyes shut. "Oh, my God. That was the last time I saw her. I didn't have a chance to give her a kiss, a hug; I—didn't tell her how much I loved her." She buried her face in her hands, her body shaking.

Before Tom could say anything, Colby appeared at the porch entryway. "Father Paul. Father Tom. What's going on? Why are you here?"

Paul stood up to shake Colby's hand. "Hi, Colby. Father Tom and I just wanted to drop by to see how you and Laurie were doing."

Colby glowered at Paul and snapped, "How do you think we're doing?" He shook his head. "Sorry. Sorry. Just a lot of stress right now. We don't need to add to it."

Tom said, "Mr. Chase, we want to help in any way we can to honor your daughter and help find the truth of what happened so she can have justice."

"Yeah, well, it won't bring her back, will it? It won't turn back the clock or change the past. I would like to change a lot of the past, but I can't. You can't. And now she's gone."

"Joline was a beautiful child of God. I know you're in a lot of pain right now, but she is okay. God has her, and I hope that time brings justice, forgiveness, and peace to you both. I think she would want that for you."

"Forgiveness?! Forgive who?" Colby left the porch shaking his head.

Tom and Paul said goodbye to Laurie and made their way back to the rectory porch. Tom sat down and studied the photos he sent from Laurie's phone.

Paul came back out with a fresh plate of peach slices. "Notice anything of note?"

"It gets a little grainy when you zoom in, but some of these photos are interesting. This photo of Joline and Ray Jordy is interesting. To be in a graduation photo, he must be close to the family, but I thought someone said he and Colby had a falling out."

Paul sat. "I think they've known each other since grade school and worked together at the shipyard."

"Wait, the man that left Mass on Saturday kind of abruptly. That was Jordy, right?"

"Now that you mention it, I think J.C. said it was," said Paul.

"Huh. Take a look at this one."

"It's a photo of Joline with the three girls we spoke with at Rollie's. What about it?"

Tom zoomed in to the background. "Is that Danny Haskell?"

"Yeah. He's there with Lizzie, so it makes sense that he's around."

Tom squinted. "I'm probably just seeing things, but are his eyes fixated on Joline?"

"Joline and Lizzie were close, so she's probably been at the Haskells a thousand times."

Tom scrolled down a few more shots.

"Are you finding anything else?"

"I don't know. It's hard to make out, but isn't that the waiter from Traci's diner? What's his name, again?"

"Huh," said Paul, putting on his reading glasses to study it closer. "You mean Ralph. Ralph Cutter. If it isn't him, it's a good likeness. I don't think he has any family in the area."

Tom stared at the photo. "Whoever it is certainly has his eye on the girls. So, what's a bachelor with no family doing at high school graduation?"

Paul paused. "Who knows? A small town without much going on. I think he lives in those apartments across the street from the high school fields, so maybe he walked over to watch what was going on?"

"Maybe."

Chapter 7

Tom stepped off the porch of the rectory and onto the quiet street.

"What are you doing, Tom?" asked Paul.

He cocked his head left and then right. "Which way to the high school?"

"Why the high school?"

"Can I walk it?"

"Sure, but what are you thinking?"

Frowning, Tom said, "If Joline dropped by the school before going to the movies, I wondered which way she would go and if anyone saw her."

Paul shook his head. "I'm sure the sheriff will check all that out." Tom started heading northeast, so Paul came out to the street. "Hey, it's this way. Let me escort you so you don't get lost on me."

A quick half-mile, and they were in the center of town. Tom could see the old movie theater. "So, how far from here to the school?"

"Maybe another half-mile. Normally, we would head straight down High Street, but I think a lot of the kids cut over through old Ben Hatch's farm."

Tom nodded. "Okay, let's try that way."

Within a few minutes, they were creeping through Hatch's farm as the kids had been doing for years. A gray-haired man was rocking on the porch, wearing suspenders and a broad-rimmed hat. "You boys are goin' to be a little early for the openin' of school this fall, ain't ya?"

Paul stood up straight, face flushed as he smiled. "Hello, Ben. I, uh, just wanted to show Father Tom, here, your beautiful farm."

Ben shook a bit as he laughed. "I'm not too old to know a fib. You do know it's Sunday, don't ya, Father?"

Tom said, "You do have a beautiful spot here."

"It used to look like something when I could get to more of the chores. It's hard to find kids who will do this type of work these days. Would you like a cold drink or something?"

Tom shook his head. "That's a nice offer, but we may need to pass for today. I wondered if you happened to see Joline Chase passing this way on Friday?"

Ben's head dropped. "So sad. Such a beautiful girl, always friendly. I was just talkin' to the missus about that. I did see her come this way. She was alone and said hello. It was a little before five because that's when we eat—five o'clock on the dot." He shook his head.

"What about later? Did you see her return this way, maybe around seven?"

Ben scratched the scruff of gray beard on his neck. "No, not this way. I sit out here every night, especially this time of year. The moon was waning but still pretty bright, so I would have seen her."

Tom thanked Ben and started to turn when Ben added, "I was a little worried about her. Like I said, she's an awfully pretty girl to be alone at night and wearing what she was."

Tom took a step back. "What was that?"

"Well, like a lot of those young girls, her shorts were too short and too many buttons open on that blouse of hers. Poor girl. I hope they find out what happened to her. I heard a lot of tootin' and pickups drag racin' on the street behind, but not much goin' on in front of us. I only saw a yellow pickup drive by and those motor-bikers rumblin' along later."

"Well, good meeting you, Ben. If you remember anything else—"

"I'll let the sheriff know," said Ben with a subtle smirk.

Tom and Paul approached the Belfast Area High School athletic field, which appeared to have track and field, football, soccer, and other events. A maintenance man was cleaning up the remaining debris from graduation as they crossed the field.

Paul called out. "Ed, how are you doing? This must have been a big job."

"It's what I do, Father Paul. Almost finished," Ed replied as he leaned down to pick up a plastic cup. He was most likely in his fifties, wearing blue overalls and close to needing a haircut. "Are you taking the Father for a run around the track?" He smiled.

"If I do, don't bet on me," replied Paul with a chuckle.

Tom reached out his hand. "Hi, Ed. Father Tom. Did you start cleaning up right after graduation?"

"Yep. Breakin' down all the chairs and the podium. Teachers and a hundred grads with parents and family means five hundred chairs."

Tom raised his brow and nodded, impressed. "I hope you had help."

"I was hoping I did, too. Just me and my assistant." Ed pointed to the edge of the track, where an excessive lump of brown-furred skin flopped on the ground.

Tom stepped over to pat him as he lifted his head, and the old dog's sad eyes greeted Tom's. "What's his name?"

"Lightning."

Tom worked to hold back the sudden urge to laugh.

"Not one of your top ten guesses, I'll bet," Ed said.

"Oh, I don't know. A bloodhound like Lightning here must come in handy during hunting season, don't you, boy?" Tom stood and turned to Ed. "So, you didn't see anyone early Friday evening?"

Ed shook his head. "Just me and Lightning, oh, and Joline Chase did come through. She loved old Lightning and helped me fold a bunch of chairs. Yup, she was all right in my book and didn't deserve to die so young."

"When did she leave?"

"She was only with me for ten minutes or so. Around five, I guess. She said she needed to see someone at the school."

Tom could see the school building in the distance. "Who would be at the school on a Friday night after graduation?"

"I wouldn't think anybody, but she was in there for a while, and then they left together."

Tom glanced toward Paul and back to Ed. "They?"

"Yeah, she was with McCready. The kids call him Mr. McC. I know his truck and saw them drive down Field Street together. I figured he was giving her a ride to the harbor or somewhere. I would have never guessed that would be the last time I saw her."

Paul said, "Thanks, Ed. I hope you get a chance to relax. You keep this place looking real proud." Tom squatted down to pat Lightning one more time. "You didn't see anyone else, did you, Ed?"

Ed curled his lip, shook his head, then stopped and gazed out at the road. "I did see a yellow truck leave shortly after McCready drove off. I think that was it for the night, except for those bikers streaming through, revvin' up in town, like they always do."

Tom nodded as he took it all in. "Good talking to you. Nice to know you're watching out for the school."

Tom and Paul strode down Field Street toward the end of the harbor, where boats were tied to the docks. Front Street ran along the picturesque harbor that housed vessels of all sizes. The half-mile walk along the harbor led back to town. Up ahead, Tom noticed several boat hoists that carried large vessels in and out of the water. All kinds of boats were being worked on.

"I wonder where Mr. McCready was taking Joline that evening?" asked Tom.

"I don't know," replied Paul as they watched the boats rock with the lapping ocean waves. "What I do know is that it's getting near lunchtime."

"Is that all you think about?" Tom smiled.

"You know, we just need to walk over that footbridge and," pointing down the shore across the inlet water, "you might be able to get that lobster roll you've been waiting for."

"On you?"

Paul half-nodded. "On me. You're not going to get any fresher than Young's Lobster Pound. Nothing fancy, but really good."

"You twisted my arm." Tom pointed to his left as they headed over the footbridge across the water. "How far does this inlet go?"

Paul laughed. "You're going to make me say it, aren't you? That's the Passagassawakeag River."

Tom chuckled. "Pass-a-gas-a-what?"

"Let's just call it 'the Passy.' It's a tidal river that goes about sixteen miles inland."

At the end of the footbridge, Tom pointed. "So the tide must bring it up and down pretty far? Huh."

They made their way to Young's, and after ordering, they sat at one of the old wooden picnic tables, waiting for the lobster rolls and steamers, and enjoying the view of Belfast Harbor from across the way.

Paul said, "It's really pretty, isn't it? I never get tired of gazing at the town on the hill, the boats in the harbor, and the rocky coastline. I know you like Boston, but I always feel blessed to be at this parish."

"I may be a city boy, but I can see why you do." Tom's eyes widened as a waiter set down their rolls and bucket of steamers. "I can definitely see why you do!"

The sun was warm on their faces as they ate and talked about their seminary days. At one point during the meal, Tom had to decide how generous he wanted to be with a seagull who landed at his feet. He knew that feeding one would encourage others to demand their share.

After finishing his roll, Tom turned over the paper placemat and drew a rough map of the town from their unique vantage point. Down the center, he drew a line for Main Street, which sloped down to the harbor and the streets that branched off of it. Then, he drew a circle around

Chase's house. "Joline starts her day at home before meeting the girls at Traci's." His pen traces a line to each stop she made. "She goes back home, then on to the high school for graduation, before hopping from party to party and then to this mysterious trip back to the school to see Mr. McC before meeting the girls at the Colonial Theater."

Paul took a large bite of his lobster roll and, with a full mouth, garbled, "And then left the movie early."

Tom tapped his pen against the paper on the table. "Why did she leave, and where did she go?"

Chapter 8

After lunch, Tom and Paul crossed back over the quarter-mile-long footbridge and started along the harbor walkway that paralleled Front Street. Tom stood under a boat hoist's large, heavy, metal arms, its sturdy wheels straddling piers over the open water where the boats would be raised or lowered.

"Man, is this huge! I imagine they can move some impressive vessels in and out of the harbor with this," blurted Tom.

"It's pretty neat. I think it can lift 160 tons or so, and they're trying to get one that handles over 450 tons," said Paul. "They service over a hundred boats a season, so the work is steady."

"Is this where Colby Chase works? And that Ray Jordy?"

"Yep. Repair, storage, and stuff like that."

Tom squinted as he stared again at the height of the hoist. "Huh. It seems like business is good, but I'm glad it's quiet on Sunday."

As they approached the center where Main Street met the harbor, Tom felt like someone was following them. Each time he turned, he only noticed innocent-looking tourists or townies strolling along the walk, some with ice cream cones and others pointing out at different boats in the harbor. He felt foolish for being paranoid until he noticed someone in a denim shirt, baseball cap, and dark beard peering at them from the corner of a building. Tom pulled Paul to the other side of the harbor master's small shack and waited.

"What is it, now?" queried Paul.

Seconds later, Tom stepped out from the back of the building and was face to face with the man with the beard. "Ray Jordy?"

Ray narrowed his eyes. "Who are you?"

"I'm Father Tom. I believe you were close to the Chase family. I am sorry for your loss."

Ray ran his hand across his beard, let out a long breath, and stomped off without a response.

"What was that about?" asked Paul.

"He was following us along the harbor for some reason. I don't know why, but he seemed nervous or something." Tom watched as Ray quickly distanced himself, hopped into his truck, and drove off.

"Why are you still staring at him?"

Tom watched as the truck reached the top of the hill and then turned out of sight. "What color truck did Ben Hatch say was heading to the school just after Joline left his farm?"

"Yellow."

"And what color truck did the maintenance guy, Ed, say left the school parking area just after Joline and Mr. McC headed off?"

"Yellow."

"And what color truck does Ray drive?"

"Let me guess. Yellow?"

Tom scratched his head. "How many yellow trucks are in town?"

"I never thought about it before, but that's the only one I can think of," replied Paul.

Paul jumped as a voice behind them gruffed, "What are you two thinking about now?"

The sheriff, J.C., was standing with his arms crossed and lips pressed tight.

Tom said, "We were just talking about how fresh that lobster roll was that we just had at Young's. I'm sure Father Paul would have treated you too, Sheriff, if you were around."

J.C. let out a long sigh. "I don't know how they do things in Boston, but I need you two to stick to church stuff. Do you understand?"

"Understood," replied Paul.

J.C. shook his head. "I don't know if you do. Every place I've been this morning, I find out you two have already been there asking questions. By the time I get there, they seem like they don't want to go through everything again."

"We—"

"Ed at the high school even said, 'Why don't you ask Father Tom?'"

Tom smiled. "I'd be happy to answer any questions."

J.C. raised his hand. "Please, just go back to the rectory and work on your sermons or something."

Tom lowered his head. "I do understand. So you know that the girls were at Traci's that morning?"

J.C. nodded.

"And Joline went to the high school to see Mr. McCready for some reason."

J.C. nodded again.

"And Joline and the girls had a run-in with the Norsemen bikers?"

J.C. raised his head and peered into the blue sky until Tom said, "And a yellow truck was seen following her tracks that evening?"

He lowered his head and stared at Tom. "Are you sayin' that Ray Jordy was following Joline around that night?"

Tom shrugged. "I don't know. He argued with Joline at Traci's in the morning, and despite having some type of falling out with Colby, he was at Joline's graduation, at the Chases' party, and I found him following us today. Like I said, I don't know, but something seems up with him."

"Okay. Okay. I will check that out. Now you are done, Father Brown," said J.C. in a gruff voice.

"Yep—oh, and Joline met somebody at Traci's around midnight on the night she died."

J.C.'s eyes widened, signaling that this was new information for him. "Are you done now?"

"For now," replied Tom.

"Not for 'now' but for good. Please," mumbled J.C. as he headed back up the Main Street incline to the small station.

Paul chuckled. "I hope you had an easier time working with the police back in Boston!"

Tom shook his head. "Nope."

They climbed the hill as cars filled the parking spots and people were out shopping or grabbing lunch. Paul led Tom down a small side street and stepped into an old bookshop called Bella Books. "I think I need a cup of coffee and a cookie." He smiled.

Tom held the creaky wooden screen door open as he peered inside the quaint shop of books and antiques. "Coffee?"

"Yeah, yeah. In the back, they have a great little café called the Free Verse Café."

Tom said hello to the older man at the book counter, who sported wire-rimmed reading glasses and a friendly smile. "I hope you're having a good day, gentlemen."

Paul pointed to the café and said, "Gary, is the café open?"

"If you're thirsty or hungry, it's open," said the owner with a smile. "Kim's not here, but Megan's working the counter."

A panicked expression came over Paul's face. "Does she have any of her orange-molasses cookies left?"

Gary shrugged, and Paul quickly hurried into the tiny café.

Tom spied several large cookies behind the glass case, hoping Paul was in luck. He stared at the chalkboard before noticing Megan Connors was working behind the counter.

She smiled. "How can I help you, gentlemen—ah, Fathers?"

Tom laughed. "We do try to be gentlemen but fail way too often. I think Father Paul here is salivating over the sight of those cookies, and we'll have two of your best coffees to go." He smiled. "Have you worked here long?"

Her eyes widened, and her cheeks turned pink as she shook her head. "Oh, no. This is my first day, and you're my first customer, so I have no clue what I'm doing."

As Megan poured the hot coffee into the large paper cups, Tom asked, "Sorry to ask about a tough subject, but you said you were at breakfast with Joline on Friday morning." He noticed that she had filled the cup up to and over the brim. Tom pointed, "Ah—"

Megan quickly caught herself and stepped back as the excess coffee ran down the side of the counter. "Sorry." As she wiped the spilled coffee, she composed herself. "Yes. It was the four of us."

"And you sat in a booth in the back area?"

"Oh, we did end up there, but we started at the counter. That creepy guy, Ralph, was eyeing each one of us. I know it's not nice to say, but he makes my skin crawl."

Tom placed a cover on the coffee she handed him. "Did he talk to you?"

Her shoulders tightened. "Who could stop him? We tried to ignore him, but he put his hands on the counter and leaned forward, staring mainly at Joline, almost like he thought she would kiss him or something." She shook at the very words. "That look in his eyes when he smiles scared me, but Joline just stared back at him and grinned."

"Was that it?"

"Almost. I don't know what he said, but he whispered something to her, and that's when Joline tipped her coffee onto his hand. I don't think he was very happy, calling her the B-word, and then we moved to a booth. Joline acted as if nothing had happened, but it freaked me out for the rest of breakfast." Megan wrapped up two of the cookies Paul was eyeing.

Tom handed her a twenty, and as she made the change, he asked, "Did she talk with anyone else?"

Megan pursed her lips. "Oh, that Mr. Jordy guy. Yeah. She went outside to talk with him, but I could tell they were arguing more than talking. She didn't mention it when she came back, and we were on to other stuff. I could tell it bothered her, though."

Megan handed him the change, and Tom placed a five-dollar bill into the tip jar. "Thanks, and good luck with your job. You're doing great."

She blushed and smiled as Tom and Paul wound through the stacks of books and out into the sunshine and the ocean air. A handful of steps later, Paul pulled out one of the large cookies, split it, and handed Tom a half. One bite, and he understood Paul's anticipation for that orange-molasses flavor.

They took it easy that afternoon, reading or chatting on the porch until it was time to make a salad and cook some trout from the Co-op. A bottle of wine, their dinner, and two comfortable chairs on the porch made for a great summer evening until the sheriff's cruiser pulled up along the curb.

J.C. pushed his sunglasses down the bridge of his nose and tipped his head. "It must be nice to have time for a quiet dinner. What do they call that—al fresco?"

Paul jumped up. "J.C. Come on up. We've got plenty of fish for the man who protects our community."

Tom stepped off the porch and approached the open window of the cruiser. "It's bachelor style, but the fish is fresh."

J.C. peered up into Tom's eyes. "I value my life too much to take that kind of risk."

"Have you talked with Ralph Cutter at the diner? He had a bit of a run-in with Joline on Friday morning."

Shaking his head, J.C. sighed. "Thanks for the tip, but I thought we had an understanding about your retirement from amateur detective work?"

Tom's face felt flushed.

"I wanted to check up on Bill McCready. According to his neighbor, it appears that he took his family on vacation early Saturday morning, but he didn't know where they were staying. He took his dog for an early morning walk and saw McCready packing his truck and boat. The neighbor said McCready seemed too preoccupied to talk, but he did notice a bruise and gash under McCready's left eye."

"Wow. He might have been one of the last people to see her that night."

J.C. didn't respond.

Tom leaned on the open window of the cruiser. "Sheriff, if you want me to stay clear of this case, why are you telling me this?"

Pushing his sunglasses back up to the bridge of his nose, the sheriff put the idling car in drive and started to roll away from the curb, saying, "God only knows."

Chapter 9

After being trounced at a chess game, Paul turned in early. Tom found himself sitting on the porch, watching the moonlight shimmer on the large maple tree in the front yard as a light breeze played with its leaves. He loved breathing in the invigorating air and listening to the crickets of a summer night. Shifting in his chair, he saw the church's front door was slightly ajar. Curious, he walked over and slowly pulled the door open wider; he saw the silhouette of a figure sitting in a pew by the candlelight. The crack of moonlight that streamed in must have startled the person—a woman, who turned quickly toward the open door.

Tom said, "I'm sorry. I didn't mean to interrupt."

The woman stood up. "No, no. I'm sorry. I hope it's okay."

Tom stepped closer. "Laurie?"

She moved into the stream of light, leaving half of her face in the dark. "Father Tom? I didn't mean to bother anyone. I don't even know why I'm here." Her eyes squeezed shut, but she couldn't hold back her tears.

Tom pulled a handkerchief from his pocket and handed it to her as she began to sob. "You can come here anytime."

Laurie dropped back down into the pew. "Before Saturday, I hadn't been in here for two years, and before that, I don't know how long it had been. I couldn't trust it. I couldn't trust Him." She glanced up at the large, shadowy wooden crucifix over the altar. "And now, He let this happen?"

Tom sat next to her and let silence fill the space.

"How could He let this happen?"

Tom glanced up at the figure of Christ on the cross and saw nothing but love. "I felt the same way when I lost the dearest person I have ever known. Her name was Corlie. She was just nineteen, only a year older than Joline, and she was everything to me. I felt angry at God but angrier at myself."

Laurie turned toward him. "Why?"

"Why was I angrier at myself?"

She nodded.

"I could have loved her more. I should have saved her, been less selfish, held her more, not had that fight, listened, been a better person—you name it. Someone so loving, so beautiful, and so wonderful was dead because of me, and God didn't stop it."

Laurie reached over with a tissue for the tear on his cheek. "Here. I'm so sorry to hear that. It sounds as if the pain never leaves."

Tom gazed upward toward the darkness of the arched ceiling that was dimly lit. "It's less raw. It's bandaged and healed on the outside but never leaves me. I might be hanging onto the pain to hold onto her."

Laurie sighed. "She wasn't older."

Tom furrowed his brow.

"Your friend was not older than Joline. Joline turned nineteen in the spring. The same age Colby and I were when we got married. I held her back from starting school to hold onto her for just a little bit longer. It sounds selfish, but I never wanted to let her go. She was so little, and I was deathly afraid of her leaving me, abandoning me. Isn't that sad?"

"I don't mean to pry, but was she the first person you felt loved you unconditionally?"

Laurie's face tightened, and her breathing shortened as tears streamed again. "I loved her so much. She would gaze right into my eyes as if no one else in the world existed or mattered. How did you know? How did you know that I felt that way?"

"I can see it in your eyes. Your mom probably felt the same way about you."

An uncomfortable silence filled the space as Laurie shifted awkwardly in her seat without responding.

"I'm sorry, Laurie. I hope I didn't say anything to—"

She shook her head. "Ahh, it's, um. I'll never know how my mom felt about me. I found out I was adopted when I was about six, and I couldn't process it. I couldn't understand why she didn't want me, why she's never tried to find me. My adoptive mom and dad told me not to tell the other kids I was adopted so they wouldn't look at me differently. That was the day I started to keep secrets, to believe there was something wrong with me. Like I wasn't good enough. I couldn't talk about it to anyone, so I made believe it wasn't true to keep from—to keep from—"

"From hating yourself?"

Laurie closed her eyes and nodded as she wept. After a few moments, she stood and stepped out of the pew. "I have to go, and please don't tell me that God loves me. He can't."

He listened to hurried taps of Laurie's heels on the tile floor of the church until the door opened and then shut, leaving Tom in the dark with only the flicker of a few lit candles. He knew he hadn't handled the situation well but breaking through dreaded feelings instead of trying to outrun them our entire lives never goes well.

Tom knelt and prayed for Joline's soul, for Laurie and Colby to find the strength and grace to heal, and for the town to find some meaning in this tragedy, if only to think about the priorities of life that often get lost in its busyness.

After some time, he left the church, closing the heavy door and breathing in the summer air before heading back into the rectory to get ready for bed.

But sleep came slowly as he wrestled with the mystery behind Joline's death or murder. Finally, he did drift off, only to sink into a dream.

Tom saw himself closing the heavy church door and locking Laurie inside for safety while she cried to be let out. In the quiet of the night, a loud rumble from bikers' Harleys raced by, and he had to leap backward in an attempt to avoid being run over, but he was struck and knocked over by the biker with the red-white-and-blue bandana who then stopped and peered down at Tom. "Serves you right for not saving that poor girl." Then he revved his engine and was gone. Tom stood up to brush himself off and was suddenly by the docks, where Solly waved him onto the boat that rocked with the waves in the night. He could hardly see the dark water as he hauled up the lobster trap line and then jumped back in panic when he saw Corlie's face break the ocean surface. Suddenly, the blue-green face changed to Joline's. Her eyes popped open—waking Tom, sweating and gasping for air. "Noooooooo!"

In the morning, Paul found Tom having a cup of coffee in the kitchen. "Were you all right last night?"

Tom shrugged. "Sure. Why?"

"It sounded like you had a nightmare or something."

Tom's eyes narrowed as he took a sip of coffee. "I did have a dream that woke me. I hope I didn't keep you up."

Paul poured himself a cup. "No, but it sounds like it kept you up. I got up around five or so and thought I saw you out talking to someone in front of the house. Was that you?"

"It might have been."

"Well, who the heck were you talking to that time of the morning?"

Tom raised his eyebrows but didn't offer a response.

Chapter 10

After morning Mass, Tom ran an errand and returned with their meals and the morning paper. He and Paul sat on the porch, eating breakfast and sharing sections of the newspaper.

"Sox won again last night. I know it's early, but—"

Tom interrupted with a smile. "It's very early. Talk to me at the end of August." He turned the paper over and stared at the front-page headline:

MYSTERIOUS DEATH OF BELFAST GRAD IS STILL UNDER INVESTIGATION

There was a graduation photo of Joline, which conjured up the unsettling image of her in his dream compared with this picture, so full of life and promise. "*Why?*" was the question Laurie kept asking the night before and the question that wouldn't leave his own mind. He reached down, slipped a manila folder out from under the newspaper, and pulled out several sheets of paper, staring intently at each until Paul's voice startled him.

"What are you looking at? Medical Examiner? Where did you get that?"

They were staring at a close-up photo of Joline's face—hair soaked, skin blue-green, and the top part of her partly torn blue plaid blouse opened to show bruising around her neck. The second was a photo of her upper torso, arms by her side on the table, with colored bands on each wrist. The third photo was of the wound in the back of her head, and next to it was the report from the Chief Medical Examiner of Augusta. Tom didn't respond.

"Tom! Tom, is that what I think it is? Did J.C. bring you a copy? Is that who I saw you talking with so early in the morning?"

Tom put the sheets back into the folder. "I didn't mean for you to see that. They aren't officially from the sheriff."

"I don't understand. Who gave them to you?"

Tom ran his hand over his head, staring into Paul's eyes. "I told my guardian angel that we needed to know what happened to Joline. This was the preliminary report, so I can't tell exactly what the cause of death was, but seeing these photos of her certainly makes this whole thing very real."

Paul sat down, shaking his head. "You're not making any sense. I'm starting to get worried about you. I thought you helped solve crimes, not commit them."

"I didn't take them. This folder was inside the paper on the front stoop. I had a conversation with Laurie Chase in the church last night. She was in so much pain that I felt a strong need to help her."

Shaking his head, Paul said, "I understand. I just don't think priests should be committing felonies."

"I didn't take them."

"Sure. Sure. Now, the paperboy delivers autopsy reports for extra cash?" quipped Paul with a pause. "So, what do you think happened to Joline?"

Standing up, Tom leaned against the porch post with his cup of coffee. "I don't know. The strangulation bruises might point to someone she knew and was face to face with, but the wound to the back of her skull might say the killer surprised her, or maybe someone she knew surprised her." Tom gazed out onto the empty street. "Let's see. We have a confrontation directly with one of the Norsemen bikers. We have a teacher she meets at school and then, maybe again, very late at the diner shortly before she dies, who disappears the next morning. We have Ralph at the diner, who would have seen her that night and claims not to have seen the girls that morning, which we know is not the truth. So, what is he hiding? Joline argued with this Ray Jordy that morning, and we know that, for some reason, he's had a falling out with Colby." He held up his index finger. "Why then would Jordy have his picture taken with Joline at the graduation and abruptly walk out of Mass on Saturday? It's a lot to sift through, and why would anyone want to kill a girl like Joline?"

Paul stood up and locked his gaze on Tom. "It's a good thing Belfast has a sheriff to figure that out."

"It is a very good thing," said Tom as he carried his plate and cup into the kitchen and then returned, asking, "Paul, who owns the cinema in town?"

"The Colonial? Therese Bagnardi and Michael Hurley. Why?" Paul scratched his head.

Tom stepped down from the porch and started walking toward town.

Paul quickly caught up to Tom with his half-eaten breakfast sandwich in hand. "Let me come with you."

Tom turned toward Paul with a quizzical expression.

"Just in case you need anyone to bail you out."

Tom laughed, appreciating how Paul always maintained his sense of humor in any situation.

Within minutes, they were standing in front of the art deco marquee over the Colonial Movie Theater that had stood in the heart of the village since 1912. The glass-front doors were locked as they peered into the darkened vintage lobby with its ticket booth and concession stand.

Behind them came a voice. "You boys are a little early for tonight's show."

"Hey, Michael. I was just showing Father Tom around town," said Paul. "Tom, this is Michael Hurley. He and his wife, Therese, bought and renovated the theater, and it's been a great part of the community."

Hurley reached out his hand and shook Tom's. Slightly balding, his hair was gray, as was the goatee he sported. "The sheriff told me to watch out for you."

Tom tilted his head. "It's good to be a topic of conversation already. You should be proud of this beautiful theater. Were you here on Friday night?"

Hurley glanced toward Paul and back to Tom. "You can ask anything you want. The sheriff already questioned me about Friday. I was here early to make sure everyone showed up for work, and things were all set for that night."

Tom nodded. "Did you notice Joline and her friends at the theater that night?"

"Ahh. I saw the Haskell girl with Jenkins and Connors waiting outside. I didn't see them come in, though. They kept talking to the boy at the ticket booth." He pointed to the small booth. "And I had to tell them to let the others in line get their tickets. You know, boys and girls at that age. I think that Lizzie girl likes Nick Campbell, who worked the booth that night. When things were all settled, I left the theater to get a bite to eat at Darby's, next door."

"Nothing unusual that night?"

Hurley rubbed his graying goatee and shook his head. "No, not really. Why are you asking? Don't they think the Chase girl drowned?"

Tom raised his brow. "I don't think they know for sure yet. I was just curious if you noticed anything out of the ordinary. Thanks for talking with me, and I hope to check out your theater one of these nights."

Hurley nodded and started to turn, then faced him again. "I don't think it's anything, but there was one thing."

Tom took a step toward Hurley.

"After dinner, I checked back in on things, probably around 10:30 or so. Nick wasn't at the ticket booth or helping out behind the counter, so I asked one of the girls where he was. She hesitated for quite a while. I don't think she wanted to squeal on her classmate, but she said that Joline entered the lobby halfway through the show and started talking with Nick. Well, she said it seemed like a little more than talking, and then Joline left the theater. Right after that, Nick asked the girl at the counter if she could cover for him for a few minutes. I didn't stay at the theater, so I don't know how long he was gone."

"Huh," said Tom with a nod. "I appreciate it, and it was good meeting you."

"Same here. So, are you heading back home soon, Father?"

Tom glanced at Paul. "I don't know. Belfast is starting to feel a bit like home."

Chapter 11

Tom stood in front of the theater, staring up at the marquee that read *HANGOVER 7 & 9* and *MY SISTER'S KEEPER 8 & 10*. "Part of me wants to support small-town theaters like this, but I don't think I could enjoy it very much right now."

Paul glanced up. "Tom, we don't know what happened, and I think the sheriff was right about letting him do his job."

"I think you have a point, and I don't intend to get in his way." Tom started making his way down High Street.

"Where are you, or should I say where are *we*, going now?"

"You don't have to come, but I just wanted to take another walk along Front Street and the harbor." Tom took a left onto Main Street, which wasn't Boston-busy but bustling with a crowd suited to the small-town shops, restaurants, art galleries, and events that had gradually been added to attract tourists and build a close community.

Paul shook his head. "I want to believe you, but I know you well enough to wonder if this is a ploy to get me to buy you another lobster roll."

"Paul! What kind of friend do you take me for?" He paused. "Monday is more of a fried oysters-and-clams kind of day. Maybe a pile of onion rings to top it off."

"Yeah. Yeah. I know exactly what kind of friend you are."

Tom imagined Joline in different spots as they strolled along the paved pathway of the harbor. Cars were parked overlooking the harbor, and along the way, there was an ice cream shop, the Front Street Pub, and then the shipyard up ahead, where boats sat in various stages of repair. A giant boat hoist in front of the shipyard was ready to lower a two-masted schooner into the harbor waters. Colby Chase, wearing working overalls and his worn baseball hat, was standing by the hoist, instructing the operator.

Tom and Paul watched as Colby signaled the operator by slowly lowering his hand. The ship was gently being lowered beside the pier until it was safely in place. He glanced over and then back to give the thumbs up to the operator before approaching them.

"All due respect, but what are you two doin' here?" asked Colby.

Paul pressed Colby's shoulder. "I was going to ask you why you were here. Don't you want to take some time off? To take care of Laurie and yourself?"

"You'd think. We are down two guys with a ton of catch-up work to do for a lot of rich people anxious to get on the water this summer. I think it's good to stay busy instead of gettin' sucked into things." Colby sighed. "I don't know what you said to Laurie last night, but she was pretty upset when she came back. Look, Father Paul here knows we haven't been goin' to church for some time. God doesn't seem to have us on his radar, and I don't think stirrin' things up is goin' to help things any. You know what I mean?"

Tom knew Colby's last line wasn't intended to be a question. "Mr. Chase, I want to honor you and your family. I just tried to listen, and it seemed as if Mrs. Chase needed someone to talk to."

Colby pursed his lips, then said, "Laurie has no trouble findin' people to fill her needs. Let her be. Let *us* be."

Ray Jordy approached Colby. "We've got another one to launch if you're done chatting."

Colby's jaw worked back and forth, eyes glaring at Ray. "You focus on your job, and I'll take care of mine. I'm ready when you are."

Ray continued staring at him. "If you took care of things, Laurie wouldn't be miserable, and Joline would probably still be al—"

Suddenly, Colby launched himself at Ray. Tom and Paul strained their muscles to pull the two men apart.

Paul shouted. "Colby! Ray! This isn't right. How are you going to solve anything this way?"

Colby threw down his gloves and strode off. "Something we should have solved a long time ago."

Ray stood, shaking his head.

Tom snatched Ray's hat from the ground and dusted it off. "I think this is yours," said Tom, handing him the hat.

Ray rubbed his beard and took the hat. "Thanks."

Tom peered into Ray's eyes. "Someone told me you two were close friends for a long time until recently."

"Well, he was probably a better friend than I, but it don't matter now."

"Laurie showed me a photo of you with Joline at the graduation. I think she still felt like there was an important connection."

Ray shrugged and avoided eye contact.

"I'm sorry, very sorry, for your loss. Someone said you had spoken with Joline that morning outside of Traci's. Was everything okay between her and Colby?"

Ray scowled at Tom. He dusted off his hat some more and trudged away without a word.

Paul leaned closer to Tom. "I don't think you are making many friends in this new profession. Don't worry, though; I'm still hanging in there with you—for a little while longer."

Tom headed farther down the harbor walk, replaying what had just happened. Obviously, a lot of raw emotion existed between Colby and Ray, but he shrugged it off as not being unusual after the death of someone so close to both of them.

Tom stopped by the small boats tied to the docks closer to the walking bridge across the inlet.

An older man, busy scrubbing down his boat, glanced up when Tom's shadow stepped aboard. "Father, if you're searching for work, you'll have to check elsewhere. I'm strictly a one-man operation."

Tom quipped, "You wouldn't be the first to sail that boat."

"Hey, I haven't had a mutiny yet."

"How is the fishing around here, Captain?"

"Mike's the name. Fishing is very good if you know what you're doin'. Striped bass, trout, herring, and mackerel are running. Bluefish and sea bass if you head out a bit."

"Do a lot of guys go out from here?"

"Mostly part-timers on this end. Weekenders and after work. Teachers in the summer. Most just because they love bein' on the water and fishin'." Mike took a seat on the gunwale. "Are you two thinkin' of givin' up fishin' for men, or am I gettin' lured in?"

Tom glanced at Paul. "Who said old fishermen are too salty to be witty? Hey, speaking of teachers, do you know Bill McCready?"

Mike eyed Tom for a moment. "Sure. Sure. Bill's a good guy, and he loves to fish."

"Does he keep his boat down at this end?"

Mike took off his cap and scratched his thinning white hair. "Yep. He's here somewhere." Glancing around, he said, "Huh. It looks as if he's out. Not a great time for fishing right now, though. The tide is out, and he likes to head up the Passy."

"Do you ever go out late at night?"

Mike smiled. "Oh, sure. If the tide's right. This past weekend, I was out at night and had a nice haul."

"Friday night?"

"Oh, sure. Let's see. I had a drink with a few other guys at the Front Street Pub, and we probably headed out between midnight and one."

Tom glanced at the boats tied to the docks. "Sneak up on the fish while they're sleeping, huh? Did you see anything unusual?"

Mike scratched his beard. "You know, I've been thinkin' on that. That's the night Colby's girl drowned. It's sad. Such a pretty girl with a ton of personality. I can't say I saw her or anythin' unusual outside of those bikers rumblin' past on this walkway. It's not meant for motorcycles, but since when do those boys care about anythin'? Other than that, it was pretty quiet. Usually is at that time of night around here."

Tom gazed out. "It must be peaceful on the water. Do you know if Bill McCready was out fishing around then?"

Mike squinted. "You boys seem real interested in Bill. Any particular reason? I didn't see him out there. Um, I do remember his boat wasn't on the docks when I went out, so maybe he did. He loves goin' out late at night when the tide's right."

Mike pointed to a brush on the dock, so Tom squatted down, grabbed it, and handed it to him.

"Well, Captain Mike, it's been a pleasure. Good luck with your fishing. Maybe you could take me out sometime if you aren't—"

"Strictly a one-man operation." Mike laughed. "Maybe a drink sometime, though," he said as he returned to scrubbing his boat.

As Tom and Paul headed back to town, J.C. Coombs was making his way toward them, and he wasn't smiling. As he approached, he grumbled, "Do you know who just called me?"

Tom shrugged. "Publisher's Clearing House?"

"Very funny. Councilman Hurley."

"Huh. We were just talking to Michael. It is a small town," said Paul.

"Yeah, well, that's what he called me about. He said you were askin' him questions about Friday night. Everyone I talk with about the case has already talked to my two Father Browns." J.C. tilted his head at the sky, possibly to make an appeal to God.

"Just being friendly, Sheriff," said Tom.

"Well, I hope that being friendly doesn't include breakin' into the police station."

Tom shook his head. "I can swear that neither Father Paul nor I have made any early-morning break-ins to your office."

J.C. shook his head as he turned to leave. "How do you know it was early morning, and why did someone see the light from the photocopier flashing in the window in the dark? Last time—please, stick to your vocation, and I'll stick to mine."

Chapter 12

As Tom and Paul approached St. Francis of Assisi Church, they could see a woman standing in front of the rectory. Laurie Chase wore a fitted yellow blouse, a red skirt, and black heels emphasizing her tanned legs.

Paul said, "Laurie. I've been thinking about you."

Laurie glanced from him to Tom. "I appreciate that. I mean, I don't know what I should be doing for Joline—for her funeral. I don't know when the medical center will be releasing her." She wiped at welling tears with a handkerchief. "I was wondering if I could talk to Father Tom?"

"Oh, sure. You can use my office."

When Laurie hesitated, Tom interjected, "Or would you like to sit in the church?"

She nodded, and he opened the door for her, then followed her into the quiet space. Sunlight streamed through the stained-glass windows, and the air held the slight scent of burning candles. "I don't know why I'm here or why I wanted to sit in the church. God hasn't been in my life for a very long time."

Tom followed behind her. "I've felt like that at times but realized He's always in our lives; we just don't always want it or see it."

She glanced around, then turned awkwardly to face him. "Well, I don't know. I wanted to apologize for being so emotional last night. I can usually keep it in check. It just seems as if a lot of stuff is comin' up. The focus should be on Joline, but my mind is full of so many things. I feel overwhelmed."

Tom motioned for her to sit in the pew, then genuflected before sitting beside her. "That's perfectly understandable. We often spend our lives running away from uncomfortable feelings, and they can resurface when we are experiencing a loss. I have found that these thoughts and feelings can be clues to things inside us that want to be acknowledged and addressed."

Laurie shook her head. "I can't. It's too much."

Tom turned his eyes to the altar and crucifix.

Within seconds, she followed his gaze and sat still for a moment, absorbing the peace before whispering, "I feel like I've been runnin' for so long."

Tom listened without saying anything. As in other situations when a person has lost a loved one, he made it a point not to judge.

She lowered her head, remaining silent for a moment, then she took a deep breath, sighed, and began in a whisper. "You know, I married Colby to be my rock, to feel safe. But things have always been a struggle, and the last few years have been so hard between us and between me and Joline. It felt like a switch got flipped, and my girl disappeared and rejected me somehow. Each day, I'd wake up hopeful, then she'd give me just one snide comment, and I'd be crushed, then angry. I just wanted to love her, to be close like we used to be. I don't think I helped it any, but I felt powerless. The routine, the predictability, the relationship was suddenly gone." She paused. "I don't know if I'm makin' any sense at all."

Tom nodded. "More than you know. You need to be heard and understood."

Her face tightened, and her breaths shortened as tears streamed. "Understood? All I feel is shame and ugliness. Like trash that no one even bothered to take away." She gazed upward at the high-vaulted ceiling. "I don't know why anyone would want to understand me."

Tom quietly said, "I would. I would like to understand you."

"I was never a good person." Laurie laughed softly. "I remember my father, my adopted father, taking me to Sunday school, and they would always say, 'Jesus loves you,' and I would think that He couldn't love me. He would judge and condemn me, and I thought He'd be right."

"Laurie, I've talked to a lot of people who believe they're broken, not worthy, but something very deep down still hopes they are worthy of love. Despite all the pain and struggle, it keeps them hanging on. It may sound childish or cliché, but Christ *does* love you. He comes to all our hurts, traumas, and pain with tenderness and love. He never comes to shame or reject us, and He was willing to die to save us, to spend forever with us because He knows how whole and beautiful we are made to be."

Laurie stood up, shaking her head. "I'm sorry. That's childish, happy talk. It's not real. If He loved me, He would have come for me long ago. He would have stopped—" She paused and closed her eyes. "He would have been there!" She stepped over Tom's legs and strode out of the church, leaving Tom sitting alone again, praying for guidance.

After more than a half-hour of prayer, Tom found Paul in the kitchen. "What are we cooking up, Chef Paul?"

Paul held up a knife and jar. "I can do peanut butter and blueberry jam sandwiches, or I can do—no, I think that's the menu for today."

"That sounds fine. Gourmet peanut butter always works in a rectory."

While Paul made the sandwiches, Tom cut up a few peaches and opened a new bag of chips.

"Laurie wasn't here very long. How is she faring?"

"She's really struggling. I think there are a lot of layers of past pain and self-rejection in Laurie. She mentioned having a hard time being adopted and feeling rejected by her birth mother, but I sense there was more. Has she ever approached you with her feelings?"

Paul shook his head. "No. Neither Laurie nor Colby comes to Mass. They had Joline receive the sacraments, but that ended a few years back. I haven't had a lot of interaction with either one outside of town events. I'm surprised she came here since my last conversation with her about faith was far from positive."

"Was it about Joline?"

"Yeah. How did you know?"

Tom bit into a peach slice. "It's possible that she believes she's given up on herself in many ways but may have also projected everything onto Joline to save herself. When Joline began pushing Laurie away, she probably reached out to you to help fix or understand it. Was it about two years ago when you spoke to her?"

"That sounds about right. Just after her Confirmation."

"She mentioned that things have been a struggle between her and Colby. Maybe she was disappointed that he had his own issues and weaknesses. I wonder if the friction between Ray Jordy and Colby fits into this? And why was Joline arguing with Ray on Friday morning?"

Paul took a bite of his sandwich and stared at Tom.

"What?"

"You really care, don't you? I've always admired that about you, Tom Fitzpatrick. You sincerely care for people you meet, and they know it. I know it."

"You know, speaking of caring..." Tom smirked and handed Paul a napkin, motioning with his hand to wipe the peanut butter off his right cheek.

Given the few hours of sleep Tom had the night before, he decided to take a late afternoon nap on the couch. The light breeze through the window felt relaxing as he drifted off, while Paul ran a few errands and house calls. After several hours, the sounds of cooking from the kitchen and the tantalizing smell of something he couldn't figure out woke him. Given how good it smelled compared to Paul's usual fare, he figured he must be dreaming.

When he reached the kitchen, Paul glanced up from the kitchen table, raising his glass of wine. "I hired a cook!"

Tom smiled broadly when he saw his old friend, the short, wiry, bald-headed Italian whose rough exterior showed the tough life he had lived in prison until he was finally saved by his cellmate of thirty years. Almost eight years earlier, Angelo Salvato had joined Tom's parish, St. Francis in the South End of Boston, and worked as the parish's all-around handyman. "Angelo! You've come to save my stomach and probably my life."

Angelo stood by the stove, stirring a pot. "I will have to say that Father Paul's kitchen was clean and uncontaminated with any food fit to eat. I had to stock the shelves with some real food."

Tom laughed. "Whatever it is, I'm in. It smells great." He turned. "No offense to Father Paul's peanut butter sandwiches."

"Hey, peanut butter *and* jam," replied Paul as he took another sip of merlot.

"Tonight, some lamb ragu on linguine, freshly baked bread, and a summer salad to start you men off. If you clean your plates, I might part with some of that tiramisu cooling in the fridge."

Tom broke off a piece of baguette, dipped it into the sauce, and joked. "That is good. I had my doubts about making it through the week on this bachelor's menu."

At dinner, the three bantered back and forth and talked about everything going on in their lives in Boston and Belfast. Tom and Paul shared stories of life in the seminary, and Angelo answered Paul's questions about what life in a maximum-security prison was really like. By the time they had polished off their dessert, they all leaned back in their chairs, smiled, and groaned.

Tom said, "You see? That is what food tastes like."

Paul laughed. "That was really, really good, Angelo. Would you ever consider switching parishes? There is plenty of handyman work and cooking to keep you busy."

Angelo smiled, rubbing his hand across his large nose. "I don't think you could match the pay."

Tom waved his finger. "He won't take a penny and insists on living in a converted shed next to the rectory."

Paul narrowed his eyes and steepled his fingers across his lips, deep in thought. "You're right. I don't think I could outbid you." Everyone chuckled. "Wait a minute. Was that Angelo I saw you talking to in the dark shadows early this morning?"

Tom's eyes shifted toward Angelo and back. "I think you were dreaming, Father Paul."

"You were the one dreaming." He turned. "Angelo, don't tell me this so-called servant of the Church talked you into robbing the sheriff's office? This is not good."

"Hey, I didn't take a thing, and nothing was moved," quipped Angelo.

"You didn't take anything except a few pictures of federal property. This is not good," replied Paul, shifting in his seat.

Tom glanced at Angelo.

Paul raised his brow. "There's more?"

Tom nodded to Angelo.

Angelo replied, "Okay, I haven't had a lot of time, but we have a few things that may help. The autopsy report confirms that Joline died before being placed in the water, but it doesn't pinpoint the actual cause of death. Since her body was floating a quarter-mile off the harbor area, my guess is that someone with a boat took her out that far, or she may have been tossed into the river and carried out by the outgoing tide, which has been running pretty strong."

Tom said, "That makes a lot of sense. You said that you found some things that might help."

Angelo nodded. "A few things, so far. I found some dried blood on the footing of one of those large boat hoists down near the harbor."

"Angelo, that could be huge. We've got to get that information to the sheriff before anyone washes that off by mistake."

Paul said, "Or on purpose."

Angelo gathered the nearly empty dishes and carried them to the sink. "I took care of that. I scraped a small sample into an envelope and left an anonymous tip at the sheriff's office as to where they could find the possible evidence."

Tom asked, "You went back to the scene of the 'non-crime?'"

Angelo nodded. "I kind of miss being at the police station. Don't worry; they thought I was a lost visitor looking for a good fishing spot. Oh, speaking of fishing, I found out where Bill McCready and his family are spending their vacation. The cottage owner said it was a last-minute request, and they would be there for at least a week. I guess McCready likes to go there to do some lake fishing and stays at this same cottage. The owner was working on the roof, so he hadn't planned on renting it out during June. McCready said he didn't mind renting while the work was being done."

Tom stood up. "Angelo, that's great stuff! How far is it from here?"

"He's on Swan Lake in Swanville. It's maybe ten or so miles from here."

Tom's eyebrows lifted. "Paul, you don't mind if Angelo and I take a little trip, do you?"

"Don't you think you should just give this information to J.C.?"

"We will, once we know there's something worthwhile to give him."

Chapter 13

Tom opened the door to his old Honda hatchback. It was a slightly different color blue than the rest of the car, which was held together mainly with duct tape and constant prayers, but it still ran. They buckled up and rattled across the Passy River on Route 1 and then followed a fairly straight shot up the windy Route 141 to Swanville, where they parked at the landing for Swan Lake, with a few more hours of daylight.

"This is beautiful," remarked Tom. "Now, what do we do?"

Angelo pointed to the boats for hire—small fishing boats, each with oars and a small motor to get around the good-sized lake. No one was there to rent the boats, which were locked with heavy cable wire. Angelo reached down and picked the lock open.

"Angelo, we can't do this!"

Angelo glanced up at him. "We can leave them the rental fee and take good care of the boat. Unless you don't want to see McCready?" Without waiting for a reply, he separated a boat from the others and relocked the padlock.

Tom stepped onto the rocky boat. "One of these days, you know you're going to get us arrested, and you're still on parole, in case you forgot."

Angelo pushed the boat away from the slip and started the small outboard engine. The low puttering broke the peaceful silence of the lake as they passed several cottages, some with docks for swimming and boating and others just with chairs to sit and enjoy the view.

Finally, Angelo pointed ahead. "That's it. I remember the yellow siding and the flagpole from the online photo."

"I'm impressed that an old-timer like you uses the latest tools."

Angelo slowly guided the boat to the empty dock. No other boat was there, so Tom assumed McCready was likely out fishing. As they pulled closer, a woman in her early thirties stepped out onto the dock with two small children by her side. "Are you gentlemen lost?"

"No. Well, maybe," replied Tom. "Is this your home? It's a great spot."

She glanced back at the house. "We like it, but we rent. We actually hadn't planned on coming this week, but my husband got a sudden urge to drop everything and come. He's a teacher. I think the first day of summer got him antsy, although he does a lot of fishing at home. We're only in Belfast."

Tom gazed out at the calm waters of the lake. "It is a pretty spot. I'm surprised you don't have to give more notice to get a place like this."

"You would think, but Bill knows the owner, so we lucked out. One quick phone call early in the morning, and we roused these little ones out of bed. Bill already had the boat ready to go. He seemed so wound up; I think some time to relax will do him good." She glanced up. "Speaking of the devil, there's the man now."

His eyes wide when he glanced at them, McCready maneuvered his boat alongside the dock so that his son, who must have been around seven, could hop out first.

"Did you two have any luck?" Tom asked.

The boy sported a huge smile, pulled out three decent-sized trout, and struggled to hold them up as high as he could. "I'll say! Look at these!"

His mother clapped while Bill half-laughed while eyeing Tom and Angelo.

Bill stepped out of the boat and tied it to the dock before turning toward his visitors. "To what do we owe the pleasure?"

Tom held out his hand in greeting. "I'm Father Tom, and this is Angelo. We were just looking to do some fishing and stopped to get our bearings. That's some catch you and your boy have for dinner tonight."

Bill glanced at his wife. "Anne, why don't you take the kids up to the house? I'll be up in a minute to clean those up." He patted his son on the back. "Really nice job, son. Those look like tasty ones to me. Head up to the house with your mom."

As Anne climbed the incline with the three kids in tow, Bill turned back to his guests. "If you boys are looking to catch any fish, I think you should start with some rods and bait. It usually works better than talking them onto the boat."

Realizing there were no fishing rods on the boat, Tom's face turned a deep shade of red. "We appreciate the advice. We were actually just getting the lay of the lake tonight. I would love to come back out to do some actual fishing, though."

Bill rubbed his chin. He was probably close to forty, solid build, slightly thinning, dark hair, sporting a pair of horn-rimmed glasses held together with tape, off-kilter, with a recent gash and bruise under his right eye. "There should be enough fish left to give you boys a good day out. You might want to get that rental back since Rick doesn't usually rent out after six."

Tom noticed the large printed letters on the side of the boat that read, RICK'S BOAT RENTALS SWAN LAKE. "Good idea, Mr. McCready."

Bill's head snapped as he stared at Tom. "Wait. What's going on here? How do you know my name?"

Tom replied, "You teach at the high school, right?"

"Yeah, and...?"

"I was curious if you heard about that girl, Joline Chase?"

His eyes narrowed, glancing back and forth between Tom and Angelo. "What about Joline? What's this about?"

"I apologize, Mr. McCready. Her death was so tragic, and you must have known her from school."

Bill shook his head. "What are you talking about? Is this some sick kind of joke? Who are you two, and why are you here spying on my family and making up stories?" He grabbed a fishing gaff from the boat and shook it at them. "Get back in that boat and stay clear of my family! I mean it. I don't want you talking with them."

Bill's wife and son stood at the screened doorway of the cottage. The kitchen light was on as the sunlight started to wane. Tom held out his hand. "We are so sorry to bother you. I thought you would be aware of the sad news."

As Bill clenched the gaff tighter, Tom and Angelo stepped into their boat and headed back to the town landing where they had "borrowed" their craft.

On the car ride back to Belfast, Tom said, "And what did we learn tonight?"

Angelo paused. "Don't go fishing without any fishing gear?"

"Yes, I got that one, loud and clear."

"Don't bother a history teacher on his first day of vacation?"

Tom turned down Route 1 and shook his head. "What did we learn that could help solve this case?"

"That Bill McCready didn't know Joline Chase was dead, or he's a very good actor. And that was a failed attempt to obtain some useful information."

They pulled into town and down the street to St. Francis, where Tom parked in front of the rectory and sat. "Something doesn't add up. McCready is seen hanging around with Joline twice that night and may have been the last one to see her alive if that was him at the diner around midnight. Captain Mike thinks he may have been out with the boat late that night, and by very early morning, McCready has a sudden need to get out of town, his boat ready, pulled out of the water, and his bags packed. You'd think he would have, at least, heard the news. I don't know if I buy it, especially with that gash under his eye."

Angelo glanced at Tom. "Whatever happened to trusting your fellow man?"

"I met a man who carries around a lock pick set for 'just in case,'" replied Tom with a smirk.

Chapter 14

Tom and Angelo sat with Paul on the porch as the sound of peepers filled the summer night, and the radio played the Red Sox game in the background. They talked about their shortened visit to Swan Lake, the argument between Colby and Ray, the odd behavior of Ralph at the diner, and the distinct possibility that there were suspects they didn't even know about yet.

Angelo smiled as he watched a pair of rabbits race across the grass in front of the porch. "We don't really know a lot about the girl, do we?"

"Not enough to know who might have posed a risk to her. Her mom is broken up, but her dad seems more angry than anything, although it's not fair to judge from the outside how a parent should react."

The street was quiet when the police cruiser pulled up slowly in front of the curb. Tom expected Sheriff Coombs to come to the porch, but instead, he sat in his cruiser, leaving the car running as if trying to decide if he truly wanted to stop.

Tom approached the curb, and J.C. rolled down the window.

"Nice evening, Sheriff, but I'm guessing you didn't drop by to talk about the weather."

J.C. stared down into the half-filled paper cup of coffee in his right hand, hesitating. "Nope. This is one of those nights when I wish I was a cop in a big city where I didn't know anyone." J.C. held up his hand as Angelo and Paul approached, and they backed off.

Tom leaned forward on the cruiser door. "Look, I know you want us to stay in our lane and out of the case, but we saw Bill—"

J.C. nodded. "I know you saw McCready. He called me and was a bit ticked off about that but more shaken to hear about Joline's death." He took a deep breath. "I don't know why I'm sharin' this, other than it is the only way to get you to stop playing detective. This goes nowhere, but there was evidence of semen found in Joline's autopsy report, and it matches a used condom found near where Angelo found that bloodstain."

Tom started to interrupt.

"Yes, I know your mate brought in the sample. Thank him because it matched Joline's."

"Okay. Do you have a match for the semen?"

J.C. nodded.

"Is he a suspect?"

"Yep. He was seen with her that night and was seen with a pretty good shiner the day after, so we'll be pickin' him up for questionin' in the mornin'. I'm hopin' you and your sidekick, Watson there, are thinkin' about headin' back to Boston soon since we may be close to an answer."

Tom rubbed his chin as he thought about the revelations J.C. had just shared. "I hope you are close, and the Chases can find some peace."

J.C. put the car in gear and glanced up at Tom. "Please don't share any of this with the Chases. I'd like to avoid gettin' ahead of ourselves or any vigilante response before we know what's what. And I need you and your partner to stand down. Understand?"

"I do," Tom replied firmly.

"I hope you do, and *please* stay in tonight."

As the sheriff drove off, Tom stepped back on the porch and could tell that Angelo and Paul were anxiously awaiting an update. "I think they have a suspect, but the sheriff didn't let on who it might be. I guess we'll find out more tomorrow."

Their shoulders quickly dropped.

The news made Tom antsy. "I think I'll take advantage of the evening and go for a stroll. Anyone interested?"

Paul decided to catch up on some work, but Angelo nodded and joined him. They walked neighborhood streets in the quiet of the night as the lights inside the houses they passed gave a fleeting glimpse of families sharing dinner, kids running from one room to another, and some couples chatting on their porches.

"You care about this girl, don't you?" asked Angelo.

Tom nodded. "I know that I'm still feeling responsible for Corlie after all these years, but I don't think that Joline or her parents can rest until the truth comes out. I hope the sheriff is on the right path, but I feel unsettled. Like you said, we don't really know much about Joline. That doesn't make her any less real or her death less tragic."

They turned down another street and were approached by the large woman Tom had met in line at Traci's for breakfast. She was walking a small Jack Russell terrier who jumped up to greet Tom enthusiastically.

"Rascal!" scolded the woman. "I'm so sorry, Father."

Tom smiled as he squatted down to rub Rascal's bobbing head. "I love a friendly greeting. It is good to see you again, Mrs.—"

"Anderson. You can call me Ginny. Father, I just can't stop thinkin' about that Chase girl. I'm scared walkin' Rascal here. I won't feel safe until they know what happened. I can't imagine the stress on Laurie and Colby."

Tom stood up. "I understand how you can feel unsafe. Oh, Ginny, this is my friend, Angelo."

Angelo greeted her and leaned over to pat Rascal. "Are you living up to your name, boy?"

Ginny sighed. "Father, I'm a bit worried about the Chases. I've gone by the house with Rascal several times and have heard pretty loud arguing going on. Just now, I saw Colby slam the door and storm down the street. It's sad to see after what's happened and all."

"You're a good neighbor, Ginny. I'll try to see if I can help."

Ginny smiled and tugged on Rascal's collar. "Come, now. It's time to be gettin' on home, Mr. Raz." She labored off into the night as Tom and Angelo passed by the Chases' house to see if there were any signs of life. With the front door open, they could see Laurie Chase in the kitchen through the screen door.

Glancing over at Tom, Angelo smirked. "You know you want to see how she is. This might be a good time to talk without her husband around."

"I don't know, Angelo, but she may feel we are intruding, especially after a heated exchange."

Angelo looked at Tom without a word.

Tom sighed. "Okay. Okay."

Tom tapped softly on the screen door and then more firmly until Laurie peeked out from the kitchen with a dishrag in hand, squinting.

"It's Father Tom, Laurie. I was just passing by and wanted to see how you were doing."

Laurie wiped her hands and approached the door cautiously before opening it. "It is you. Come in. Come in."

"Mrs. Chase, this is my friend, Angelo. He came up from Boston to visit, and we were just out for a summer night walk. I hope we aren't interrupting anything."

Her lips pursed for a second, and she shook her head. "No. It's just been another emotional day, but—" She paused and motioned them into the living room. "It's okay. Can I get you something to drink? Iced tea or lemonade?"

"No. No. We won't stay long." Tom glanced around. "You have a beautiful home."

Laurie squeezed her eyes tight, but the tears still made their way through. "I'm sorry. I just—"

Tom handed her a handkerchief. "Please don't apologize."

Laurie lifted her head and gazed around at all the photos of Joline, the family, and her wedding. "I never thought I would have a home, a family. I didn't deserve it, but what's a home when there is nothin' left of your family? I'm in there cleanin' the counters, but what's the point?"

Angelo stepped toward the mantle and stared at the photo of Laurie and Colby on their wedding day. "It is a beautiful photo. You look very happy, Mrs. Chase. Both of you do." Angelo reached out to hold the framed photo. "May I?"

Laurie nodded, holding the wet handkerchief against her cheek.

Angelo said, "I never really had a family. No one to love me or to love back. It made me bitter and hard, and I turned to a very bad and dark life. It took a long time to let some light into all that pain. My hope for you is that all the pain you feel right now will ease to let the memories and love stay in the picture." He peered up into Laurie's eyes with a sincere kindness. Next to the wedding picture was a photo of the three of them when Joline must have been about six years of age. Tom smiled, comparing her early grade-school grin with two missing front teeth and sparkling eyes to her more serious senior-smiling photo next to it. While Joline was stunningly beautiful, the makeup and sophisticated expression on her face didn't seem genuine, nor was her smile as authentic and joy-filled as her younger image. Tom thought about her childhood journey and wondered how she lost her joyful self and grew such an artificial pose. How different had Laurie's journey been up to her wedding day when she was the same age her daughter would be today?

A small painting hung on the wall to the right of the mantel, catching Tom's attention.

Laurie noticed. "She had a talent for art. Maybe a love-hate relationship with expressing things inside."

Tom stepped closer to the watercolor of a girl sitting on the edge of a cliff. The sky was an intense blue, and the flowers on the ground were stunning, but a cloud in the shape of a dark figure hovered above. The girl looked as if she could soar into the sky with her wings, but she was sadly curled into herself, holding her head against her knees and missing the beauty and potential of the moment. "I have to say that this is quite good."

Taking a step forward, Laurie sadly gazed upon the painting for a short time. "I think so. The walls of her room are covered with her drawings and paintings."

"I'd love to see them sometime," replied Tom.

"Well, you're here now." Laurie motioned Tom and Angelo up the stairs and down the hall to Joline's room. She took a breath before slowly pushing the door open. The walls were indeed covered with pencil drawings and paintings, primitive to more sophisticated.

"Oh, my gosh. This is wonderful." A bed was neatly made in the corner beside a window, a large slanted desk with pencils and a jar of brushes, and an old curl-up style upholstered chair with a stack of books next to it. On the wall over the desk was an elaborate doodle design with a distinctively drawn J at the bottom and a painting of a simple flag with four colors and four connected rings.

Tom and Angelo, respectively, moved around the room. Marveling at the extent of her artistic talent, it certainly seemed that Joline found art as a way to express what she felt and thought. Her earlier drawings of wonky houses, lollipop trees, and her family of three made Tom smile with their sweetness and innocence. As her art became more sophisticated, Tom noticed a change in her pictures, colors, and mood. One dark painting was of a man with his face blurred; his back turned next to a woman and a girl standing in the distance. The joy in the early work seemed to have gone.

Stepping outside the room with Laurie, Tom said, "Thank you for sharing that. I know it's personal. Paintings are like a visual letter. She was quite a beautiful young person in so many ways."

"I can't believe she's gone," whispered Laurie with deep sadness in her voice.

"She may be in a different place, looking forward to seeing you again, but she is still loving you."

"I wish I could believe that. I really do. But I'm afraid my hope for love and happy endings didn't start very well and has left me for good."

Out on the front stoop, Tom and Angelo paused to say goodbye. "Mrs. Chase, I will keep praying for all of you, and please know that I'm available to talk anytime," said Tom.

Inside the screen door, Laurie stood with arms folded as she nodded. "Please call me Laurie."

Tom smiled. "Of course. Laurie, did Joline have any boyfriends?"

She shook her head. "Not really. Lots of boys liked her. She did go to prom with Rudy Jenkins, and I know that he thought of himself as her boyfriend, but I don't think she saw it goin' anywhere. Why do you ask?"

"Just curious. Please take good care of yourself. I think the sheriff will have answers soon."

Laurie sighed. "I hope so. Colby has been pretty frustrated at the lack of progress. He's been ready to fly off the handle at the drop of a pin. I don't know what he might do these days."

Paul was still at work on his homily when Tom and Angelo reached the rectory, so they sat on the porch watching the fireflies dancing and flickering in the twilight. The tiny lights had fascinated Tom from childhood as his eyes widened with each series of flashes. "Did you know that certain female fireflies are nicknamed 'femme fatales' because they lure unsuspecting males of other species to their deaths? They mimic the flash patterns of other firefly species to draw the unsuspecting males in closer, then bam; he's the entree for her dinner."

"Did you know Joline had several paintings of fireflies with human features on her walls? A sad irony."

Tom tilted his head as he turned to Angelo. "Angelo, you look like one of those teenagers staring at your phone. What has you so engrossed in that thing?"

He turned it so Tom could see. "While you were talking with Mrs. Chase in the hall, I stayed in Joline's room to take pictures of her artwork to see if there might be some clues."

"Great idea, but what is this?" inquired Tom as he pointed to the handwritten text on several of the photos. When Angelo hesitated to respond, Tom pressed. "Come on. What are these?"

Angelo leaned toward Tom and replied, "When I scanned the room to see if anything stood out. I noticed something on the wood-paneled wall beside Joline's bed. There was a section of panel that appeared a bit darker, and I wondered if it opened to a small hiding place behind the wall."

"And?"

"It was well concealed but easy to pull the cut piece of panel open, and there was this floral-covered journal inside with a lock as they have on those diaries."

"Angelo, we can't be prying into someone's diary," rebuked Tom, returning the phone to Angelo.

"I know, but we can't ask her for permission either, and a killer may be permanently on the loose if we don't get a better picture of Joline's world."

Tom sighed. "I know. I know. Was the lock open or locked?"

"It was locked when I found it, and it's locked now. I did put it back but quickly took pictures of a few entries. I think we can keep her confidence and maybe offer justice to the family."

Tom stood up and paced the porch to think about the right thing to do. Paul broke the tension when he opened the door and asked if anyone was up for a chess game.

An hour later, during the final game between Tom and Angelo, just as Angelo was ready to move Tom into checkmate, Tom said, "Let's wait until Sheriff Coombs comes back with his findings before we do anything with those notes."

Angelo nodded and tipped over Tom's king as Paul sat with a confused expression on his face.

Chapter 15

Tom wrestled for much of the night, wondering about who J.C. was bringing in and what might be on the pages of Joline's journal that Angelo had photographed. He finally drifted off early in the morning, but the smell of something delicious wafting from the kitchen woke him, clearly indicating that Paul was not the one cooking. Running his hand through his hair, he entered the kitchen to see Paul happily digging into Angelo's breakfast special of soft-cooked eggs simmered in a tomato sauce flavored with garlic, herbs, and red pepper flakes. Angelo pointed Tom to the empty chair as he set down a fresh cup of coffee and his plate of food. "Ah, the famous 'Eggs in Purgatory,'" said Tom as he sat and lifted his coffee to Angelo.

"Whatever it's called, it's good!" said Paul.

Tom laughed. "Paul, even though you set a low bar for comparison, Angelo's cooking always pleases the tastebuds."

Angelo sat. "So, what's on tap for this morning?"

"I know I'm being a nuisance, but I think I'm going to head over to the station to see who the mystery suspect is," replied Tom, sipping his coffee.

Paul shook his head. "I don't know, Tom. I really think we've been pushing J.C.'s patience."

"I know. I know. I just feel so unsettled about this." Tom glanced up at Angelo and then Paul. "No one will even know I'm there. I'm guessing he'll bring the suspect in around nine a.m., so I should get going."

As Tom approached the station, a car pulled alongside the curb, followed by J.C. in his patrol car. Out stepped a man and woman in their late thirties to early forties and then a young man from the back seat. The boy seemed familiar, but Tom couldn't place his face. As he got closer, he spotted a bit of yellow and blue discoloring under his eye, and then it hit him. He was in one of the photos of Joline's graduation. The couple must be his parents.

The woman glanced down the street and spotted Tom approaching them. "Father…"

Tom nodded. "Father Tom. Is everything okay?"

Shaking her head, she let out a deep sigh. "I don't know what's happening. You were with Father O'Connell at the Mass the other night for Joline, right? Oh, I'm Kate Campbell. Nick's mom. Can you—"

Tilting his head, Tom said, "Anything, Mrs. Campbell. What do you need?"

Her eyes rolled upward to stop the tears that began to flow. "Can you please, please, say a prayer for my son? I really don't know what is happening."

"Kate!" called out her husband, waving as he walked with Nick toward the station door.

She turned quickly toward Tom. "Thank you."

J.C. motioned to Kate to follow her son as he glared at Tom before disappearing into the station, presumably to question Nick Campbell.

Sitting on the front steps of the station, Tom tried to imagine a scenario where Nick might be responsible for Joline's death. *Let's see, he worked the ticket booth that night at the movie theater but disappeared without explanation after Joline left the movie. That was probably around ten o'clock or so. One of the theater owners—what was his name?* Tom shook his head a few times before it came to him—*Hurley. Michael Hurley said he didn't know when or if Nick ever returned to work that night. Also, Nick had a bruise under his eye that was healing. I thought one of the girls said he was dating Lizzie, but Laurie Chase certainly made a point of saying how handsome he was. Huh. Did they have a fight? Was there an accident?*

Tom glanced up and spotted someone marching toward the station—a tall, athletic-looking young man with broad shoulders who appeared enraged as he approached the front door. Tom stood in the way to slow down his stride. "Are you okay?" He recognized the face, but it took him a second to remember from where. "It's Rudy, right? From Traci's."

There were beads of sweat coming from Rudy's brow, and his dark, wavy hair didn't look as if it had been combed that morning. He tried to edge around Tom as his eyes were clearly fixed on the police station door. "I need to get in there."

Tom placed his hand on Rudy's shoulder. "Okay. I'm pretty sure the sheriff is busy at the moment."

Eyes glaring, Rudy turned his shoulder to escape Tom's hand. "He better be! I can't believe it. Why did I let him go?"

Tom raised his hand to calm him down, "Rudy. What happened? Is this about Joline?"

Rudy's eyes squeezed tight as he shook his head. "Who else? She's dead, and someone needs to pay for it." He dodged around Tom and took two long strides toward the door, opened it, then headed inside.

Tom followed him. "Rudy! I wouldn't charge in there."

But Rudy opened the door with the name *Sheriff J.C. Coombs* painted on it and did just that.

Sitting at the table in front of J.C.'s desk were J.C., Nick, and his parents, who all quickly turned to see Rudy sweating, eyes bulging from their sockets. He pointed angrily at Nick. "He was there! He was with her, and now she's dead. He knows what happened!"

J.C. jumped from his chair to get between Rudy and the Campbells. He didn't touch Rudy but held his hands up in front of him. "Jenkins! You don't belong here right now. I need you to calm down and sit outside the office. I promise you that we'll find out what happened to Joline. Now, I need you to leave." He glanced up at Tom. "And you, too."

Rudy leaned to get in Nick's face. "You were with her. I saw you!"

Ignoring Rudy, Nick lifted his chin, glanced at his parents, and then dropped his gaze.

J.C. escorted Rudy and Tom down the hallway and closed the door to his office. "Rudy, look at me. I want to know everything you saw. Everything, but you have to let me do my job."

Rudy raised his head. "Isn't your job to protect people from getting killed?"

"Can you just focus on telling me what you saw?"

He took a deep breath and nodded. "Okay. I walked by the theater sometime around ten or later, and Lizzie Haskell shot out of the main doors, glancing up and down the street. She was crying and said she thought Nick had gone somewhere with Jo. I told her to go back into the theater, and I would find them." Rudy bit his lower lip as he composed himself. "I finally found them, all right. They were arguing, so I had it out with Nick, but Jo started pushing me away. I'm her boyfriend—or was, and she's ordering me to leave."

"What did you do?"

Running his hands through his hair, he replied, "I left. I was so angry that I left, and it's my fault. I should never have left."

J.C. tilted his head to stare Rudy in the eye. "Did you see Nick strike or choke Joline? Did you see him kill her?"

Rudy shook his head, then dropped his gaze, staring at the floor. "No, but that doesn't mean anything. He was still with her and then she was dead. He was hiding in his house for three days. Why was he hiding if he wasn't guilty?"

J.C. sighed. "Let's not get ahead of ourselves. Why don't you go home and calm down and let me figure out what happened?" The sheriff turned toward Tom. "You, too."

Tom accompanied Rudy outside. Rudy remained agitated seemingly lost about which direction to head.

"Rudy, was that everything you remember seeing? Did you see either of them after you left?" asked Tom calmly.

Rudy glared at Tom and strode down the street, leaving Tom with only the additional fragments of Joline's last moments alive.

Chapter 16

On his way home to the rectory, Tom wondered if Nick Campbell was mentioned in Joline's journal. What could have happened to make a situation escalate to the point that someone was killed? The temptation to read the pages of the diary Angelo photographed was getting harder to resist. To ease his inner tension, he decided to take a walk. After a mile, he could feel himself relaxing when a car pulled alongside him, and the passenger side window rolled down.

Tom leaned down to see the driver. "Sheriff."

J.C. motioned for Tom to open the door. "You can sit in my mobile office."

Tom slid onto the black vinyl seat and gazed ahead at the row of trees lining the sidewalks and modest homes. "You weren't with Nick too long."

"Nope. He made his statement, and the parents both said he was home shortly after eleven p.m. They were surprised because he would normally be cleanin' up the theater after the last show, but he went to his room. Joline was seen alive around midnight."

Tom shifted in his seat. "Do you believe his story?"

Pursing his lips, J.C. let out a deep sigh. "I want to, but I don't know. I know he didn't want to admit to havin' sex with Joline while his mom was in the room, and he seemed to be hidin' somethin'. Rudy is right that it's odd he hasn't been out of his house since Friday night. Maybe he was letting that shiner under his eye heal, but you could still see the discoloration, so it must have been a pretty good hit."

"Do you believe his folks are telling the truth?"

"Who knows what you might do for your own kid? Nick Sr. has plans for his son's future college and all. He might be willing to hedge the timin' of things. They're fillin' out their formal statements, and we'll see if anythin' conflicts. I wanted to know if Rudy Jenkins said anythin' else to you outside the station."

Squinting, Tom thought about their brief exchange. "Nothing, really. He's pretty angry with Nick. He seems convinced he's guilty, but I don't know that he actually witnessed anything. He had a good reason to be jealous and angry with both Nick and Joline, so he's running on emotion, and I don't know that you can rule him out, either."

"For murder?"

"Who can you rule out based on witnessed facts?"

Tightening his grip on the steering wheel, J.C. shook his head. "Nobody, so far. I've still got people to talk to."

"Bill McCready?"

J.C. glared at Tom. "People. Let's leave it at that."

Tom reached the rectory but hesitated to go inside. *Why can't I just let this go?* he thought. *If Nick was responsible, he certainly isn't going to offer any details about why he was with Joline, why they were arguing, and if he killed her. I guess Rudy could have acted out in a moment of passion but, in some twisted way, blames Nick for his actions. I don't know.*

"Are you talking to yourself or God, Father? You never know with a priest."

Tom spun around. "Angelo. I didn't hear you. You know, you would make a great—"

"Yeah, I know. Very funny. What are you trying to figure out?"

Tom described his trip to the police station and conversations with Rudy and the sheriff. "Tragic as this is, maybe the answer is not that complicated. Maybe the sheriff is right, and we should stop trying to figure this one out. You know?"

Nodding, Angelo smiled. "Sure. You've always been good about turning that inquisitive brain of yours off when you care about people. No problem."

Tom glanced down and noticed sheets of paper in Angelo's hand. "That's not what I think it is, is it?"

"It is, but I haven't looked at any of them. I just printed them out in case you changed your mind and want to help find some justice for that girl."

Tom sighed. "I did say to wait on it to see what happened today. I'm as curious as you, but I'm struggling between Joline's privacy and doing the right thing by her. I don't know." He sighed. "Are some of those the photos of the drawings and paintings in Joline's room?"

Angelo nodded.

"I think it would be okay to look at those since Laurie Chase showed them to us."

They sat on the wicker chairs on the porch and spread out the photos but kept the ones of her journal turned over. There were several minutes of silence as they studied the images of her artwork.

Finally, Tom pushed one of the photos closer to Angelo. "What do you think of this painting? Compared to the others, it seems she spent a lot of time on it."

Angelo nodded. "Yeah. Notice the beautiful girl at the center, but below her are all these men gazing up at her. My guess is that she's smiling because she has their attention and is up on a pedestal."

"Look closer. I don't know if it's a genuine smile. Her eyes look vacant, maybe from fear. See the dark all around her. I think it creates an optical illusion; the longer you look, you can see she's actually in a dark pit, and the men are staring down at her as their prey."

"Huh, okay, I can see that if I stare long enough, but how do you know which one is what she intended?" asked Angelo.

"Good question. Maybe that's the point. She was torn between feeling or experiencing both. Joline was a stunning girl, so she probably had a lot of men staring at her, even if just to appreciate her beauty. How could she know what they were thinking?" Tom pointed to another painting. "See this one. The girl is dressed like a princess, her face is radiant, and her eyes are closed as if she's waiting for a kiss to wake her."

"How do you know that?"

Tom pointed. "I don't, but there is a lot in this picture. The girl is in a tower, and remnants of burned spindles are in the corner. If you know the story of Sleeping Beauty, she was cursed by an evil fairy to die on her sixteenth birthday with a prick of a spindle, so her father, the king, ordered all the spindles burned, but one was left. So, of course, she pricked her finger and fell asleep for a hundred years."

Angelo shook his head. "I thought you said the curse was for her to die?"

"Ah, it was, but a good fairy lessened the curse to a deep sleep for a hundred years for both the girl and everyone in the kingdom. See the fairies in the corners? Joline painted one nasty-looking and the other one kind. So a prince does come along and falls in love, kisses her, and she wakes."

"Okay, so they live happily ever after," said Angelo with half a smirk.

"In the story, they do, but this painting is odd. The girl has one eye open, and the prince at the door doesn't seem to have an expression of genuine love. There is light coming in from behind him, but he is almost all in shadow, hunched over. I don't know what she was trying to say."

Angelo pointed to another piece. "This one is a pencil drawing similar to the Sleeping Beauty painting, but there is no one at the door. She signed this one with a fancy 'J' at the bottom."

Tom nodded. "It's hard to tell which are more recent. I would think that the quality would improve as she continued, like some of these paintings. They're more sophisticated but have similar themes of a beautiful girl catching a man's eye or several men's. In this one, I think she tried to paint that party scene from *Gone with the Wind* when Scarlett had all those beaus surrounding her and trying to win her favor."

"I've never seen it. The girl in this painting has certainly won over all these men, but her face doesn't seem very happy. I wonder, what made Joline happy? You said people were telling you how full of life she was."

Tom nodded. "What's going on inside isn't always what we show the world. I would imagine it's a tough road for young girls today to believe their self-worth comes from so much more than how attractive they are to others. How many men are out to use them as objects instead of women of dignity? I don't know." Tom picked up one of the photos. "Here's another, which she signed with that fancy '*J*.' It's a drawing of an empty room except for an unmade bed. The door and windows are closed, almost like a prison cell."

Angelo sat back in the white wicker chair. "Do you think these are helping at all?"

"Not without more insights." Tom let out another sigh and glanced at Angelo. "I know. I know. Maybe there's something in her journal."

Chapter 17

The dilemma of whether or not to read Joline's journal was put aside when Tom spotted Kate Campbell approaching on the sidewalk with her son. He wondered what Nick's world must feel like right now. His private moments with Joline were now not so private. His girlfriend, Lizzie, probably wasn't talking to him. He was a possible suspect in a murder investigation, and his mother was hauling him to church as if he were a seven-year-old she couldn't control any longer.

Kate stopped in front of the rectory porch. "Father Tom, Nick would like to see you about something, if this is a convenient time for you." She pulled on her son's sleeve for him to take a step forward to face the music, but his head remained down.

Tom stepped off the porch and onto the sidewalk, not saying a word until Nick lifted his head, his eyes tired and red, the remnants of the bruise hung on his left cheekbone. "I'm very open to talking, but it is really up to you, Nick."

"Talking?" interrupted Kate. "He needs to make a confession."

"It's still up to you, Nick."

Nick closed his eyes, nodded, and followed Tom into the church, where they sat together on the wooden pew silently for five minutes before Nick uttered any sound. He breathed deeply and muttered, "Is this an official confession?"

"Only if you are coming of your own free will and want to be forgiven for something you truly regret. Everything you say is confidential, and you must know that we have a merciful God who only wants to love us."

Nick leaned forward and rubbed his forehead with the tips of his fingers, pausing before asking, "Sex is a sin, right?"

"No."

Nick quickly turned his head toward Tom with a furrowed brow, obviously confused. "Then, why am I here?"

"Nick. God created each of us with love and for goodness. He also has a plan and a purpose for our lives. Sex also has a plan and purpose. Even if you didn't believe in God, it's easy to see the biology of attraction and sex are geared toward finding a healthy mate and desiring to be close in every way, including physically. If we are honest, we also know that sex is geared in every way for creating a new life, so it makes sense that God created it for a committed and responsible couple in love—for the sacrament of marriage. God creates the miracle of new life through us, and we are called to care for and love a child just as He loves us. That's a very short version of it, but does that make any sense?"

Nick half-nodded.

"Hey, God has amazing plans for us, but we humans tend to like our own plans better. The problem is that those plans are always less than His and never work out. The devil tempted Adam and Eve with a plan less than God's, and they gave in. They were weak. Imagine having sex with a girl you liked, and she was suddenly pregnant. Remember that contraception fails a lot more often than they tell you. What would you be thinking right now?"

With a shrug, Nick replied, "I guess I'd be in a panic."

"So, why are you here today?"

He rubbed his hand across his mouth. "I had sex, and I'm not married."

"And?"

"And, what?"

Tom didn't respond.

Nick exhaled. "And, I was weak. I gave in to temptation and took a chance with a baby's entire life to have sex without any commitment, responsibility, or love. I gave into my plan over God's. Is that what you mean?" Suddenly, tears streamed down his cheeks. His hands covered his eyes as his face tightened. "I didn't mean it. I didn't mean for any of it to happen. I am so sorry. Joline would be alive if it weren't for me." His body began to shake, and he turned toward the exit. "I have to go. I'm sorry, but I have to go." Nick sprang up from the pew, reaching the door with three long strides, and as he opened it, the light from the outside streamed in for a moment before it shut behind him.

By the time Tom opened the door, Nick was gone. Halfway down the street, he could see Kate walking quickly after Nick. He stood watching, trying to figure out what Nick's true confession really was before he left without any absolution. He suddenly noticed that Angelo was now by his side, someone he could always count on.

"I won't even attempt to ask you," said Angelo.

"And you know it wouldn't do any good, but I am getting a strong message that we need to understand Joline's life better."

Angelo didn't turn, but his eyes rolled in his direction.

"Yes. Let's take a look," said Tom as he stepped back onto the porch.

Angelo pulled out the photocopied pages from Joline's journal and sat with Tom. "I only got a few pages from different spots, so we may not get what we're looking for."

"What are we looking for?"

Angelo smiled. "I thought you knew."

Just as he put down the first page, Paul stepped onto the porch from the side door and leaned over. "What's going on? Is this something I don't want to know about?" When Tom and Angelo glanced up at him, he quietly turned around. "I think I'm going to work on Sunday's homily and pay some bills."

"He's a good man, Angelo. I wish we were, too, but I feel a need to see if we can learn anything from the journal entries," said Tom as together they read the handwriting on the first sheet, a style that was half-cursive and half-printing, depending on the letters.

April 25

Finally! A nice spring day. I can wear that dress I've been dying to show off. In an odd way, I guess the one thing I learned from MC is how to finally have power and control. The biggest, strongest, and most intimidating boys become like Jello when they see me looking attractive. The priest at church keeps telling us that our value and worth come from inside, but I've never felt like that was true. I always feel better when I can turn a boy's head, especially when he is with someone. And then, I come home and feel depressed again, powerless, worthless—ugly!   J

"Wow," said Angelo. "I'm guessing she's between fourteen and fifteen when she wrote this. I wonder how many girls feel this way?"

"Probably too many. We should focus on one, though. I feel as if something happened in her life to make her feel what she is expressing here; the lack of control and sense of self-worth seem more extreme than a normal teenage girl's struggle. The temporary high and control she expresses might be like a person who takes drugs to avoid the pain inside, even if for a moment."

Angelo placed his finger on the paper and pulled out one of the photos of the walls. "The *J* is the same as on these two drawings on Joline's wall."

"Definitely the same. Okay, let's see the next one."

Angelo placed the next sheet down. "I think this page was earlier in the journal."

I wish I could go to Mom. I wish we were close like other moms and daughters, but she's never been like that. Sad. Funny, I can talk to MC. The last thing I want to do is share my feelings with a guy, but he's different. He looks me in the eye and listens. He holds me when I feel lost. No one has ever held me like that. I don't know. I feel confused. It feels good, but I don't know. I keep thinking that I shouldn't let him do those things, but I think he's the only one who knows me or cares about me. Why do I feel so ugly and empty? I wish I could talk to Mom. Somehow, I think she knows.   J

Both Tom and Angelo leaned back in their chairs. "What do you think?" asked Angelo.

Tom felt too frozen to answer. His mind was quickly bouncing from one thought to another, and none of them were good. "I don't know. MC shows up in both of these journal entries, and I don't know what to think about his relationship with Joline. I'm not getting a good feeling about it."

"C could be for Chase. Maybe there's a family member whose name starts with an M?"

Tom sighed. "It's certainly a possibility. How many more entries did you take photos of?"

"I only got one more. I think this one was later in the journal."

"Okay. Let's see if it helps to fill in any pieces."

Angelo set down the last sheet.

September 13

I don't know how I feel today. I don't know if I feel anything, like I'm drowning in the dark of the ocean—then I'm flooded with emotion, stuck in the middle of a huge tornado, sick and dizzy. If I were dead, this would all go away. All these years of never feeling good about myself, there is another life in me. Half of it is me, and half of it may be RJ. Should I tell him? Should I keep it? Should I keep me? I don't know how I feel today.   J

"Wow. There is a lot of turmoil going on inside that girl. I wonder what happened with the baby?" asked Angelo, stacking the other sheets together as he stared at the last journal entry.

"I hope it was a mistake or something natural. She seemed to indicate that RJ was the father, but not with much certainty."

"Sounds like she was sleeping around."

"I don't know how much sleeping was involved, but who is RJ?" asked Tom, rereading the journal entry to himself.

"Who was the kid that wanted to take out Nick Campbell at the station?"

"Rudy. Rudy Jenkins. Joline's boyfriend. RJ."

"What did you say he looked like?" asked Angelo, now staring across the street.

"Tall, athletic, dark mop of hair—" Tom turned to see what Angelo had his eyes fixed on and spotted across the street a young man making long strides in the direction of Nick's home. "Kind of like him," replied Tom as he hopped off the porch and crossed the street. "Rudy!"

Rudy didn't break his stride or turn until Tom caught up with him. "I've got somewhere to go," bristled Rudy as he veered past Tom.

"Rudy, can you hold up just for a second?"

Rudy picked up speed. "If you can keep up with me, we can talk."

Tom was in good shape but worked to keep up with Rudy. "Sorry to ask, but how long were you and Joline dating?"

Breathing deeply, Rudy replied, "Off and on for two years. Why are you asking? I don't get what your deal is."

"You cared about Joline. I think you may have even loved her."

Rudy came to a sudden stop and stared at Tom. "You don't have to think it. I did love her."

"I believe you. She had a lot of deep feelings going on inside, too."

Rudy nodded, staring off as if deep in thought before letting out a deep sigh. "Yeah, she did. She was hard to figure out. I never knew if she was going to love me or hate me from one day to the next."

"Sorry to ask this, but were you two physically close?"

Rudy shot a dagger of a glare at Tom. "That is no one's business." He squeezed his eyes tight as if to hold back tears. "She always loved giving everything she had, but I don't think any one person could be enough for her."

"I know you are hurting, but were there others?"

His eyes bulged with anger. "How can you ask that?"

"We need to know who might have been—"

"What? Angry enough to kill her and dump her body in the ocean?"

Tom tilted his head, trying to catch his eye. "Rudy, why do you say she was killed and then put into the water? How do you know she didn't drown?"

Rudy gave a piercing glare. "Because I know. She didn't drown or kill herself. She died at that boat hoist. She was reckless with herself and with others, and it cost her." He turned and paced off. "I'm done talking to you. I'll leave the soul-saving business to you."

Chapter 18

Tom pulled his phone from his pocket. "Hi, this is Fr. Tom Fitzpatrick. Is Sheriff Coombs available?"

"Oh, hi, Father. Not at the moment. Can I help you?"

"Do you know how I can get in contact with him?"

"He had an emergency at home, so I don't know."

"Does he live close by?"

She gave him the address, and Father Tom got in his car and drove.

J.C. lived on the other side of the Passy River at the end of a dirt road. His house was a modest cabin in the woods with a stream running by it. The spot was peaceful, but the woman racing out of the front door with a white plastic box and towel in hand looked anything but peaceful. She grabbed a bottle of water from a cooler and headed toward the woods.

"Mrs. Coombs?"

She didn't stop. "Sorry for being rude, but I need to tend to a medical situation."

Tom rushed after her. "I hope everything's okay. I'm Father Tom, and I need to speak with the sheriff."

"Well, right now, he's being a dad. Our son fell from a tree and has a gash on his leg that we need to take care of."

After a few minutes, they reached a small clearing with a birchbark structure that resembled a teepee. J.C., holding his son, was trying his best to calm him down as he reached for the wet towel from his wife to clean the deep wound.

He glanced up. "Sorry, Father. Let me get this bandaged up."

"Sure thing. Let me know if I can help." Tom looked into the boy's eyes. He was a good combination of his mother and father, with beautiful bronze-colored skin, longish dark hair, and holding back impending tears. He was about eight or nine years of age and had a colorfully beaded strand tied to his hair. Tom gazed into his eyes as he winced with each dab of the towel. "You are a brave man. I love your teepee. Did you build it?"

The young boy took a few short breaths to steady himself and nodded. "It's a wigwam!"

"Joseph," said the mother as J.C. applied the antiseptic ointment and bandage to his son's knee. "Be polite to Father Fitzpatrick."

"Listen to your mother," said J.C. in a calm voice as he tended to the bandage. "This is my wife, Beth, and my indestructible son, Joseph."

Tom smiled at Beth. "So good to meet you. You have a good man there—or, should I say, two good men." He squatted down to be eye-to-eye with Joseph. "You are being very brave. What happened to you?"

"Nd-akuadawephue abaszik."

J.C. rolled his eyes and glanced up at Tom. "He's very into his heritage. Not a bad thing, but sometimes a little, well— tell Father Fitzpatrick why you were climbin' a tree."

"Nadadiali moulsem," replied the boy, wide-eyed.

J.C. smiled. "He knows a few native Penobscot words." He tilted his head toward his son. "So, you were huntin' a wolf from way up in the tree, were you?"

Beth pursed her lips, her eyes narrowing. "What did we say about climbing alone?"

"But the wolf would have eaten me," rebuked Joseph.

Tom glanced over at the mask of a wolf's head on one of the trees and a fishing spear on the ground. He smiled. "It was a good thing he didn't get you."

As J.C. picked up his son and carried him back to the cabin, Tom followed.

On the way back, Tom told J.C. about his encounter with Rudy and his concern that he was going to Nick's house.

Beth offered Tom some tea and raspberry bread, which he gladly accepted, while J.C. called the station and ordered an officer to make sure things were okay,

Tom peered around the homey cabin with an eclectic mix of modern appliances, a computer, and signs of traditional native items: woven baskets in progress, hunting weapons, historical photos on the walls, and a bear's fur hide on the floor. "Do you do the beautiful work on these baskets?"

She blushed. "When I can. I do accounting work for two businesses, but I like to keep up with tradition. We have a baby girl napping right now. I hope to pass this skill on to her."

"That's wonderful."

"There are only a few thousand of the Penobscot tribe around, so we do the best we can."

He sat at the table with Beth, sipping his tea and taking a slice of the bread.

"I feel blessed to be in your home. Your husband has an important job protecting the community," said Tom.

"I know. I worry about him as much as I do that young man over there, especially if a potential killer is on the loose. I mean, there is so little we know right now. That poor girl was so young. My husband says that you've been interested in the case."

Tom scratched his head. "I'm trying to stay out of his way, but I would like to see justice for Joline."

"Did you know her?"

"No, but I feel some sense of connection and want to do right by her. I think it is a complicated case so far. Maybe the answer is simple, but there are no clear clues at the moment." Tom sipped his tea and ran his hand across the old wooden table.

"Well, it's certainly kept him up at night, thinking about it. He takes his job so seriously sometimes. He's such a smart and strong man, but I worry when he's out at night or—I just worry. I always worried when he was in Afghanistan, but it's almost tougher now because I'm with him every day. It's more real, but then I think of Laurie Chase and what she must be going through. I didn't know her well in school, but I always sensed that she had a tough life behind her outgoing personality. I can't imagine losing my daughter so young."

J.C. came into the room and picked up his teacup. "What are you two chattin' about?"

"What else?" replied Beth with a half-smile.

He ran his fingers through his hair and turned to Tom. "Um, do you mind if we sit out on the porch?"

Settled on the front porch, Tom scanned the area. The light breeze in the trees and the sound of the running stream made for a peaceful moment. "Sheriff, you are blessed with a beautiful home and family. Really."

"I am. Thank you. Now, let's talk about why you're here."

"Oh, yeah. Well, after your interview with Nick and his family, his mother dragged him to church to talk to me." Tom paused.

"And?"

"I can't really say anything."

J.C. dropped his head and tapped his foot. "Are you sayin' he made a confession to you, and you can't let me know what he said?"

"Sort of."

Shaking his head, J.C. asked, "Sorta?"

"Well, he sort of gave a confession, but I still can't break the seal of confession. The way he left, I couldn't tell if he was embarrassed by his mother knowing what he did or if there was something more he was struggling with. I spotted Rudy Jenkins hoofing it toward Nick's house a bit later. He seemed angry and bent on revenge, and I wanted to let you know. I think Rudy loved Joline but got angry when he caught Nick and her together. He said she was reckless and that no one person would be enough for her. He was definitely still angry and blaming himself, so I'm not clear what he feels guilty about."

"Did Nick seem like he felt guilty?"

"Ah, I really can't get into anything he said. We know they were both with her close to her death, and there are a lot of unanswered questions." Tapping the arm of his chair, Tom paused, hesitating. "Nothing you don't know, but Joline's timeline that night needs to account for every second. It's like pieces are filled in, but so many are missing."

"You're tellin' me. A night owl told me that you visited Laurie Chase last night. You and your Italian sidekick."

"Yeah. We were walking—"

"Just so happens by the Chases' house."

"Right. Well, we were told that Colby and Laurie had a loud argument, and Colby charged off, so we did drop in to see if she was doing all right. Laurie's obviously very shaken by this, but she seems to feel guilty about something. I'm getting the sense that she and Joline drifted apart during the past four years or so. She appeared to be battling some of her own demons in her life, and when you don't have a parent you can go to, you usually seek out someone else."

J.C. pursed his lips a moment. "How do you know she was battlin' her own demons, as you put it?"

Tom stood up and handed J.C. his empty cup. "You're not going to like this, but I really can't say. Please thank your wife for her hospitality, and I hope your son heals quickly. You did a nice job on that bandaging."

Standing up, J.C. eyed Tom. "You know, if the puzzle has a lot of important pieces, I'm goin' to need all of them to see the whole picture. All I'm askin' is if you manage to find some pieces, don't hold onto them. Who knows if someone else is in danger?"

Chapter 19

On the way back from J.C.'s home, Tom glanced into the rearview mirror, adjusting it to peer into his own eyes. *What are you doing?* he thought. *You're a priest. You're a guest in your old friend's home and consumed with this girl's investigation?* He asked himself, "You know it's not your job, don't you?" The eyes in the reflection just stared back as if they didn't hear a word. Instead of heading straight to the rectory, he turned down Main Street and drove to the pier, bustling with activity on a busy workday. The air smelled of salt and fish bait, and the sun glistened gently off the small waves on the ocean water. He parked his car and watched volunteers helping to man the sails of Captain Jack's schooner as it headed out for a two-hour tour.

Tom stepped out of his car, sighed at the refreshingly cool breeze on his face, and slowly trod down the harbor walkway. He passed the Front Street Pub and an ice cream shop before approaching the boat hoist where Angelo had spotted the bloodstain from Joline. He tried to imagine what it felt like that Friday night, pitch black at midnight in Joline's last moments of life. He thought about the possibilities. *Maybe she enticed Nick to leave the ticket booth, and they came here? Maybe parked in the dirt lot and sat in the car staring out at the harbor that night, and they got carried away, or maybe Nick lost control and forced himself on Joline? That might explain the bruise under his eye that he was trying to hide.*

Tom strode over to the parking area where they had found the condom. *Did Rudy see them in the car together and then argue with her afterward? How long was he here before he couldn't take it anymore and intervened? He's still pretty angry three days later, so how angry was he that night?*

Did he come back? After he left, did the fight between Nick and Joline escalate? Maybe there was an accident, and he panicked, trying to cover it up.

Tom moved over to the area next to the boat hoist. It was so close to the parking area that it made sense that they might have ended up there during an argument. Then he had another thought. *Wait. Wait. The guy at the diner, ahh Ned... Ned Parker... said he saw Joline later that night. It had to have been later, and she was talking to someone older.* He shook his head because the timeline didn't make sense unless Rudy or Nick waited for her to leave the diner— or it was someone else entirely.

He strolled down the walkway to think and noticed the lobster boat, *Miss Lizzie*; he had gone out early that Saturday morning with Paul. Solly was busy scrubbing down the deck. Tom approached. "Ahoy, Captain."

Without turning, Solly replied, "I know you didn't really say that."

"Sorry, Solly. It's Father Tom."

Solly turned and gave a half-smile, hiding the number of teeth that were missing. His well-worn jacket was soiled with oil and salt stains, and his face was rough with deep wrinkles and small brown blotches from years in the sun. What caught Tom's attention were Solly's eyes. They didn't look old or worn, but young and blue as the ocean he spent most of his life fishing.

"I saw you walkin' around over there. I hear you're thinking of turning in your collar for a detective's license."

Belting out a laugh, Tom said, "Don't believe everything you hear."

"Or see. What's on your mind if you aren't trying to figure out this sad mystery?"

Tom stepped past the bulkhead of the boat where Solly was standing. "You're too smart to fool. I was thinking about Joline's death and what might have happened that night."

Putting his brush into a bucket, Solly shook his head. "I wish I could say that it would bring the Chases peace to know what happened, but I doubt it will help their grief any." He paused. "The missus and I never had any children, but I can't imagine anything taking away the pain of losin' a child."

Nodding, Tom said, "So true, but I would want to know. How have you and Danny been?"

"Well, I'm doin' fine. Danny, ahh—Danny is Danny. The missus doesn't like me out too far without a mate aboard."

"Has he been sick?"

"Only of his own makin', I suspect. I think he took that girl's death real hard. He despised Colby, ever since I've known him, but he's always talked about Joline. He took her out with us a few times. Nice girl. Curious about everything." He scratched his beard. "I don't know if somethin' particular happened, but he's been actin' kinda strange for several weeks now."

Tom watched as a seagull landed on the stern's washboard. "Huh. Like how?"

"Just strange. I did see him talkin' with Joline a few weeks back. Come to think of it, they did have a pretty good row about somethin'. Seems about the same time he went into that funk of his." He shook his head. "Well, I've gotta get finished here and get home to the missus—" He glanced up. "Before she puts one of those APBs out for me."

"Thanks, Solly. Take care of yourself. Your wife's a smart woman who loves you so much that she wants to have someone with you when you head out to pull those traps. Love's a good thing."

Solly nodded as he grabbed his scrub brush and bucket. "You be careful, too. Whoever's responsible for that girl's death and took the time to bring her body out to sea isn't playing games."

"If you promise, I promise," replied Tom with a smile as he turned and headed back to his car.

Driving up Main Street, he slowed as he noticed Danny Haskell entering Rollie's Tavern. Tom raised his eyes and said, "Lord, what do you want me to do here?" The tug inside of him was to stop and attend to a man in need, but he couldn't deny his desire to put more pieces of the puzzle together. As he pulled into an open parking spot, images of his past flooded his mind. *He was entering the apartment he shared when he was in college, calling out, but no one answering. He reached the bedroom and saw pills on the nightstand. A sense of horror and panic overtook him as he tried to wake Corlie's lifeless body.*

His eyes squeezed tight at the clarity of the scene, still blaming himself as tears flowed.

When he finally opened his eyes, he tried to shake off the memory. As a young girl passed in front of his car, he refocused on Joline and who might be to blame for her death and unceremonious burial at sea. He decided to go into the tavern, where a handful of patrons were sharing beers and conversation.

At the end of the bar sat Danny, alone, taking a noticeably long gulp of his draft. His soiled baseball hat sat tightly over his scraggly hair; his tee shirt was wrinkled and in need of a wash.

"Mr. Haskell, how are you doing today?"

Tom's approach startled Danny. He shrugged and took another gulp, perhaps hoping Tom would continue without the need to reply. He finally motioned toward the open barstool.

Tom sat down. "Are you sure? I don't want to intrude."

Turning, Danny eyed Tom with a raised brow.

"Thanks. I could use a beer. Hey, I talked with your daughter, Lizzie, the other day. You must be proud of her."

Danny sat motionless, staring into the bottom of his empty beer mug.

The bartender set down a foamy Guinness draft in front of Tom and another ale for Danny.

Tom took a sip and let a few beats settle between them before launching into a conversation. "It was such sad news about Joline. I hear she was so close to Lizzie. I'm sure you knew her well. I wanted to tell you how sorry I am for your loss."

Danny rubbed his hand across his eyes, possibly wiping away a tear. He nodded and took another swig of beer. "She was—" He paused and nodded again. "I can't believe she's gone."

"Do you have any gut feelings about who could have done this?"

His pause was uncomfortably long before he shook his head. "No. She was a beautiful young woman. I don't know anyone who didn't like her."

"She did seem quite talented and friendly, from what I've heard. Did Lizzie ever mention her struggles or issues with anything or anyone?"

Rubbing his hand across his mouth, Danny shook his head slightly. "Everyone has something they're dealing with. She was a strong girl, but—" He took another drink. "I don't know. None of this makes any sense. Life has never made any sense to me. We just go from day to day, trying to get by and not think about things too much. It's almost too overwhelming when you think about all the crap we tolerate. Maybe she's better off not having to face a lifetime of it?"

Tom placed his hand on Danny's shoulder. "You haven't had it easy. Father Paul told me that you lost your wife to cancer and have had to raise Lizzie on your own for some time now. I admire you for that. Fathers are so important."

Narrowing his eyes, Danny shook his head again and gave a half-hearted laugh. "Father of the year, huh? I wanted to be a father to my daughter, but I, um, I don't know. Life never is what you hope for, is it?"

The question made Tom pause to think about the pain and grief that must be deep within Danny, not just a momentary bump in the road but a lifelong struggle to find hope and an ultimate purpose to it all. He knew that his own suffering had strengthened him and allowed him to know pain intimately and understand the suffering of others, but its sting still remained inside. He didn't know Danny, his daily struggle, his disappointments, and betrayals, or if he believed in God and His loving mercy. What could he say that didn't sound cliché or preachy that would actually help?

"I've felt the same way at times, but I've found that there is hope in everything, even if we can't see it. Despite the tragedy, I think Joline is in loving hands right now, and her gift may be to help people stop and think more about life beyond this one. Danny, what was your wife's name? I want to say a prayer for her, too."

Danny glared at Tom. "Kristie? Can you pray for someone if they are in hell?" He drank the rest of his beer and dropped a twenty-dollar bill on the bar before sliding off his stool. "Do you want to do something good, Father? Just leave well enough alone. We don't need any white knights or angels from heaven to save the rest of us sorry souls in Belfast. Don't the folks in Boston need you?"

Tom watched Danny amble out of the tavern. He felt more confused and no closer to solving the mystery of Joline's death.

Chapter 20

Tom spent the evening with Paul and Angelo, enjoying dinner on the porch and several rounds of chess. When Paul retired early, Tom and Angelo returned to their conversation about the case, which was getting more uncomfortable with each day.

Tom recounted his conversations with Solly and Danny to Angelo. He caught that familiar expression in Angelo's eyes. "Okay, what did you find?"

Angelo frowned. "Who said I found anything?"

"Because we're like two old spouses who know each other far too well. Is it anything good?"

Angelo bobbed his head. "I don't know. Remember when we saw Bill McCready that night, fishing with his son?"

"Yeah. What about him?"

"Well, if he'd been fishing the night before and was in a rush to leave for the lake in the morning, you'd think your favorite fishing shirt wouldn't look so clean. There are a lot of possibilities, but it did strike me at the time."

"Okay, so?"

Angelo rubbed the remaining short hairs on top of his head. "So, I dropped by McCready's, but they were still at the lake, and no one was home. His next-door neighbor was washing his car in the driveway, so I acted as if I were a friend dropping by and struck up a conversation. He told me McCready likes to go fishing often after school and late at night. Then he mentioned that Joline had passed by McCready's house one night and that McCready had turned as white as a ghost when he saw her."

"How long ago was that?"

"He said a few weeks ago. McCready quickly accompanied Joline down the street a bit, out of the sightlines of his house, and had a 'lively conversation' with her, as he put it, not so that he could hear what they were saying, but McCready's body language was very animated. When Joline finally left, McCready headed straight into his house without a word to the neighbor. He thought it seemed very odd for McCready."

"Huh. Was that it?"

Angelo held up his hand, entered the rectory, and returned with a brown paper bag. "After my conversation with the neighbor, I was able to sneak into McCready's backyard from the other side without being seen."

Tom smirked. "Are you expecting me to be surprised?"

Angelo shrugged. "Once in a while might be nice." He opened the bag. "I noticed a firepit in the back of McCready's yard. I lifted the cover, took a stick to move the ashes, and noticed a piece of a collared jersey."

"And?"

"I had some gloves, picked up the corner, shook the ashes off of one of the pieces of fabric, and noticed dried blood on most of it. It hit me that his shirt was so clean on that Sunday night we saw him. And it's kind of odd for a high school girl to be dropping by her teacher's house, especially when the teacher reacted the way he did."

Tom examined the fabric more closely. "That definitely could be dried blood. I guess it is possible that Joline was posing some sort of threat to McCready and forced the meeting at the school. We don't know if that was him with her around midnight at the diner, but if it was, that was very close to the time of her death."

"And he had the boat to take her body up the river with a strong enough tide to carry her out to sea that night. Next day, he's suddenly in a hurry to get his boat and his family out of town early that morning and not happy that we dropped by the lake. If it was him, how do we prove any of that without witnesses?"

Tom mulled it over for a few minutes. "Well, if her blood is on this piece of fabric and any traces are found in

McCready's boat, that might be enough proof, along with the circumstantial stuff, to bring him in." He pointed to the fabric Angelo was holding in his hand. "And you'd be holding evidence, there."

Nodding, Angelo said, "There are other pieces with blood, but I'll return this to the firepit late tonight and leave a friendly note at the station for the sheriff."

Tom went to bed around midnight, and Angelo headed over to McCready's place while Tom tried to sleep. Tom had been tired earlier, but his mind was racing about the possible suspects. He had so much energy that he unsuccessfully tried to pace his room. Wondering if the sheriff caught Angelo at McCready's house, Tom decided to get dressed and go to the police station to find out. All the lights were out except for the front desk when he reached the station. There was no sign of Angelo. Tom sent him a short text: *Are you okay?* Angelo quickly returned a "thumbs up" emoji.

It was a pleasant summer night, and the town was quiet at that time on a weeknight. There were no cars on the street, only a handful of shop lights to keep the street lamps company. Tom strolled down the steep grade of Main Street, thinking about McCready and his shirt. He hated to get too far ahead of himself without some validation of a theory. Far too often, he'd been surprised by people and events to lock in too tightly on a guess and a few clues. He laughed to himself about Angelo noticing a clean shirt on a fisherman, which was an unusual coincidence when the counter guy's white apron on top of his grease-stained tee shirt seemed more curious to him.

As Tom approached Traci's Diner, he tried to remember the waiter's name. He stopped outside the lit windows of the diner that appeared to have only one patron at the counter and a couple in one of the booths. *Cotter?* He thought. *Nope. Wait, Cutter. Ralph Cutter. That's it. Your brain isn't completely gone yet, Thomas Fitzpatrick.* The bell over the door rang as he opened it, and Ralph lifted his chin, his two hands on the counter as he leaned forward. Sitting at the counter was Ned Parker, the man Tom and Paul had spoken with over breakfast that past Sunday.

"Ah, priests prowl the streets with insomnia, too, do they?" quipped Ned as he scratched his scruff of a beard.

"You've got that right tonight. It's Ned, right?" Tom sat on the stool beside him. He glanced up to see Ralph still in the same position with a nervous half-smile and edgy intensity to his black eyes.

"Can I get you anything?" Ralph asked, standing up and wiping the counter with the wet rag, his apron now as grease-stained as his tee shirt.

"Sure thing. I'll have a cup of coffee and a piece of that raspberry pie."

Ralph poured a cup of hot coffee and slid over a small bowl of creamers before pulling out the lone remaining slice of red raspberry pie, holding it up to his pock-marked face. "You know, I usually save a piece of this pie for the sheriff, but he didn't drop by tonight."

"Oh, I don't know if I want to steal anything from Sheriff Coombs. I've been more of a thorn in his side this week."

Ned tapped Tom on the arm. "Never mind, Ralph. He gives everyone a hard time about that last piece of pie because he wants it for his break, don't you, Ralph?"

Ralph glared at Ned and placed the pie down in front of Tom before heading to the back room.

With a broad smile, Ned said, "I'll probably be on pie probation now. Traci does make a good one."

Tom pressed his fork into the flaky crust and baked raspberry filling and took a bite, savoring the pleasure of its taste. "You are a man who tells no lies. It's delicious. Did Ralph disappear on us?"

"He's probably out the back door taking his smoke break. Traci doesn't want any smoking inside, and Ralph doesn't mind the excuse to get out from behind the counter."

"Ned, you said you were here on that Friday night the Chase girl died, right?"

Ned took a sip of his coffee and nodded. "Such a shame. I was here, probably from eleven or so to maybe one-thirty. Years ago, I would have been at the tavern drowning myself in something other than coffee, but I almost killed a boy one night and haven't touched the stuff since. It was me, Ralph, Mike over there—" Ned turned and called out, "Hey, Mike. You were here last Friday night, weren't ya?"

Mike nodded. "Yup. I was trying to figure out this crossword I'm still working on with Julia."

Ned turned back as Tom asked him, "You said that Joline was here, as well."

"Yep."

"And there was someone with her?"

"She came in alone. Oh, yeah, around midnight. I remember hearing the clock on the wall chime, and Ralph said, 'Hey, Joline.' I think he creeps out most of the girls, but she never seemed to let him bother her. Ralph eyed her up and down. If she wasn't over sixteen, he could get arrested for how he gawks at a girl, but Joline ignored him and checked around till she saw someone in the back booth. I'm guessing she was expecting to find him here."

Tom scratched his head, wishing Ned had seen the person she was meeting, maybe the last person she ever saw.

"Hey, wait a minute," said Ned. "Mike was in the same booth." Ned turned again. "Mike, you were sitting right there on Friday, right?"

Mike nodded. "Always am."

"Do you remember when Joline Chase came in that night and sat with someone in that back booth?"

"Yup."

Ned rolled his eyes. "And can you tell us who it was?"

"That teacher, fellow. Bill somethin'," replied Mike.

"McCready?" asked Ned.

"That's it. He came in the back door and sat in the booth for a few minutes, and then she showed up. Joline was doing most of the talkin', and McCready seemed to be gettin' more uptight the more she talked. I don't know. He just seemed uncomfortable and suddenly stood up and left by the back door. She followed right after him, still talkin' at him."

Tom listened intently. "Can you remember what she said?"

"Nah. Oh, wait." Mike squeezed his eyes tight as if it would help him remember, then blew a breath out through his pursed lips, shaking his head. "I don't know. Somethin' like, 'I'm not afraid to tell,' or somethin' close to that."

Ned whispered to Tom. "Now we know why he's still working on the same crossword."

Tom smiled. "Thanks, Mike. I appreciate it." He turned back on his stool to finish off his pie. "I was guessing it was McCready she'd met with but I didn't know for sure." He stared into his empty cup. "Ralph must smoke those extra-long cigarettes."

"Funny, he took his break right after I heard Joline leave by the back door that night. The place was quiet, so you could hear everything."

"Ralph took a break and went out back when Joline left?" said Tom.

"Yeah, and come to think of it, he was gone for a while."

"Were you here when he got back?"

Ned smiled. "Where else am I going to go these days? Yeah. He came back. I could hear him running the water in the sink. He had a wet rag in his hand when he came out, wiping his hands and neck with it. Then he grabbed an apron and was quiet the rest of the time I was here, which was odd because you usually can't shut him up."

Tom ran his fingers across his lips, trying to put together the picture. "Ned, does Ralph normally take his apron off when he takes a break?"

Ned paused in thought. "Nope, but I don't think he had one on when he came back from his break because he grabbed a new one. He must have tossed the other in the laundry. It was kinda weird seeing him in a clean white apron."

Tom stood up, put a twenty-dollar bill on the counter, and grinned. "I hope that covers mine and yours. You've been a great date."

At the door, he paused and approached the booth where Mike and Julia sat. Julia must have been ten years younger, and her eyes were closed as she slept, leaning against his chest. Tom reached out to shake Mike's hand and whispered, "It was good almost meeting both of you. One quick question. Did McCready have a gash under his left eye when you saw him that night?"

Mike paused and shook his head. "Naw. He stood up at one point to look out the window, and I could see his face pretty good. I think I would have remembered somethin' like that."

"Thanks," said Tom, glancing down at the table. "Revenge."

"What?" asked Mike with a furrowed brow.

"Nineteen down. R-E-V-E-N-G-E."

Mike bore down as he filled in the boxes on the crossword. "Thanks. It looks funny spelled out."

Tom smiled to himself as he proceeded to the back booth, staring at it for a few moments before exiting out the back door that Joline and McCready had used on Friday night. The back grade behind Traci's was steep and too dark to see. His eyes needed a minute to acclimate to the darkness before he slowly stepped down the embankment to the path leading to the harbor walkway. He noted that it was close to the same time of night that Joline must have taken the same steps. He felt a nervous twinge in his gut as he followed the dark walkway with only the salt waters lapping against the piers and the periodic clanging of sail lines against their metal masts, breaking the eerie silence.

He couldn't figure out why Joline was talking with McCready. *Why was McCready so uncomfortable at the diner and outside his home? Was Joline threatening him? What if she pushed his patience too far?* Without a sound or warning, Tom felt a sudden spike of pain that seared across his shoulder blade and he dropped hard to the paved ground. His instinct was to raise his arm to avoid another blow from the shadow looming over him, but there was another thud as two figures hit the ground. Tom could barely distinguish the forms wrestling on the ground until he heard the footsteps of one of them running away.

"Are you all right?"

Tom struggled to stand. "Angelo? Are *you* all right?" He reached out a hand and helped him up.

Angelo brushed himself off. "Yeah. Yeah. I'm fine."

"I know you are my guardian angel, Italian-style, but how did you know I would be here?"

"If someone is trying to knock you off or scare you out of town, we should get moving," replied Angelo.

They proceeded back to the town pier on Maine Street. "Huh."

Tom rubbed his shoulder with his other hand. "What's the 'huh' about?"

"Probably nothing. When I came down the street here to find you, there was a yellow truck parked on the street. Now it's gone."

Chapter 21

Tom glanced up as Paul entered the kitchen. Angelo was tending to the welt on Tom's shoulder.

"What are you two doing up at this time of night—are you okay? What happened to you?"

Tom grimaced as he put his shirt back on. "Fell out of bed."

"Right, and I'm Larry Bird."

"I'm okay. I couldn't sleep, so I went to Traci's diner for a piece of pie and then strolled along the harbor for a bit, and someone didn't want me there. Luckily, Angelo showed up to save my bacon."

"Whoever it was, I think they were trying to scare you off from poking around in Joline's murder," said Angelo.

Tom shook his head. "We don't really know that, but let's assume it's true. Who could it be?"

Paul waved his hands. "Shouldn't we be calling J.C.? If there is a murderer out there attacking young women and priests, we need to call this in."

Tom put his hand on Paul's shoulder. "I appreciate your concern, but I don't think we need to wake J.C. up in the middle of the night. We can catch him in the morning. We just need to figure out who might have done this."

Shaking his head, Paul admonished, "Tom, I think you need to stop with this. We're not talking about a game here. J.C. has asked you to let him do his job, and I'm asking you, as a friend, to let him do it. I'm worried about you." He turned. "And you, too, Angelo. You could have both been hurt or worse."

Tom and Angelo nodded and let Paul head back to bed before they sat at the kitchen table to write out a list of possibilities while keeping their voices low.

"I guess Ray Jordy would be one. He followed you the other day, and I think that was his yellow truck that suddenly disappeared," offered Angelo.

"I agree. I'm guessing McCready is still at the lake, but it's possible he could be retracing his tracks to remove any evidence. And Ralph from the diner went out the back for a smoke just before I went down that embankment. He could just be awkward, but he gets highly uncomfortable if I ask any questions, and he would have been one of the last people to see Joline alive. Maybe her rejection of his advances didn't sit well with him?"

Angelo wrote their names down. "I haven't met him yet."

"People said he flirted with Joline when she came into the diner, and he appears oddly lurking in that photograph at her graduation. It was also odd that morning at breakfast, his tee shirt was grease-stained, but his apron was almost spotless."

Angelo tapped his pen on the table. "That Rudy kid or even Nick Campbell are still in the picture. Crimes of passion are pretty common, and then there is panic to cover up. And we haven't even talked about Colby."

"Colby Chase?" queried Tom with a raised brow.

"Well, we heard that he's had arguments with Joline, some possibly physical. He's been pretty hot-headed and at odds with Mrs. Chase. Most murders are committed by people close to the victim. I just don't think we can rule him out or—"

"Or who?"

Angelo tilted his head. "Someone we haven't even met yet."

After a few hours of sleep, Tom awoke to the sting in his shoulder. Paul was up and still very much concerned about Tom's safety and felt better when Tom agreed to pay a visit to the sheriff's office. "You know he won't be happy about this."

"I know," replied Paul. "I just don't think you should be playing the caped-crusader in the middle of the night or putting yourself at risk. Look at yourself. I can tell *that* doesn't feel good." He pointed to Tom's shoulder.

With a half-smile, Tom patted Paul's shoulder. "I think I'll survive, and I appreciate how much you care. I'm heading to the station now. Okay?"

Paul smiled and nodded, and Tom made his trek down the sidewalk. Halfway to the station, Tom heard a pickup truck slowing down behind him and finally pulling alongside. Tom turned and lowered his head to see Colby Chase.

Colby stared without a word for a few seconds. "Are you still around?"

"Hello, Colby. How have you and Laurie been managing?" replied Tom, leaning on the door with his forearms. "I'm keeping you both in my prayers."

"Look. I know you mean well, but we can't bring Joline back, and getting everyone in town riled up isn't going to change that. Laurie seems like more of a mess every time she talks to you. Do you hear what I'm saying?"

Nodding, Tom replied, "I do. I want to respect you and your time of mourning."

"Good idea."

Tom sighed. "Don't you want to know who is responsible?"

Colby put his truck in gear and only stared into Tom's eyes in a way that was hard to read. "Let it go. You're a priest!"

Tom lifted his arms from the door as Colby rolled away and disappeared down the street. He stood conflicted, wanting to be empathetic with the impact of the tragic loss of his daughter, but Colby's anger seemed to be about more than that. As he approached the station, he spotted J.C., who glanced back at him with a look of disbelief as he escorted a man to the door. It was Bill McCready.

J.C. stopped and had an officer bring McCready into the station as Tom approached slowly. He seemed highly uncomfortable, taking off his police hat and wiping his forearm across his brow before sighing.

Tom approached and tilted his head. "Are you okay?"

"Yeah. Why are you here?"

"Well, I couldn't sleep last night and stopped by the diner for a bit."

"I heard."

"Afterwards, I took a stroll down to the harbor walk and.."

J.C. raised his head with interest. "And?"

"I was attacked from behind. Struck pretty hard with a board or pipe or something that knocked me to the ground." Tom motioned to where the blow had struck.

"What? Who was it? Was he tryin' to kill you?"

Tom shook his head. "It was too dark to see. I don't know what he would have done next because Angelo showed up and knocked him off of me. Then he took off."

J.C. paced back and forth. "Damn! Did you see which way he ran?"

"I think back up the embankment or toward Main Street. Why?"

"I don't know. This is crazy. *Wawôdokawa.*"

Tom tilted his head. "What?"

"Sorry. I was wonderin' if it was more of a warning for you to stop pokin' around versus tryin' to kill you. It would mean that you're hittin' on some sensitive turf, maybe gettin' too close for comfort. We need to talk."

Nodding, Tom replied, "I'll help in any way I can."

J.C. rubbed his forehead with both hands, pausing before responding, "I'm crazy. I really hate to do this. I shouldn't be doin' this."

"What are you thinking, Sheriff?"

J.C. glanced around. "Look. You know that Bill McCready is staying at Swan Lake this week. Well, he was spotted in town last night, down by the harbor, just after midnight. He won't say why, and I don't know if he could be your attacker or if he was retracin' his tracks from last Friday or he just wants to make things more interestin' for us, but he's got to answer some questions. My office is next to our interrogation room, and you can hear everythin' between the two rooms, from talkin' to a polite fart."

"What do you want me to do?"

"Father, I need you to listen to the questionin', especially his answers. If the answers don't jibe with your conversation with him or your situation last night, I want you to write them down. You have to promise me that everythin' is completely confidential. I need to know if his answers seem kosher or not."

"Okay. I did confirm that McCready was the person Joline met at the diner around midnight on Friday. They left out the back door after a tense conversation."

J.C. glanced up and then nodded.

Tom sat by the partition in J.C.'s office and could hear the shuffle of chairs and the voices loud and clear from the interrogation room. He regretted he wouldn't be able to see any of the nonverbal reactions, which were often more telling in these types of situations. The difference in each of their voices made it easy to tell who was speaking.

"Please take a seat, Mr. McCready."

"I don't understand why I'm here."

"We are talkin' with everyone and anyone who knew and saw Joline Chase on her last day. We understand you saw her several times that evening, includin' a meetin' only moments before her time of death."

There was the sound of tapping on the table. "Joline was a student of mine and was saying her goodbyes. There was nothing more." A moment of silence followed.

"Okay. The records show that you didn't have Joline in your class for the past few years. Why would she take the time to meet you at school and then again at the diner on the same night just to say goodbye?"

Again, a pause. "I don't know. Graduating can be a scary time for kids, and they can get very sentimental. She was going through some things when I had her in class, and maybe—I don't know."

"Okay. So you met with her at school, said your goodbyes, and then drove her down to the harbor near where you keep your boat. What happened then?"

"She left, and I went fishing."

"Hmm. I know you like fishing upriver, but the tide was pretty low around then. How did you know to meet her again at Traci's around midnight?"

"Ahhh. I don't know. We ran into each other near the town pier, and she said she wanted to talk about something, so I agreed."

J.C. asked, "And what did you talk about?"

"It was really nothing. She was scared about what to do next in her life and wanted some advice. I told her to go to college and figure it out, and she got angry. I didn't know what she wanted from me."

"That gash under your eye. It looks like it was a nasty injury. When did that happen?"

"Friday night. I was hauling the boat in to take it to the lake and tripped on a block of wood or something."

"Hmmm. From what I understand, this vacation on the lake was a very last-minute thing. After midnight, you called the cabin owner, hauled your boat in, and woke your wife and kids early to take them to Swanville. No plans. No notice. Just a sudden urge to get out of Belfast. Is that right, Mr. McCready?"

"The school years are long and hard. I just wanted to get away, and the lake is a peaceful spot to fish with my son."

"Interestin'. There was still testin' for the Freshmen and Sophomores so you had to call in a sub to cover for your absence, and then you had another sub pack up the room for the summer."

There was no response.

"Last question for now. If you wanted to get out of town for a vacation, why were you seen lurking in the area behind Traci's after midnight last night?"

No response.

Tom could hear a loud sigh and the scrape of a chair along the linoleum floor. "Bill, we need the truth about this girl, the whole truth. I don't know what to think, but your answers seem like you're holdin' somethin' back. I need you to think long and hard about them and let me know what you're not tellin' me."

"Can I go now?"

After the interview, Tom stood as J.C. entered his office. "You're the psych guy. Is he tellin' the truth?"

"I don't know, but my guess is that he's definitely hiding something. Do you have any evidence to disprove anything he said?"

J.C. pursed his lips. "Nothin', but we're doin' forensics on his boat as we speak. If he hauled her body out to sea that night, maybe we can find some evidence he hasn't cleaned off. What I need is a witness. Someone who saw Joline after she left the diner that night. McCready could have easily brought his boat down to where she died and gotten her on board. If we find no further evidence or a witness to the murder, I don't know how we prove this damn case."

Chapter 22

Tom exited the station and stopped as Angelo approached from across the street. "Did you miss me already?"

"Only at midnight when you're out on the prowl. Speaking of which, I found out where Ray Jordy lives, so I stopped by his house."

"What made you curious about Ray Jordy?"

"You mentioned that he was following you and Father Paul a few days ago, and he seemed a bit testy. You also said he was driving the only yellow truck in town, possibly the same yellow truck seen following Joline to and from the high school on Friday night, and—"

"And possibly, the truck you saw last night when I became acquainted with a less-than-friendly blunt instrument." They began to walk, and Tom added, "It was pretty dark, and how do we know it was the same truck?"

Angelo replied, "When I passed by Jordy's driveway and saw the truck, I remember seeing the stack of two-by-fours on the back rack, and they were still there. Kind of late to be cruising around town when you're working the boatyard early the next day."

"Hmm. He did have that unexplained argument with Joline on Friday morning and then the heated fisticuffs with Colby Chase on Monday. He has some definite connection with Joline that we don't understand and a falling out with Colby a few years back after being best friends since their school days. We may have to check him out a bit more."

Angelo rubbed his hand across his head. "Well."

"Well? What did you do, Angelo?"

"I didn't touch a thing," replied Angelo with a pause. "But I did see an envelope inside the book's pages on his bedroom bureau. No letter was in it, but it was addressed from Veritas Laboratories."

"What do they do?"

"Drug and alcohol testing, but they mainly offer DNA paternity tests. I found a yellow slip inside that read, *Paternity DNA Test Results Charges, $850, Paid.*"

Tom stopped in his tracks. "What?"

"What are you thinking?"

"I don't know. I guess I'm thinking about Joline's journal entry. What was it? *All these years of never feeling good about myself, and now there is another life in me. Half of it is me, and half of it may be RJ. Should I tell him? Should I keep it? Should I keep me? I don't know how I feel today.*"

"Right. We were thinking of her boyfriend, Rudy Jenkins, but this certainly raises some questions about who RJ is, why Jordy was arguing with Joline and at odds with Colby, and if Colby knows. Maybe he didn't want anyone to know, burying his secret at sea. And now you are trying to bring it to the surface, so he panicked. Maybe it was an accident, and he did care about Joline. Colby may have had his suspicions, and Ray may have thought Colby should have cared for her better?"

"Angelo, you certainly have a way of complicating a case—" Tom rolled his eyes toward Angelo. "Or making it clearer to see."

"Hey, I wouldn't rule anyone out, including Rudy Jenkins."

"I know. There are probably many more clues or answers in Joline's journal, but I'm not comfortable getting it or telling Laurie we found it. It's a tough call."

"It wouldn't be hard to get."

Tom smirked. "I like you better on this side of the metal bars. Remember the food."

Angelo nodded. "That is a very good point." Glancing up, he added, "Speaking of Colby."

"Hello, Father. Angelo," said Laurie Chase as she approached them. "You're still in town, I see. They're releasing Joline's body—" She squeezed her eyes tight for a second and pressed her hand over her heart. "For the funeral. We're thinkin' of Saturday. Could you tell Father Paul?"

Nodding, Tom replied softly, "Of course. If there is anything I can do, please don't hesitate to ask. I mean that."

Laurie pulled a tissue from her pocket and dabbed the edges of her eyes to dry them. "I appreciate that. I really do. I appreciate that you took an interest in Joline and her art the other night. Most people don't know or appreciate that side of her. At least, they never did with me."

"We all deserve to be noticed and appreciated. Can I ask you a question? Was Joline dating Rudy Jenkins?" asked Tom.

Laurie shrugged. "Off and on. Rudy was crazy about Jo. What boy wouldn't be? But she wasn't ready to commit to anyone. She wanted to experience the world and would spend hours in her room writin' and paintin'. I was hopin' she would go out with a boy like Nick, but I guess she, um— well, she liked to know she was attractive. I think she longed for love but was deathly afraid of it, I guess. Who isn't?"

"How have you and Colby been doing?"

"I just feel numb. I think I'm in complete denial, but Colby has been—I don't know. We've been havin' a tough time of it for a while, but he seems unhinged at the moment."

"Do you think he suspects someone in particular?"

"Hmm."

"He had a fight down in the boatyard the other day with Ray Jordy. Do you think he would suspect Ray in any way?"

"Ray? Ray would never harm Joline. He couldn't. He's always been close to her. I think he's just, well—Colby looks for reasons to be jealous. He's not secure when other men are around me, or Joline, for that matter. He's either smotherin' you or angry and detached."

"I don't mean to be too personal, but has Colby ever been physically abusive when he gets jealous?"

"Well, that's pretty personal." Laurie shot Tom a glaring stare. "Please let Father Paul know I will give him a call later."

Tom nodded. "I will, and I'm sorry. I didn't mean to infer anything. I care about you and Joline, and I just wanted—"

Laurie let out a sigh and pursed her lips. "I know. Joline was all I ever had in life. She's the only real love I've known, but I felt as if I lost that a few years ago, and now I've lost any hope of havin' her back. I am so confused." She turned to leave. "I'm sorry."

Tom called out, "I'm here to talk anytime." He and Angelo watched her disappear down the sidewalk. "I'm worried about her."

"And I think she's worried, too," murmured Angelo.

"I know. I know. We could find out more from the journal. I think I need a cup of coffee. There's a bookshop down the road here that has some great coffee. I just want to call Father Paul to see if he needs anything." He pulled out his cell phone and hit a number on his contact list. "Hi, Paul? What do you mean, 'Who's this?' I know. We were supposed to play golf this week. If I get you some of those cookies from the bookshop, will it make up for my being a bad guest? They're big, you know? Okay, I'll see if they have three." Tom hung up and smiled as he headed with Angelo to the bookshop and opened the creaky wooden door.

The old man who owned the shop finished putting a handful of books onto a shelf before turning. "Ahh, you did come back."

"Gary, right? This is Angelo. I told him about your great coffee and cookies. We were wondering if there were any left."

Gary pointed toward the small café in the back. "I would usually say, 'If you're lucky.'"

"Why is that?" asked Tom.

"Things have been slow. Who wants to bring their families to town if they think a murderer might be on the loose? I don't mean to make light of that poor girl's death, but did you ever see those mystery series on public TV? The whole town sits around while everyone gets knocked off one by one."

Tom nodded. "I always wondered why people in those shows weren't more worried."

"Well, what are we doing differently? Running our shops as if nothing has happened, but what if it was murder?" Gary shook his head as he opened up a box of the newly delivered books.

Tom and Angelo entered the tiny café area with the old pastry counter and a few small tables and chairs. The girl turned and smiled. "You came back!"

"And you're still here, Megan," said Tom with a smile.

Megan stood on her toes and peered through the café doorway, whispering, "They haven't fired me yet."

"That's good. Could we have three of your best hazelnut coffees and three, make that four of your famous orange-molasses cookies I see there in the jar."

"Oh, they're not mine, but they are addicting." She fixed their coffees and added, "That Ralph guy comes in every day and has two of them. He stands there and just watches me working, talking with his mouth full half the time. He makes me nervous."

"What does he say?"

Megan tightened her shoulders as if to shudder at the thought of being alone with him in that tiny area. "I don't know. He's always bragging about this or that. He seems to have a thing for teenage girls. I don't know why. None of us have a thing for him. Ick."

Tom replied, "Well, I hope there's always someone else in the shop with you. Gary said it's been pretty quiet."

"Yeah, except for the creep. He seemed exceptionally happy when he came in here just before you arrived. He said he had a big opportunity in the works. He wanted to know when I finished work, and I told him he was the last person I would tell that to. That's when he got angry like he used to with Joline. She never took any of his crap—sorry for the language, but I could think of worse things to say. She kind of pushed it with him, but I got really pissed—sorry—when he said she probably deserved it. Those black eyes and his sarcastic smile scared me, and I told him to get lost. Now, I'm afraid of what he might do." She handed Tom the tray of coffee cups and a bag with the cookies.

"I will see what I can do. I would let Gary know that you don't want him alone with you in the café." Tom gave her a twenty and said to keep the change and take care of herself.

When they reached the rectory, Paul was standing at the entrance with a smile at the sight of a full bag from the bookshop and his companions, seemingly in that order.

<h1 style="text-align:center">Chapter 23</h1>

At close to noon, Tom made a phone call. "Sheriff Coombs, it's Father Tom. I've been thinking about things, and I feel as if I owe you lunch and an apology...oh, did you get new evidence...sure, I'd be up for that. I'll see you in an hour."

Paul lifted his eyebrows. "What was that all about?"

"Ahh. They brought Bill McCready back in."

"For questioning?"

"No. They arrested him for the murder of Joline Chase. They had forensics do a check on McCready's boat and a piece of fabric Angelo pulled from the ashes. It looks as if they found traces of Joline's blood on the gunwale and helm of his boat and also on the fabric. That, combined with his being seen with her a very short time before her death, his suddenly urgent getaway vacation, and lack of answers, pointed to him being a strong suspect."

Paul's gaze drifted off, and Angelo interjected, "Being arrested makes you more than a suspect. It's hard to argue with the sheriff's logic. Even if it was a moment of passion, I wonder what would have gotten him that angry?"

"Or afraid," added Tom.

"Why do you say, 'afraid?'" asked Paul.

"Well, fear and anger usually go together, two sides of the same coin for many people."

An hour later, Tom approached the police station door, which opened before he could reach the handle.

Exiting was Ralph Cutter, who shot Tom a wary glance. His eyes only seemed to grow darker as he squinted, gave a nervous smile, and snickered before heading off.

Tom entered the lobby, and a police officer tipped his cap, pointing toward J.C.'s office. Tom approached, and knocked on the door jamb. "You got your man, Sheriff?"

J.C. glanced up and waved him in as he finished putting some papers into a folder. "Come in, Father. Yes, I think we have him. He's not saying very much, but there is too much evidence pointin' his way to ignore. By the way, you were apologizin' to me, but I think I should be apologizin' to you, *niddbc*. I may have felt a little stressed about havin' a potential killer on the streets and, as my wife, Beth, said, a little gruff with you."

"It has to be stressful trying to protect an entire town when a tragic death is unsolved, so no apologies necessary." Tom smiled. "Thank your wife for me, though. You are a lucky man to have her and your son, Joseph, to share life with. What is that word you used—*nidbik*?"

J.C. gave a broad smile. "*Niddbc*. It means, 'my friend.'"

Tom felt moved by the sincerity in J.C.'s eyes and gave a slight nod and smiled back.

"Speaking of wives, Beth just brought this warm lunch. She always brings twice what I can eat, so you are welcome to try some authentic Penobscot food."

Tom watched as J.C. pulled out containers from the thermal bag. Before he knew it, he was handed a plate filled with grilled trout, a colorful dish of multiple layers of freshly cooked vegetables, and cranberry-nut cornbread. He closed his eyes, said grace, took a bite to savor the herb-flavored fish, and nodded. "This is excellent."

"Simple but always fresh and healthy. You should come over when we do a full-out Sunday dinner."

Tom took a forkful of the vegetables, and his mouth curled into a smile as he let the taste linger on his tongue. "Do you eat like this every day?"

"I wish. Pizza, Kentucky Fried Chicken, and hamburgers on the grill are regulars on the menu," J.C. said with a laugh. He definitely seemed more relaxed.

"You said that McCready wasn't talking much?"

J.C.'s demeanor became more somber again. "Nothin'. Darndest thing. No comment about the blood on the boat or the remnants of his shirt in the firepit ashes. No explanation for Joline seein' him twice that evenin' or why he left Traci's upset or why he was in the area you were attacked. No believable story for his panicked need to get out of town late that evenin', pullin' his boat in after midnight and wakin' his family early in the mornin'. And no explanation for why we found Joline's missin' pearl earring on his boat, the boat he claimed she never set foot on. Maybe it wasn't her feet on the boat, but that earring matched the one she was wearing that night."

Tom took a sip from the paper cup. "That is a lot to explain. If I didn't do it, I would be working pretty hard to help explain something, but he's not saying anything."

"Nope. Nothin' other than a shake of the head or a blank stare. A guilty stare, if you ask me."

"Huh. I saw Ralph Cutter leaving the station as I came in. Anything going on with him?"

J.C. scratched his short, thick black hair and pursed his lips. "Yeah, I don't know what that was all about. He came in after we questioned McCready, requestin' to see him. For some reason, McCready agreed, and they spoke for no more than a few minutes. I have no idea what was said, but one of them seemed happy."

"I take it that Ralph was the one smiling?"

Squinting, J.C. replied, "How did you know that?"

"Just a hunch. So, did you really only ask me here to feed me a great meal and apologize for giving me a hard time? I'm sensing there's more."

J.C. stood up and grabbed the large key on the wall. "McCready made a request. He asked to see a priest—and he asked specifically for you. You don't have to see him, but that's the deal."

Tom grabbed a piece of cornbread. "I'd be happy to talk with McCready if you're okay with it. One question: are we still *niddbcs*?"

"Very funny, *wagabit*. Very funny," replied J.C. as he led Tom to the back area where two jail cells stood, one with a hunched-over Bill McCready sitting alone in his otherwise empty cell. "McCready, did you still want to talk to a priest?"

McCready stood up, not a spark of hope on his face, nodding.

J.C. turned to Tom. "I can get a chair for you to sit outside the cell and close this door so you can talk in private."

Tom shook his head. "I'd rather sit inside with Mr. McCready if he's okay with that."

McCready nodded, and J.C. paused as if to assess how comfortable he was with leaving Tom alone in the cell with a suspected murderer. He let out a long sigh and turned toward McCready. "One peep from him, and I'm in here like it's nobody's business."

He inserted the large key into the cell door and opened it for Tom, who whispered to J.C. as he stepped by him. "What's a '*wagabit*'?"

J.C. shook his head. "Just make sure you yell at the first sign of danger."

Tom faced McCready, who remained seated on a metal bench. "Is it okay if I sit?" Tom pointed to the thin cot covered by a worn and tattered blanket.

McCready nodded, and Tom sat down, forearms resting on his knees as they both remained silent.

"Can I ask why you wanted to see me?" asked Tom.

No response.

"Did you want to talk or—"

"Or. If I talk to you, is it confidential? What do they call it?"

Tom leaned forward. "Mr. McCready, do you want to make a confession?"

"If I do, is it confidential? Can you tell anyone what we talked about?"

"If you are truly making a confession, it's called the Seal of Confession, and, no, I'm not allowed to divulge anything we talk about. Did you want to make a confession? Do you repent something you did?"

McCready raised his head. "Father Tom, is it? We don't have the time for all the things I regret in my life."

Tom turned and scanned the cell. "Are you going somewhere? I've got all the time you need. Are you Catholic?"

McCready bobbed his head. "I was baptized Catholic, but my family never really went, and I've never checked it out."

"Okay. Have you ever been to confession?"

McCready shook his head.

"Tell me about yourself. You have a wife and three kids. I imagine they mean a great deal to you?"

He nodded, and Tom spotted a teardrop make its mark on McCready's pant leg. "I didn't kill Joline." Raising his head to look directly into Tom's eyes. "I would never try to hurt her."

"I believe you would never try to hurt her, but did you?"

He nodded.

"Can you tell me how you hurt her?"

He shook his head.

"Mr. McCready, I feel as if you want to tell me something. You know that God knows everything. He knows our hearts. There is nothing we can do that He won't forgive if we are truly sorry and confess."

Tears now streamed down his cheeks as he trembled. "I can't. I just can't."

"Mr. McCready, I understand this is very hard, but the police are going to need answers. Why did Joline come to see you at the school and later that night? What happened when you left the diner? Did she threaten you? Why did you suddenly need to leave town? If you didn't kill her, you need to give people a reason to believe that."

"Don't you think I know that? Sorry. I need to be alone to think."

"Okay, Mr. McCready. Please have them call me anytime if you need an ear or anything."

Tom stood with McCready and reached out his hand.

Seemingly surprised, McCready took it and shook it. "Call me, Bill."

"Okay, Bill. Um...I don't mean to pry, but why would Ralph Cutter come to visit you? Are you close friends?"

Suddenly, McCready's face flushed, and his eyes filled with panic, but he didn't say a word.

Outside the jail cell area, J.C. stared at Tom, possibly for any signals he could discern, but Tom offered none.

"Did he tell you anything?"

"You know those conversations are confidential. It doesn't matter what he tells me; as a priest, I can't pass it on to you."

"Are you sayin' he made a confession, and you know whether or not he is guilty? If he murdered that girl and said he was sorry, would you absolve him from his sin? He's free and clear. Is that what you're tellin' me?"

Tom made eye contact with J.C. "I can't tell you anything he said. Just so you know, being sorry for your sins is what God asks of us, and He is a God of love and infinite mercy, but—"

"But!"

Tom put his hand on J.C.'s shoulder, "But there is always justice to be paid, and we are responsible for those we hurt. I can tell you that I did ask him why Ralph Cutter visited him. He seemed panicked by the question. I don't think it was a friendly visit."

J.C. ran his hand through his hair. "You told me you wanted to help. Let me know when that help is comin' 'cause I need to solve this thing. People need to know justice matters and that they're safe sleepin' in this town at night, includin' my family."

As Tom returned to the rectory, J.C. stood in the police station doorway, appearing as confused as he did when Joline was brought in on the *Emily Lauren*.

Chapter 24

Back at the rectory, Tom sat on the porch steps as Paul and Angelo came out with their cups of tea.

"Does the sheriff have his man?" asked Angelo.

"I'm not sure," replied Tom. "Do you want to take a ride?"

"Not I, said the real priest," joked Paul.

Tom and Angelo climbed into Tom's Honda Accord, both making the Sign of the Cross as Tom turned the key to start it up. Relief came with their prayers being answered as Tom drove out of town, heading north.

"Are we going fishing?" asked Angelo with a smile.

"You are a smart man. I'm assuming McCready's family is still at the Swan Lake cabin. I didn't see McCready's car in their driveway back in Belfast."

Finding the rutted dirt driveway leading to the cabin where the McCreadys were staying took a while, and Tom slowed down to see McCready's son playing in the yard. Tom stepped out of the car and approached the boy. "How is the expert fisherman?"

The boy glanced up, but Mrs. McCready stepped out onto the cabin porch before he could answer. "Will! Come here, please." She waved him over.

Will took a step and turned toward Tom. "You were here before, on the boat."

Tom nodded and approached the cabin with Angelo. "Mrs. McCready, I wanted to let you know that I spoke to your husband today."

"Will, can you go into the house and take care of the girls?"

"Mom."

"Please. I need to speak to these gentlemen, and I'm sure they will be on their way in a few minutes." Reluctantly, Will plodded into the house, and Mrs. McCready turned back to Tom and Angelo. "They came and took the boat, the car, and then my husband. I don't understand what's going on." She collapsed onto the wooden bench outside the cabin door.

"Mrs. McCready, I am sure the truth will come out. If your husband is innocent, we will make sure—"

She raised her hand and bit down on her bottom lip. "I told Bill that the truth had to come out. He looked horrified when I said it. I know he couldn't have killed that girl. He couldn't kill anyone. He's a history teacher. He loves history and teaching. That's not the description of a murderer. Why do they think he could do this?"

"Mrs. McCready, did your husband ever talk about Joline Chase? Or any of the other students at school?" asked Tom.

"He always talked about one student or another, especially those who came to love history. I remember him talking about Joline several years ago. She would come for help after school, and he was worried she might have a schoolgirl crush on him. He wanted my advice on handling the situation, but I think it took care of itself, and I never heard him mention her again. I don't think she was even in his class again. Why are you asking?"

Tom replied, "No particular reason. What about Ralph Cutter? Did he ever mention him?"

She rubbed her mouth. "Cutter? Bill would go to the diner sometimes when he was doing night fishing. That guy always bothered Bill because he would hang around school events despite having no wife or kids. Why would he be there? Bill thought he lived across the way from the track and football field. Oddly, he came by here earlier, looking for Bill. I don't know what it was about, but he wasn't too quick to leave after I told him he wasn't here. He started asking about the kids and me. He just has a way of making you feel uncomfortable after a while. Do you know what I mean? Then, finally, he left."

"So, they weren't friends or business associates of any kind?"

She raised her brow. "No way. Bill didn't like or trust him in the least."

"Mrs. McCready, was there anything else that seemed unusual recently?"

Her eyes drifted off toward the lake. "Everything seems unusual right now. I don't know what end is up. This sudden trip seemed unusual. Bill wanted to get away for a peaceful week, but he seemed agitated the whole time, disappearing for periods of time during the day or late at night. You two showed up that day on the boat, and then, out of the blue, Bill wanted a new boat and started working on a home equity loan the other day. Nothing about the week seemed peaceful—like then the police came and arrested him. What am I to think?"

Tom nodded. "I can imagine how confusing this must be for you, but I still think the truth will find its way. I promise."

She gave half a smile.

"Well, Angelo and I don't want to bother you anymore. Is there anything we can do for you?"

She stood up. "Thank you for offering. My older sister is coming by to take us to her house. Funny, she never wanted me to marry Bill. I was a freshman when he started teaching down in Portland. He was fresh out of college, and I thought he was so smart and mature compared to the other boys."

"You were a freshman in college. Where were you attending?"

"No. High school. Bill's eight years older than me. I never had him as a teacher, but we would see each other in the hallway, and I felt like he was the kind of guy I wanted to be with. He always gave me a look that made me feel better about myself. Well, we met again when I was a junior at USM, and he was teaching a night class to make extra money. My sister thought I was too young and too pretty for him. She used to say that men who like much younger women were just wired to always be attracted to younger women and get tired of anyone they are with, but Bill's been a great husband and father."

"A good man is hard to find," said Tom, handing her a card with his number written on the back. "If you need anything, please don't hesitate to call."

"Thank you. You know, there was one strange thing. Bill had left an envelope on his bureau, and now it's gone. I don't know if he took it when the officers came or if that Cutter guy from the diner grabbed it somehow."

Brow raised in curiosity, Tom asked, "Did Cutter go into the cabin?"

"I didn't think so, but something about him makes me want to wash."

Angelo asked, "Mrs. McCready, do you have any clue what was in the envelope?"

She shook her head. "No idea. There were initials on the outside, but they were crossed off. I think *RJ* or *RJC* or something like that."

"Okay. Take care of yourself and those precious kids of yours."

As Tom and Angelo drove off, Angelo asked, "So, do your heavenly instincts tell you if McCready is a guilty man or not? A double life that fools even his wife?"

"I don't know, Angelo. If we assume the sheriff is right, but he's actually innocent, we're taking our eye off the other possible suspects. If McCready is guilty, I don't know if the circumstantial evidence would be enough to convict him. What's his motive? Were there any witnesses? Those initials on the envelope—"

"Um. *RJ,* or she said it could have been something like *RJC.* I vote for the latter since you don't normally recall letters that weren't there. Do you think there is any connection to the *RJ* in Joline's journal?"

Tom glanced over. "That's right. Potentially the father of her baby, but I've never heard anything about her having a baby. I really hope she didn't have an abortion. Maybe we should be talking to Ray Jordy about his connections with

Bill McCready. You did find that paternity test bill in his house.”

Tom parked at the town pier, and as they headed toward the boatyard, Angelo pointed toward the worn, gray-shingled Front Street Pub. “Isn’t that Jordy heading into the pub?”

“Could be. It’s around quitting time.”

Inside, it looked like an old small-town pub, with a wooden bar, stools and booths, and lots of local beers and ales on tap. Ray Jordy had taken a stool at the bar, but Tom noticed the fisherman he had spoken to days before. “Captain Mike. Do I have that right? My memory is fading in my old age.”

Mike turned from his half-empty mug with a laugh. “Ah, Father, if you’re old, then what does that make me?”

“Wiser than me?” Tom smiled as he caught the bartender’s attention and pointed to both Mike and Ray. “Can you get these gentlemen whatever they’d like, and what would you recommend for a local draft?”

“If it’s your first time, welcome. I’d recommend a flight of different beers so you can sample some good ones,” replied the tall bartender as Tom and Angelo sat down on their stools.

“Sounds good.” Tom turned to Ray, sitting to his right as Angelo talked with Captain Mike. “Mr. Jordy, I feel as if we’ve gotten off on the wrong foot.”

Ray didn’t look up but stared into the cold beer set in front of him. “Thanks for the beer, but it doesn’t change anything.”

“The last thing I want to do is cause more pain for you or the Chases. Joline deserves some justice and Laurie and Colby some peace.”

Ray took a sip and then shook his head. “This isn’t the *Bells of St. Mary’s*. You don’t know this town. You don’t know me or Laurie or Colby, and you certainly didn’t know Jo. If you want peace, stop stirring things up and sticking your nose where it doesn’t belong. No offense intended.”

The bartender set down a flight of eight beers in front of Tom and Angelo, quickly pointing to each one to let them know the name and type.

Tom leaned toward Ray. "Which one should I try first?"

Ray pointed to the second one from the right. "If you like a Guinness—"

"And I do." Tom took a long sip. "That is very good."

"Look, Father—"

"Tom."

"Okay, Father Tom. We can't bring Jo back. Talking with Laurie will only bring up more pain and hurt. She's been trying to move forward in her life. I just think you need to let things go."

Tom nodded. "Understood, and I appreciate your insights. It sounds as if you care quite a bit. You've known Laurie for a long time, right?"

Ray stared down and nodded; the reddish-brown in his beard stood out more than ever to Tom. "Yeah. Ever since I can remember." He gave a slight laugh. "It was kind of like a club for misfits. None of us had our real dads around growing up. Laurie had her stepdad, but I don't know if that was a good thing."

"So, you knew Colby and Laurie at the same time?"

"Yep. And Danny. He was an honorary member only because his dad was alive but not really around much. He spent more time with the bottle than his family. That might be the only thing he left to his son."

"So, Laurie had a tough childhood?"

"She was fun, beautiful, and great to be with, but underneath, she really struggled to cope with life. Sometimes, I think Jo tried to be like her mom, you know, thinking you are only worth something if a boy likes you or finds you attractive. I should talk."

Tom leaned a bit closer. "What do you mean?"

"I'm not a good person. I empathize with girls that have, what do you call it, low self-esteem, but then—" He paused and then took a long drink from his mug. "I'm just avoiding life as much as anyone. If I believed in God or the devil, there would be no contest. I'm way too easy to tempt, and it takes no more than a light breeze to collapse this house of cards."

"Well, I can't make you believe, but both God and the devil are real. The devil is okay with you not believing in him, and he is very cunning, dragging you down and making you think you're not good enough for God, so why bother?"

Ray squinted. "You really believe in that stuff, huh?"

"Yep. And I haven't met too many people who are happy and at peace who don't. Can I ask you a few questions?"

Ray shrugged. "Shoot."

"Don't take any offense at any of these. I'm just curious. You own a yellow truck, right?"

He nodded.

"Did you follow Joline to the high school and then down to the harbor that Friday night?"

"Nope."

"So, what was your relationship with Joline?"

Ray stared at Tom for a second. "None of your business. No offense intended."

"Okay. Why did you and Colby have a falling out a few years ago?"

"Like I said, none of your business, Father."

"Hmm. Understood. I won't ask why you abruptly left the church service on Saturday, but can you say what your conversation was with Joline that Friday morning outside of Traci's Diner?"

Ray finished his beer and dropped a ten on the counter. "Please mind your own business. You don't know us, and you aren't helping." And he stomped out of the pub, leaving Tom with Angelo and Captain Mike.

Tom shifted his stool. "I hope your conversation is going better than mine did."

"You say that as if you're surprised." Angelo chuckled. "We were just talking about trout fishing and his wife's laundry business."

Tom smiled. "Ah, so your boat is a one-man operation, but home is a different story. I guess you heard that Bill McCready was arrested for Joline's death."

Mike nodded. "And I'm guessin' that's why you were askin' so many questions about Bill the other day. I would never have guessed. Do you think he did it?"

"I don't know, but it doesn't sound as if you believe he did."

"Who knows what to believe anymore? I'm too old to be surprised by anythin' or anyone these days. I guess he did kinda hightail it outta town that night. What happened with Ray Jordy there? Usually, he's here for a few hours after work and never leaves after only one. Was he all right?"

Tom pursed his lips. "I don't think he appreciates me poking my nose where it doesn't belong. He's right. I don't really know the people in town, their history, or their relationships."

"Well, there's somethin' to what he says," replied Mike.

"I know," said Tom.

"Those kids were a little on the wild side, if you know what I mean."

Tom narrowed his eyes. "Joline and her friends?"

"No, Jordy, Chase, Haskell, and Clarke. I guess you always worry when you see kids too young to know better actin' like they're too young to know better. You know what I mean? Of course, no one ever gave them much to hang onto or believe in. We seem to go round and round, makin' the same mistakes from generation to generation. It's sad, you know."

Angelo said, "It is sad because it's so true. Hey, you mentioned the name Clarke."

"Laurie Clarke, before she got hitched to Chase. Usually, when I see a girl actin' out like that, somethin's not right inside. Her girl, Joline, seemed to be goin' down the same path. They ought to think more of themselves and want to be treated with respect. Girls seem to just want to be like 19-year-old boys these days." Mike finished up his drink and stood up. "Thanks for the refreshment, boys. I'd have another, but I've gotta catch me some dinner."

Tom sat with Angelo, thinking about what Captain Mike had said. "The impact a missing dad can have on a person's whole life is no small thing."

Angelo nodded as he took a sip from another beer. "Tell me about it."

Chapter 25

As Tom and Angelo passed the police station on their way back to the rectory, Tom recognized the woman sitting in the driver's seat of the parked car outside the front door—Mrs. McCready with her children in the backseat. If she was visiting her husband, Bill, why was she hesitating to go inside? Before he could consider the possibilities, J.C. Coombs escorted Bill McCready out the front door to the car. They shook hands, and McCready got into the passenger side. As the McCready's drove off, J.C. glanced up at Tom and shook his head.

J.C. stepped off the curb to greet them. "You did say you weren't sure he was guilty."

Tom replied, "What happened? Did you unarrest McCready?"

J.C. nodded. "A witness came forward and said he saw McCready and Joline leavin' Traci's diner and making their way down the harbor walk before eventually partin' ways when some of the Norsemen gave them a hard time. Supposedly, McCready warded them off, and then they chased him down the path on their bikes, and he narrowly escaped on his boat."

"Huh. Did McCready confirm that scenario?"

J.C. nodded. "Yep. I got independent testimonies, and they matched. That's how McCready got the gash under his eye and why he felt he needed to get his family out of town that morning."

"Some of that makes sense, but it doesn't explain Joline's earring and the remnants of her blood on the boat and his shirt," said Angelo.

"McCready said that he drove Joline from the school down to the harbor earlier that evenin', and she got on his boat and may have cut her finger or somethin'. I guess it's possible, but this witness will testify that McCready did not kill Joline that night," replied J.C.

"Kind of interesting that the witness didn't say anything for five days and suddenly comes forward. Can you say who it was?" asked Tom.

J.C. raised his head and glanced at Tom. "Cutter, from the diner. He said he saw them in the diner that night, arguin' a bit before they left by the side door when he was taking a smoke. The diner was slow, and he was curious, so he followed them down to the walk to see what would happen. He signed a statement, and right now, I've got nothin' more than suspicion to hold McCready."

"Huh. I wondered why Ralph visited McCready. They could have coordinated a story for something in return. Just a thought," said Tom.

"Oh, the same thoughts are rattlin' around my old head, too. I don't know if I'm back to square one or not, but I have to get goin'. When are you boys leavin' town?"

"Sometime, Sunday. You know you're going to miss us, Sheriff," said Tom with a laugh.

J.C. glanced at them and shook his head as he started back into the station. "I think I'll get over it."

Angelo stood with Tom in front of the station. "Do you smell fish?"

"Very fishy, Angelo. Very fishy."

Angelo decided to take a detour of his own as Tom returned to the rectory and spotted Paul on the porch reading. "I've been a terrible guest, haven't I?" said Tom.

Paul smirked. "How would I know?"

"I know. I know. I haven't been around much, have I?" He took a seat in the wicker chair next to Paul. "I don't know if I've been good for anyone in town."

"Now, what makes you say that?"

"That's how people have been letting me know I'm poking my nose in places I wasn't invited. Colby Chase and Ray Jordy have been pretty clear about that, and I'm not sure that the sheriff is too happy with me either. Tom broke off a piece of cookie from the plate on the small wicker table between them.

"Tom, we've been friends a long time. One thing I admire about you is your sense of people and how much you respect and care about them. I know that we share our faith in a way that we propose it versus imposing it, but I often wonder if I'm too passive with people in town who never hear about the point of life that Jesus taught us. He wanted us to at least know about God's plan to have a chance of living life with joy, and I wonder if I hold back too much for them to come to my door to ask about it. You know better than I that people find their greatest gifts when they go into the darkest places they tend to avoid the most. I think you make yourself available to help them push through those walls that keep them from living. Your instincts are good ones, Tom, so I wouldn't be too hard on yourself. The fact that you're even asking the hard question means you care about them more than yourself."

"You are very kind, my good friend."

Paul glanced down and noticed that the rest of the orange molasses cookie was no longer on the plate. "You know that was the last one, don't you?"

Before Tom could answer, Laurie Chase approached the porch. "Hi, Father Paul. I assume Father Tom let you know that we'd like to have the funeral for Joline on Sat—" She brought her hand to her mouth. "I'm sorry."

Paul got up with Tom and stepped down to the sidewalk where she stood. "Absolutely. Whenever you are ready, we can sit down to talk about readings, music, or anything special you would like for Joline."

"I appreciate that, Father Paul. I'm sorry we haven't been to church in so long, but I would like her to have something, you know, beautiful, something meaningful. I really loved her so much. I don't know what I can do for her right now except for this." Mascara and tears ran down Laurie's face, and Tom handed her a handkerchief.

"My white handkerchief knight comes to the rescue again."

Tom tilted his head. "Actually, I wanted to apologize for my behavior this week. I was talking with Ray Jordy earlier, and he was right. He told me that I really don't know the people in this town, the history, or the relationships, and I've been poking my nose in places without invitation. I—"

Laurie held her hand out. "Father Tom, please don't apologize. Sometimes, I felt as if you were the only one who wanted to know the truth, the only one who cared to want to know Joline on the inside. I know Colby and Ray have been pushing you to mind your own business, but I don't feel the same way. You've been very kind and helpful to me, and I think Joline would have appreciated that."

Tom felt a tear making its way to the corner of his eye with the sincerity of her words coming just when he doubted himself. "That means a great deal to me. It really does. I assume you heard that Bill McCready is no longer being held?"

Laurie bit her lower lip. "I did. Joline used to talk about him all the time a few years back, and then she never mentioned him again. I never knew why or what happened, but it seems as if everything changed around then, between her and me and with Colby. It's almost as if she died twice, back then and now for good."

Paul glanced down at his watch. "Laurie, I hope you can excuse me; I have a call coming in in a few minutes. We can talk anytime you want."

When he disappeared into the rectory, Laurie turned to Tom. "Father Tom, I feel as if I failed her as a mother. I think I held on too tight and wanted to protect her. I wanted her to be loved and accepted, but I don't know if I taught her the right things. Is it a sin to be a rotten mother? I really did love her, but she deserved a better mother. I never had a real mother to love me, and I didn't know what to do."

Compassion filled Tom. "Kids don't need perfect parents. They just want to know that they matter and that you love them the best you can. How did you feel about your stepmother?"

Laurie exhaled a deep sigh. "I wanted to know that my real mother loved me. I don't know why she didn't want me. At least my stepmother adopted me, but somehow, it's not the same. She wasn't a soft or loving type, almost cold at times. I don't know if she knew how to be a mother. She would always tell me to be pretty, to be attractive because that was how I would find a boyfriend and husband someday." Tears began to stream down her cheeks again as she wiped them as fast as they flowed. "I thought that was all that mattered, and I'm so afraid that's what I taught Joline. I think Joline wanted to believe there was more to her inside, but I couldn't stop myself from commenting on how beautiful she was, what she was wearing, and asking if any boys were interested in her. Why would I do that to her when it never made me happy?"

"Laurie, you can't beat yourself up over guilt. You know you loved her and tried your best. You have to trust that she is in God's loving arms and that He will take care of her."

She glanced up at Tom with wide eyes full of fear. "That's the problem. I don't know that she is in heaven, and now I can't do anything for her. I can't fix the damage I've done. It wasn't her fault, and I can't even tell her I'm sorry."

"You can still pray for her."

Laurie shook her head and walked away in pain.

He wondered again if he had been any help.

Chapter 26

Tom stepped into the parish office just as Paul finished his phone call. Tom asked, "Are you up for nine holes?"

Paul's eyes widened. "Don't kid me, now. Are you saying that Sherlock can spare time to hit the links with a peasant priest like me?"

"It's a beautiful afternoon. The sun's out, and there's nothing I'd rather be doing."

The local golf course was small but beautiful with its green, rolling, tree-lined fairways and stone bridges. Tom felt good being out on the course and enjoyed the friendly banter and competition. As they readied to tee off on the ninth hole, Paul said, "This was just what I needed: a little fun and the chance to finally beat you at something."

Tom laughed as he drove the ball down the fairway. "No one has beaten anyone yet."

Stepping down the sloping fairway, Paul said, "I'm a stroke up, and you're using my old third-hand clubs. How can I lose? I do miss spending time with you like we did when I was in Boston, but this is good." When they reached Paul's fairway lie, he pulled out his three-iron and landed his shot right on the green. "Yes, this is very good," he added with a smile.

"That was a very nice shot, Padre Paul," said Tom as he approached his ball. "I do still have a chance if I—" His shot floated in the air, and as it approached the green, it dropped short into the sand trap in front of the green. "If I didn't do that," finished Tom.

Paul smirked and patted Tom on the back. "I see you still enjoy going to the beach." With a one-stroke lead, Paul's lie on the green, and Tom's shot buried in the sand, it appeared as if Tom would be treating Paul to a free dinner. "I'm thinking about one of those very expensive rib-eye steaks tonight."

Tom pulled the sand wedge from his golf bag and stepped into the deep bunker of sand. He couldn't even see the pin from where he was. "They do say it ain't over 'til it's over."

"Oh, it's over, and the fat lady is singing. It's definitely over," said Paul with a friendly laugh.

Tom scratched his scalp as he stood at an awkward angle on the sloping sand trap. He lifted his head to the sky and said, "Oh, Lord, have mercy on me and deliver me from this desert." He brought back his club and sprayed the golden sand as the ball barely made its way over the grassy lip of the trap.

Tom climbed the embankment, and Paul watched incredulously as the ball slowly sputtered onto the green and rolled right into the cup. Paul's club dropped from his hand, staring at the same blue sky, and said, "Haven't I been a good priest, too?"

Tom smiled when he reached the green, realizing what had happened. "You know, you are so right. It does seem like a good night for a juicy rib-eye steak."

"How about a pizza?"

As they approached the café-style restaurant tucked into the lower level of a historic building on the sloping Main Street, Tom smiled at the *Meanwhile in Belfast* name. Paul said they had tasty Neapolitan-style wood-fired pizza, Italian fare, and a good wine selection. It was perfect for a nice summer evening with outdoor seating. Angelo met them there, and he was seated at a small table already full of antipasto and warmed olives in a tasty-looking herbed oil.

"*Buona sera, padri,*" said Angelo as he lifted his glass of wine.

"*Possiamo unirci a te?*" asked Tom.

Angelo laughed. "*Solo se stai pagando.*"

Paul sat and said, "I don't have a clue what you two are talking about."

Tom motioned for the waiter as he replied to Paul, "It's Italian. I asked if we could join Angelo, and he said only if we were paying. I think that means you."

"I would love to learn Italian and have one of those men in stripes ride me down that beautiful canal in a gondolier in Venice!" exclaimed the portly waiter with dark wavy hair and a broad smile who now stood by their table. "I'm Rick, and I'll be serving and entertaining you this evening."

Paul asked, "I haven't been here for a while. How have you been, Rick?"

"I'd rather be happy than sad, so I pick happy," Rick replied as he eyed Tom up and down. "Don't tell me this one is a priest, too, Paul. That would be disappointing."

Tom reached out his hand. "Sorry, but it's a pleasure to meet you, Rick. My name is Father Tom, and this is my good friend Angelo."

"I've met Mr. Angelo already. Would anyone of you like ice water?"

"That would be great," replied Tom.

"Spring or tap?"

"Either is fine," said Tom. "Unless Father Paul gives a hoot?"

Paul shrugged. "Let's go for spring."

"The hoot's been heard!" Rick blurted out for all the tables to hear. Everyone chuckled as Rick gave a slight bow and headed to the kitchen.

As they toasted and sipped a very rich Tuscan blend, Tom noticed that he could see Traci's Diner up the street and the harbor walk across from where they were sitting.

The owner of the restaurant came to their table, pointing to Paul. "I know this one, but are you gentlemen visiting?"

Tom nodded and raised his glass. "Compliments on the wine. It's very nice, as is your restaurant, and Rick has been taking good care of us."

"Grazie. Rick is an excellent server and quite a joy to have on our staff. I hope you enjoy your evening, and let me know if there is anything I can get you."

"Thank you. Question: how late are you open on Friday nights?" asked Tom.

"We are usually closing up around eleven-thirty or so."

"I was wondering if you noticed anything unusual this past Friday."

The owner pursed his lips. "Oh, when that young girl died. *Molto triste*. Very sad. It was quiet that night when we were closing. Nothing unusual that I can recall."

Tom nodded. "Did you see Joline Chase or Bill McCready that night?"

He shook his head. "Hmmm, I did see Mr. McCready sometime after ten. He comes in sometimes for a pizza or just to say hello, but he just passed. He seemed very anxious about something. I said hello, but he must have been so preoccupied that he never responded. I guess that was unusual for him."

"*Grazie*," said Tom as the owner moved to another table.

Tom turned back to Angelo and Paul. "Do you think he was anxious about meeting with Joline?"

Paul smirked. "I guess we're back playing detectives again."

Tom smiled. "Speaking of which, where did you go today, Angelo?"

Angelo peered around at the other guests and lowered his voice. "A few tidbits. It seems as if McCready sold his boat, or I should say, gave his boat away."

"What? Is he buying a new one?" asked Tom, having a hard time figuring out what caused the sudden sale.

"Not that I could find out. Guess who he transferred ownership of the boat to?" asked Angelo.

"I don't know. Captain Mike?"

"Ralph Cutter."

"What? Why Ralph? Do you mean that when Ralph visits McCready and clears his name, he suddenly is given a boat by McCready? I wonder how much it's worth?"

"Well, it seems as if Ralph wanted to know that himself. Now he's shopping it around and already had an offer of forty-thousand dollars. One of the fishermen on the pier said that he didn't think Ralph had ever in his life been on a boat."

Tom tilted his head. "Boy, this sounds very fishy."

After the waiter took their order for two pizzas, Tom turned to Angelo. "You said a few tidbits. Was there something else?"

Angelo shrugged. "Maybe. Remember when we were at the Front Street Pub earlier, and I was talking with Captain Mike while you were having fun with Ray Jordy?"

"Yeah."

"Well, I think I mentioned that Mike's wife had a laundry business and does pickups from several restaurants on Wednesday. Well, that's today, and I helped her out a bit by bringing a bin out from Traci's."

"And?"

"And, while she was talking with Traci, I rummaged through the bin and found a greasy, stained apron with the initials *RJC* on the inside. Remember when you said his apron seemed awfully clean compared to his tee shirt at breakfast that Sunday?"

Tom seemed perplexed. "I do. *RJC*? Is that Ralph Cutter?"

"I think so. There were some stains on the edges, you know, where you would wipe your hands, and it looked like dried blood, so I took the apron and dropped it off at the sheriff's office to take some samples."

"Wow. Great work, but now things seem more complicated than clearer. When will we know about the bloodstains?"

"It may take a day or so."

Paul said, "Are we going to do detective talk all meal?"

"Well, we could talk about our golf game instead," replied Tom with raised eyebrows.

"No, let's not. So where does this lead you?" asked Paul.

Angelo pulled out a small notebook and flipped through the pages. "We can guess about motives, but I think we need to think more about Joline. Was she ever pregnant, and who might be the reluctant father? She had '*RJ*' with a question in her writings. And was she assaulted or abused in some way by an '*MC*?' Was her behavior getting more risky and bold, especially her sexual behavior? What happened to her that suddenly damaged relations with her father and mother a few years back, around the same time Colby and Ray Jordy had a falling out? What was she pushing McCready on when he left the diner, and what was she arguing with Ray about that morning? Lots of unanswered questions, for sure."

Tom said, "I agree. We may be missing someone completely, but the odds are that a victim usually knows their killer well. Angelo, maybe we can create a board with Joline's relationships, the impact she brought to those relationships, and the possible motives each person might have to—well, you know. In the meantime, I need to visit a couple of people to understand her better."

Paul poured the remainder of the wine into each of their glasses. "I don't want to know where you are getting all this information, but by the sounds of that, I'm guessing I won't be getting my revenge on the greens any time soon."

Chapter 27

Paul reluctantly paid the bill for dinner, and as they stood to leave, Tom noticed a girl across the street. "I think that girl with the flowers over there might be Lizzie Haskell. You two can head home. I want to see if I can catch her."

Tom crossed the street as he watched the girl head toward the harbor walk and followed from a distance until she stopped by the pier near where Joline may have breathed her last breath. He maintained his distance, but he could tell she was shaking as she finally tossed the flowers into the ocean waters. Slowly, Tom stepped beside her and stared down into the dark waters where the flowers floated and began to drift apart. "You miss her."

Lizzie's tears fell and disappeared into the saltwater.

Tom sighed. "Those are lovely flowers in memory of a friendship I'm sure you cherished. Hmm. I see a beautiful assortment there. Let's see. Willow and daisies symbolize forsaken love, pain, and innocence. Pansies refer to love in vain, violets for faithfulness or death of the young, and the poppy signifies death. Are those forget-me-nots I see as well?"

Lizzie nodded with quick breaths.

"You certainly made an effort to honor her memory. There is a famous painting of Ophelia from Shakespeare's Hamlet where she held those same flowers when she—well, it is a beautiful and moving painting if you've never seen it."

"I have seen it. Joline had the painting in her room. Ophelia was beautiful with her auburn hair as she lay in her watery grave, just as Joline must have been. She used to stare at that painting and say she thought she was going as crazy as Ophelia. She kept finding out stuff that made her wonder about everything. I think that's why she was getting more unpredictable. I don't know."

Tom motioned to the wooden bench on the pier. "Do you want to sit for a minute?"

Lizzie nodded, and they sat as the sun started making its move to call it a day. "I just feel so bad that she's dead. I still can't believe it."

"Well, in the most important way, she still lives. Our souls never die, and God has a plan for us that never ends. Sometimes, that helps me cope with losing a girl I loved long ago. It's hard because she didn't have to die, and I could have been a better friend to her, but we have to deal with things as they are."

"I guess. My parents never really believed in any of that stuff, so it's made it hard to make sense of it. Jo believed in God, but she was mad at Him sometimes. Is that okay?"

Tom smiled. "He can take it. He created us for a real relationship with Him. He gave us the dignity of free will so that we had the freedom to accept or reject Him. You don't have a true friendship without that. What was she mad about?"

"Oh, I don't know. Family secrets. Disappointments. Maybe a fear that she wasn't as good or wonderful as everyone thought she was."

Tom pointed to a seagull that landed on the pier. "I think he's hoping we brought some dinner for him." He paused. "Lizzie, you may have known Joline better than anyone. Did something change for her a few years back?"

Lizzie moved uncomfortably in her seat. "What do you mean?"

"Did anything happen to her? Did she find something out or see something that impacted her relationships with anyone?"

She paused for several moments.

Tom quietly waited for Lizzie to collect her thoughts as he watched the flowers drifting with the tide below as two seagulls descended to check them out.

"I know there was something that happened. We used to talk about how boys have so many ways to show their value.

Are they smart, funny, athletic, strong, good leaders, clever—things like that? It's different with girls. We can do all those things, but do they count? When we got to high school, Jo kind of came into her own. She was so beautiful, but she didn't believe it and didn't know if people thought she was anyone. Do you know what I mean? Inside, she was losing her confidence in herself but getting more attention on the outside. Not for what she did or who she was but for how pretty she was. She hated that, but it also gave her power. Where else does a girl have power? Does that sound weird?"

"Not at all, Lizzie. I think it's every woman's battle to believe her value lies in more than her looks or how popular she is. Society tells women they get the man if they are physically attractive, but believing that doesn't work for the girl or the boy."

"I'd like to believe you, Father, but it doesn't seem like that. I don't know that Joline believed that. I think she wanted to, but it was a struggle. I think her mom might have, well, not helped her there—and I haven't really had a mom around for me. So, there's that. There is nothing wrong with being attractive, is there? We want handsome boys, too."

"Lizzie, you are young and about to step away from the security of your home and into your own. It's scary. There is fear that you will be alone without love or family if you don't get picked. I understand that, but you could take the absolute prettiest woman, and if she has nothing inside, no man, even the most shallow, will want to be with her after a while. True beauty comes from within. True love is about friendship, trust, support, struggling on a journey together, and real love versus just physical attraction."

Lizzie turned. "What is real love?"

"Hmm. That's the big question. Jesus shows us what perfect love is by His willingness to give everything for us out of unconditional love. So, for us, it's wanting the absolute best for someone, not for what we get in return, but just for them because we care about them that much. It's knowing the person we love is holding nothing back and will let us show our true selves, even the ugliest parts of ourselves, and still love us even more because they know us more intimately. There is no fear of losing them just because they find out something about us. They have given themselves to us completely for life, and we do the same for them. It's an amazing journey of trust, freedom, and uncovering what true love really is."

Tears rolled down Lizzie's cheeks. "I think that is what she really wanted. I don't know if she ever knew how much she already had."

"We all want that unconditional love and championing in a spouse or a true friend. Lizzie, do you know if Joline was ever abused or if she was ever pregnant?"

Lizzie's head snapped back. "Pregnant? Why would you think that? I've never heard that. Ever. She would have told me. Do you know something?"

"No. No. I was just wondering if she was dealing with any serious issues in her world. I'm sorry for asking. What about her relationship with Rudy Jenkins?"

She shrugged. "He was crazy about her, but I don't think he was ever going to be the one for her."

"What about Mr. McCready? Did she ever talk about him? She went to see him on Friday evening for some reason."

Curling her lip, she shook her head. "Yeah, I don't know why. I remember when we had him for History as sophomores, she used to talk about what it would be like to seduce an older man, to have an affair, but it was all talk. I do think he might have liked her, though. I'd catch him gazing at her during class like she was a painting or something. He seemed harmless, though. I have no idea why she wanted to see him. She never talked about him after that year. Not with me, and we talked about everything."

"What about her mom and dad? Did she ever talk about her relationship or anything that stands out with them?"

"Oh, man. How long do you have? She loved her mom, but the relationship was complicated. She wanted to be like her, and she wanted to be nothing like her. I think it caused a lot of confusion for her. I think she found out something about her mom that really upset her. She was too embarrassed to tell me a lot. Her mom is one of those women who needed to know that men were attracted to her. I think Jo was embarrassed when her mom flirted or dressed a certain way, but then she would do the same thing. Like I said, she was attracted and repulsed at the same time by who her mom was."

"What about her dad? Was she close to him? Did they have problems?"

"Hmm. They always seemed close when we were growing up, but that changed the summer before our sophomore year. I remember her saying once that she didn't even think he was her dad. She just seemed to change, and I think it caused more friction with her dad. He would get really angry with her, but I think she, um, what's it called, agitated him. She seemed to push it with him until he got angry. I think he wanted to love her, but she made it tough. Funny thing was—" Lizzie squeezed her eyes tight and stopped herself.

"Lizzie, are you okay? What were you going to say? I won't judge you."

She took a deep breath and blew air through pursed lips. "He, um, my dad would perk up whenever she was around. He treated her more like a daughter than me. I can't say it didn't make me jealous at times, but Joline never really paid much attention to it. It would have been an issue for me if she had, but she usually ignored him. Most of the time, Dad held onto his bottle of beer more than he ever held me. It was just the two of us, so it was hard. His sadness. His anger. His grief. I lost my mom, and he always acted as if he was the only one who lost someone."

Tom tilted his head. "Lizzie, I am so sorry to hear that. You seem to have a strength inside of you that I hope has helped you along the way." They sat in silence for several moments as Tom thought about Lizzie imagining the love her heart longed for.

"Lizzie, you've been so good to share your thoughts. One last thing. Do you remember anything that happened on Friday evening?"

She shook her head. "No. She said she wanted to leave the movie early; then she was gone. Really gone."

"Did you and the girls try to look for her?"

"We split up. I asked at the theater, but no one knew."

"Did you talk to Nick afterward to see if he saw anything?"

Lizzie glared at Tom and wiped her cheek as she stood. "I don't want to talk about him. I don't want to talk anymore about that night. We can't bring her back, so why can't we leave it alone? Why are you so interested when you never met her?"

Tom sighed and watched as Lizzie hurriedly stomped away. After a few moments, he made his way to Main Street and headed up the steep grade, appreciating the sunset, splashing the clouds on the horizon with pink, purple, and red hues. Restaurants were busy, and some shops were still open. He noticed Danny Haskell outside of Rollie's Tavern talking with Ralph Cutter, which reminded him about the initials on Ralph's apron that Angelo retrieved. *RJC.*

Tom stared at Ralph's face as he argued with Danny. *Ralph J. Cutter*, he thought. *RJC was on the apron, but Mrs. McCready thought those initials were on the envelope Bill McCready had left when Bill was arrested. Hmm. RJ are also the initials Joline wrote in her diary as being the possible father. She put a '?' after the initials, which means...*

A sudden blast from a horn broke his train of thought as a car tried to pull into the parking spot where Tom was standing. He waved an apology and jumped onto the sidewalk curb, wondering about Joline. Was she being sexually aggressive? Was she with so many men that she wasn't even sure who the father of her conceived child might be? Why the question mark? Did she go too far with someone? He made his way back down the hill to the harbor walk and made his way to the piers just before the walking bridge where Captain Mike kept his boat. There he was. "Captain Mike, are you heading out?"

Mike glanced up, smiling as he untied the line. "Oh, Father Tom. I could hardly make you out in the twilight. Yeah, I'm heading out." Still, at a distance, Tom noticed someone approaching the boat. "Bill McCready is coming out, too."

"I thought you were strictly a one-man operation?"

Mike chuckled. "You're right, but he's been like a sad puppy on the pier since he gave up his boat. I'll never know why he did that. He loves being on the water so much." Bill had stopped at the dock. "Hello, Bill. I'm ready if you are."

"Hello, Mr. McCready," greeted Tom.

Bill gazed into Tom's eyes for several moments and then called out to Mike. "I think I might stay ashore tonight, Mike. Thanks for the offer, and good luck."

"Maybe next time," said Mike as he started his engine.

As Tom watched Mike pull away from the dock, he said, "I didn't mean to take you away from your fishing."

"I feel as if you've been trying to tug me somewhere, though." Bill exhaled. "I don't know why I didn't jump on and avoid this, but I need to talk to someone."

Tom nodded.

"I don't even know what I'm going to say, but I need to *know* it's absolutely confidential."

"On my life. I have a feeling that Ralph Cutter blackmailed you, and that is why you gave him your boat. That's a pretty big price to pay for something I'm thinking you didn't do. Didn't you know that he'd have to testify, and the truth would come out, even if he promised not to tell? It seems as if there had to be something more, something else."

Bill stared over the waves, unmoving.

"I'm guessing you didn't kill Joline, did you? You tried to protect her."

Bill dropped to the bench behind him, sitting silently as the waves lapped against the pilings of the pier and the boats docked for the evening. "I don't know."

"You don't know if you killed her, or you don't know if you protected her?"

"I really don't know. How do you kill someone? Little by little, we help others live or add to their death; I don't know what you call it. I'm not a good person. My wife thinks I'm a good person. My son thinks I'm a superhero, but I'm not." He peered out at the remnant colors left by the parted sunset in the sky. "I just struggle so much."

"Bill, we all struggle. Life can be really difficult, and we often make it even more difficult on ourselves by leaving out our most important strength. The world doesn't have our best interests at heart, but Someone does. The problem is that we just listen more to the world. What is it you struggle with the most?"

He glanced upward. "I'm weak. I'm so weak."

Tom sat next to Bill. "Bill, we're all weak. It's the human condition after the Fall. We aren't sinners because we sin. We sin because we are sinners, and we can't overcome our sinful nature alone. We need the strength and grace of God to avoid the regrets of our weaknesses in times of temptation. I'm still learning to forgive myself for my own selfishness and weakness, but I've come to find I can't do it on my own or in my own head. The reason Jesus gave us the wisdom and grace of confession and being with others is to help us. There's an old Celtic term for a priest you are confessing to. He is called *anam-chara* or a 'soul friend,' someone who compassionately cares for your soul. Tell me what's on your mind."

Bill dropped his head, shaking it back and forth. "I can't. If it just affected me, I think I could finally say it, but it doesn't."

"Bill, nothing you say to me can go anywhere. If you want to make a confession or just talk to me as a counselor, I am bound by the seal of confidentiality. You can say anything to me, and I won't judge you or think less of you—only God can judge us, and He will never think less of you. I cannot and will not disclose anything you say to another soul. In the Name of God."

Bill glanced at Tom again. "I guess I'd have to trust both of you. I think I helped to kill Joline."

This admission made Tom's heart drop, and a sense of discomfort seeped through his being.

"I didn't do it intentionally, but I didn't do what any real man would have done. I think you know how beautiful Joline was. I mean, stunning doesn't do her justice, but there was so much more to her. I met her when she became a freshman at the high school. She was so full of life, curiosity, and something special. I don't know what to call it. By the time she reached her sophomore year, something had changed in her. She was as physically mature as any grown woman and seemed to be preoccupied with her attractiveness and with boys. I guess that isn't unusual, but there were times when she would stare into my eyes during class or in the hallway for the longest periods of time."

Tom furrowed his brow. "Okay. What did you do?"

"Nothing. Like I said, I was weak. I started having a sense that she was trying to seduce me by the looks she gave me, her provocative dress, and how close she would stand. I was screaming inside to move away from her or talk to her parents, but another part of me did nothing to dissuade her. This kind of thing doesn't happen to a guy like me, and it was like there were two different people inside."

"Bill, you wouldn't be the first person to be tempted," said Tom as he tilted his head, wondering what more Bill had to share.

He closed his eyes. "I wasn't just tempted. She stayed late after school one afternoon and asked for a ride home. We were the last ones to leave, and when we got into my truck, she—" He paused for quite some time. "She leaned over and kissed me. I mean kissed me, and I didn't stop her. When she opened her blouse, I lost it altogether." He shook his head.

"Did you have intercourse with her?"

Bill hesitated and then nodded.

Tom took a deep breath. "Okay. And you sound like you're truly sorry about it."

He bit his lower lip. "It's wrong. It was so wrong. How do I know what effect it had on her? She seemed to become more promiscuous after that in her dress and with the boys. I made sure she wasn't in my classes during her Junior and Senior years, but she slipped a note in my jacket at the graduation asking to meet that evening."

"What did she want?"

"She felt I had rejected her those two years and wanted to have an affair, or she would tell everyone what happened, that I seduced her when she was too young to know better. She gave me until midnight at Traci's to give her an answer."

"Can I ask what you told her?" Tom inquired.

"I told her that I couldn't. I had a wife and family. I told her it was wrong then and wrong now and pleaded with her not to make things worse for everyone, including her." He stood up. "I left by the back door, and she was right behind me, following me down to the harbor walk path."

"And? Bill, if someone else were listening to you, they would think that you are describing a strong motive to shut her up."

He turned and stared into Tom's eyes with a look of terror in his own. "You don't understand. It would have been wrong even if she were older, but she was a minor. Fifteen makes her a victim of child molestation and me a registered sexual predator. I would lose my wife, family, teaching career, and my whole life. You wanted to know why I gave in to Ralph's blackmail. Well, he somehow knew and threatened to turn me in—and what better motive for murder?"

"Man, he is a piece of work, huh? Okay, I understand this weight you must have been feeling, and I agree that it was wrong either way, but what happened on the harbor walk?"

Bill's eyes squeezed tight as he sighed. "Well, uh—we argued on the way down. I pleaded with her to not ruin my family and would do anything to repay what happened. I have a feeling she was almost playing with me. I think she felt a sense of control or power when we, uh, you know, and this was giving her that same sense of being in the driver's seat."

Tom asked, "How were you feeling at that point? Angry? Frustrated?"

"Probably more numb than anything. But then those guys came roaring down the path. I think they call themselves The Norsemen or something like that. It was too dark to see them, but there's a light above the boat hoist where we were standing, and one of them yelled out, 'There's that bitch that gave you a hard time earlier!'" He paused for a moment. "They revved their engines and came at her, and I tried to block her with my arm, and one of them clipped me with an undercut. He must have had a ring on his finger because it cut into my cheek as I fell and Joline went down. I didn't know what to do but grabbed a nearby stick and started to swing it while they circled around us on their bikes. They backed off a bit, and I knelt down to help Joline up. She yelled at me to run, and when I realized they were more concerned with getting me, I took off down the path with all three of them in pursuit. I was scared to death, but at least they weren't after Joline any longer."

"What happened?"

"I stopped and swung that stick as they got closer until I reached the dock here, jumped on my boat, and started it up. They laughed when I pulled out of the slip, yelling that they knew where my family and I lived, and then took off up the hill there." Bill pointed to the hill that led up to the high school.

"So, they didn't go back down the path to Joline?"

Bill shook his head.

"And that was when you called your friend on Swan Lake for a place to hide out for a while?"

"Yep, and why I wasn't too friendly when you and your friend were poking around and asking questions about my family."

Tom stood up, wiped his brow, and stared into Bill's eyes. "Thank you for standing up for her and for telling me the truth. I'm sure that weight has only gotten heavier over the years. Now, I do want to tell you something. I agree with you that what you did with Joline was dead wrong and shameful. You are a teacher and responsible for caring for these boys and girls, even if they make it as hard as hell on you, but I think you know that."

"I do, so you don't have to tell me. I have regretted it every day. Every day, when I look at my wife, when I hold my kids and think of the impact it may have had on Joline's life, I am as sorry as I can be, and I can't even tell her now. So, what are you going to do? Even with your promise, aren't you under some obligation to report me?"

Tom squinted and peered into Bill's eyes. "Bill, I have to leave that up to you, but I do want you to know that Joline was not fifteen when she was a sophomore. Her mother said she held her back a year, which would have made her sixteen. I don't believe that changes anything morally, but it may give you some relief from a legal standpoint."

Bill paused to take in what he had just heard. "You're right. It doesn't change anything for me, but at least it takes away some of the threat of the stigma for my kids having a child molester as a father. Now, I'm just a—well, you can fill in the blank. I'm sure many will."

"That is between you and the Big Guy," said Tom as he patted Bill on the shoulder.

Chapter 28

After McCready left the pier, Tom sat and prayed for all those involved in Joline's life and for an answer concerning her death. The sky was now dark except for the waning moon, the countless stars, and the handful of lights on the walkway to town. Despite the peaceful atmosphere, Tom felt restless with so many questions unanswered. On his way back down the walkway, he noticed Ray Jordy heading into the Front Street Pub. Possibilities flooded his head. Was he 'RJ'? Was the paternity test to see if he was the father of Joline's baby? Was his falling out with Colby over her?

By the time he turned the corner and headed up Main Street, it was just after ten o'clock, and he was surprised to spot the yellow truck parked directly in front of Traci's Diner. The surrounding shops were dark and closed, but the diner's bright lights signaled that they were open. He could see a couple sitting in a back booth but no one at the counter. *How could a small piece of that berry pie hurt?* The bell rang as he shoved the door open.

He held the door to decide if this was really a good idea, and a voice rose behind him. "These are the big decisions in life, Father. To diner or not to diner?"

Tom turned to see Ned Parker behind him. "Good evening to you, Mr. Parker. I was tempted to try another piece of pie."

Ned settled into his customary spot at the end of the counter, and Tom took the next stool.

"You really do come here every night, don't you?"

Ned half-smiled. "Ever since my wife died, I find it hardest to be alone at night. You know?"

Ralph emerged from the back room, appearing more upbeat than Tom had ever seen him. He wiped a spot on the counter, his black eyes still holding that eerie expression when he smiled. "I didn't expect such a large crowd tonight." He pulled out two mugs from under the counter and held them up. "Coffees?"

As he poured the piping-hot cups of coffee, Tom said, "Ralph, I was wondering if you had any more of that raspberry pie?"

"Call me R.J. I think my luck has been on the upswing, and how many famous Ralphs are there around?" He slid a slice of pie with the flaky crust onto a plate and placed it down in front of Tom.

"Emerson," said Tom.

"What?"

"Ralph Waldo Emerson is a famous Ralph."

"Never heard of him," said Ralph.

"Ralph Lauren," spouted Ned.

"Ralph Nader and Ralph Fiennes."

"Okay. Okay. None of them sound as good as R.J."

Tom bit into a piece of the pie and wasn't disappointed with his decision to stop in. The doorbell jingled as he took another forkful, and J.C. stood in the doorway.

"Did you save me a piece of that berry pie, Ralph?"

Ralph eyed Tom's plate, and his face flushed despite the mischievous smile that made its way to his face.

J.C. stood beside Tom's stool. "You're eatin' my pie, Father." He glanced up. "Ralph, you gave my pie to a stranger passing through town."

"R.J.," said Tom.

"Who's R.J.?" queried J.C.

"R.J. Cutter," replied Ned. "It's the new Ralph."

J.C. continued staring at the half-eaten pie piece on Tom's plate. "Speaking of R.J., I thought Ray Jordy might be here since his truck is outside."

Ralph smirked. "You mean my truck now. I'm thinking about a bigger apartment, too."

Ned asked, "Did your aunt die and leave you some money, Ralph... I mean R.J."

"Yeah, something like that."

As he swallowed another forkful, Tom glanced. at the sheriff. "Do you want a piece?"

"I did," replied J.C. with a crooked smile. He glanced at Ralph and murmured to Tom, "By the way, thank your sidekick for the package. We should know tomorrow if there's anything there."

Tom noticed Ralph glancing over with narrowed eyes, even though he couldn't have clearly heard what was said, and then disappeared out back. Tom leaned toward Ned. "Hey, last Friday night, you said that Ralph disappeared on his break when Joline and the person she was meeting left by the back door, right?"

Ned nodded as he sipped his coffee. "Ralph was gone a lot longer than usual. I was wonderin' if he was gonna come back, but he finally did. Yeah, I remember him coming back in lookin' spooked, wiping the sweat from his brow onto the new apron he was putting on. That was a long smoke." Ned leaned over for a package of oyster crackers, opened it, and popped a few into his mouth. "Come to think of it, he was kinda weird that night, writin' stuff down on a pad of paper and all the time kinda lookin' anxious, you know, lookin' out the window more than usual. He's always been an odd duck, so it's hard to say what's normal for him."

Tom and J.C. exchanged a glance, and then Tom stood and placed a ten-dollar bill on the counter. "You have a good one, Ned—oh! And thank Ralph—I mean R.J.—for the pie. It really hit the spot tonight."

When J.C. turned his back to leave with Tom, Ralph stepped back and lifted a plate from under the counter with another slice of pie he had hidden from J.C., giving Tom a mischievous smile.

Outside the diner, J.C. said, "Very funny. So, when are you leavin' town again?"

Tom laughed. "I really didn't know it was the last piece of pie or yours. By the way, what do you think about Ralph? He certainly came on to Joline. She teased and embarrassed him with a hot cup of coffee in his hand that morning when he claimed not to have even seen her. He disappears from the diner around the time of her death, comes back spooked, dumps his apron in the laundry, and then blackmails Bill McCready in return for clearing his name."

"How do you know he blackmailed him?"

"Well, McCready had an unexpected visit from Ralph at their cabin on Swan Lake, and suddenly he remembers that McCready was innocent *after* he takes ownership of a forty-plus thousand dollar boat he doesn't know how to operate. He's acting like he won the lottery, and now he suddenly owns Ray Jordy's truck. How did he weasel that? It's just odd stuff."

J.C. leaned against the back of the yellow truck. "It certainly is, but I still have my sights on the teacher. People don't give up somethin' they love and costs that much if they're not guilty of somethin'. And I have a feeling Mr. Cutter is shadin' the truth a bit to line his pockets."

"Megan Connors, over at the bookstore, said Ralph was all giddy talking about big opportunities coming his way. My gut tells me McCready isn't a killer, even if things seem a little fishy."

J.C. stood back. "Things are certainly fishy, but I've got to write this truck up for a broken taillight and expired license plate."

The night felt so good that Tom decided to meander through the side streets and slowed as he approached the Chases' house on the quiet, treelined street. It was still warm out as a gentle breeze played with the leaves above, and some of the brightest stars shimmered between the openings in the branches. He brought his gaze down and stopped in his tracks when he saw Laurie sitting on her front stoop; the glow of the cigarette in her mouth grew brighter as she took a drag. It was late, and he debated whether it was a good time to say hello.

After she let out a long puff of smoke, she said, "I won't bite."

Tom stepped out of the shadows and slowly approached. "I wouldn't want to intrude."

"Nothing to intrude on. Colby's out somewhere, and my baby's gone forever. I can't protect her anymore." She took another drag and held her head up to hold in the tears. When Tom didn't respond, she exhaled. "I know you're thinking something. I can always tell when people hold back what they really want to say."

Tom shifted his feet. "Don't mind me. I always have a thousand thoughts running through my noggin'. I'd rather hear about how you're doing."

Without lifting her head, her eyes fixed on him. "Trust me; you don't. I want to know what thought just ran through your head."

With a sigh, Tom said, "Well, um, sometimes when we work so hard to protect someone, we are really protecting ourselves. There's a painful wound in there that needs someone to care about, so we pour all that need into others."

"I'm guessing it's not a longshot bet to say you've never had kids."

"Laurie, a good mom does everything to love and protect her children. It can just get more complicated if we've had a challenging childhood ourselves. It can make a punch in the gut even more painful. I didn't want to say anything, but I'm truly empathizing with you more than you can imagine."

Laurie said, "I did ask for it, didn't I? I appreciate that you dropped by. Everyone's been very supportive, but I've felt lonely. You seem to be the only one who's had a glimpse of the darkness inside."

"I think we all have one of those dark places inside."

"Yeah, but mine's a one-room house."

"Well, my guess is that you actually have a very grand house with many rooms waiting for the lights to be turned on and to be lived in."

Laurie's eyes widened, and she forced a smile.

"Laurie, can I ask you something?"

She nodded.

"When you were kind enough to share some of Joline's artwork, I wasn't sure, but was there a photo of a painting on her bedroom wall? A young woman holding flowers?"

"Yeah. She used to call it her Ophelia for some reason. It always bothered me, and even more so now. I have nightmares of Joline floating out at sea, holding those same flowers. I reach out to save her, but she sinks deeper and deeper into the ocean's dark, and I've lost her. I can't sleep anymore thinking of that. Why are you asking?"

"Not sure, exactly. The painting is of a young woman named Ophelia from Hamlet. Her death is tragic, and I was wondering why Joline liked it so much."

She tilted her head. "How did you know that she liked it?"

"Lizzie was tossing flowers into the bay in honor of Joline, and she mentioned it. Would it be okay to see it again?"

Laurie stood up and opened the door. "Sure. Come on in, and don't mind the mess. I haven't been in a good place to keep things clean for guests. I guess I need to think about Saturday and the funeral reception." She led Tom to Joline's room, opened the door, and flicked on the light.

Tom spotted the picture directly over her bed and leaned closer to notice something written at the bottom.

I would give you some violets, but they all withered when my father died.

"Laurie, this is a line from Hamlet, but would it mean anything to Joline?"

Laurie got closer, narrowing her eyes. "I've never—" She stopped short and straightened, turning away from the photo, anxiously wringing her hands. "No. I don't think so."

"Okay. I'm sorry for asking." He glanced back at the illustration next to the photo. It was the drawing of the empty room he recalled from the photos Angelo took. Tom remembered the unmade bed in the room without any windows and a closed door. It was the distinctively signed 'J' at the bottom that caught his eye. "She was as good an illustrator as a painter."

Laurie stepped over. "Oh, that. One day, she got into my sketchbook, pulled out these two, and asked if she could keep them. I did them a long time ago when I was a budding artist before I wilted."

"This is yours? It's very good. It is a very powerful drawing, but why would Joline sign it?"

Laurie gave a half-smile. "That was my signature. My middle name is Jenna. It's actually the name I was born with, but my adoptive parents wanted something different. That's the real me."

"Art can be an imitation of reality, but it can also give us a deeper picture of the human soul and help us to find truth and beauty," said Tom softly.

"Hmm. I don't know. I would find truth but not beauty when I'd draw for hours and hours in my room."

For the moment, Tom gazed into her eyes and could almost feel the intense pain and emptiness she may have felt her entire life.

Chapter 29

Wearing a pair of striped pajama bottoms and a white tee shirt that read, *Catholics: Kicking old school since 33 AD*, Paul scratched his head as he entered the kitchen where Tom and Angelo were having coffee. "You know, I used to be tucked in and sleeping like a baby by ten p.m. every night before you two showed up. What's going on with you detectives tonight?"

Tom smiled. "Grab a cup of coffee and join us."

Paul shook his head and pulled down a bottle that read *Kilbeggan Small Batch Rye Irish Whiskey* and three glasses. "I'll sit down, but then I want to go right back to my pillow and sweet dreams afterward." He poured the yellow-gold rye into each of their glasses, adding a bit more to Tom's glass to ensure everyone was even, and then lifted his glass. "To the midnight trio. May we find answers and bring peace to those in pain."

"I'll second that," said Tom as they clinked their glasses. "That's very good. A bit of old Ireland?"

"Tis. Now, what are we gabbing on about here in the middle of the night?"

Angelo replied, "Father Tom thinks we may have gotten something wrong."

Tom took another sip. "I was passing by Laurie Chase's this evening, and she showed me the pictures on Joline's bedroom walls again. When I got to one of the drawings with the fancy 'J' signature at the bottom, she told me it was her drawing and signature, not Joline's."

"Huh. What would the 'J' be for?"

"Laurie's birth name was Jenna. The drawings were hers and—"

Angelo interjected, "And, so, the journal I found might have actually been Mrs. Chase's and not Joline's."

Paul put down his glass. "Journal? What journal? How would you have Laurie's journal?"

Tom replied, "We don't have it. We just have photos of a few pages from it. We saw three entries, and they were the reflections of a troubled girl. Maybe abuse. Maybe pregnant with a baby, she wasn't sure who the father was. We've been trying to see how the entries could possibly provide a clue to her death."

Nodding, Paul said, "So, you thought it was Joline's just because of the 'J' signature?"

Angelo said, "Plus, I found the journal hidden in the wall beside Joline's bed, so we assumed it was hers. Now, if she found her mom's journal and secretly read it, what effect did it have on her?"

Running his palm across the kitchen table, Tom said, "Good question. The entry where she doesn't know who the father is and if she should keep the baby or even end her own life would be pretty upsetting for a young girl to read if she thought she was that baby. I wonder if that explains the line Joline wrote on the photo on her wall?"

"What was that?" asked Angelo.

Tom said, "It was a line from Ophelia in Hamlet. *I would give you some violets, but they withered all when my father died.* Remember when Laurie said that everything seemed to change with Joline about three years back, like a light switch flipped, and she suddenly felt as if she had lost Joline—and the relationship with her father changed, too? Maybe Colby isn't her dad, or at least, she began to believe that. The journal points to an 'RJ' as the possible father. Maybe it *is* Ray Jordy, and that explains his falling out with Colby, Laurie keeping Jordy in Joline's life, and Joline's argument with Jordy that morning."

Angelo cleared his voice. "It could also explain the paternity test invoice at Jordy's house, his argument with Colby at the boatyard, and why he was following us that day.

Also, the yellow truck followed Joline that night. Was he worried about her? Was it he who attacked you that night to keep you from digging and finding out the truth?" Angelo paused. "Now, it also looks like Ralph Cutter has something on Ray Jordy to blackmail him with."

"Very good point," said Tom.

Paul backed up in his chair. "Wait. Wait. Journals hidden in the wall. A paternity test inside Ray Jordy's house. Where are you two getting all this information?" He glanced from one to the other as they remained silent. "Do I even want to know?"

Tom eyed Angelo, and they both shook their heads. "Probably not."

Tom stood up.

Paul said, "Now, where are you going?"

Putting his hand on Paul's shoulder, Tom replied, "Why don't you get your beauty sleep while Angelo and I get some pie?"

"Pie?" Paul's brows narrowed.

Tom approached Traci's Diner just after midnight. As they entered, no one was at the counter or in any of the back booths.

When the bell of the door rang, Ralph stepped out from the back, and gave a nervous half-smile as he tossed a towel over his shoulder. "You're back again? Trouble sleeping?"

Tom rubbed his hands together. "Actually, I just had another hankering to taste that pie you have hiding under the counter. I was telling Angelo about it, and we dropped by to see if you still had a slice left."

"I'll, um, I'll take a look, but the sheriff wasn't all too happy when you stole his piece earlier." Ralph awkwardly attempted a muffled laugh. Tom and Angelo took to their stools as Ralph leaned down to check. "I got one piece of the mixed berry left, so you better hope Coombs doesn't drop by after I told him we were all out."

Tom glanced at Angelo. "I guess we can take that chance. Ralph, can you pour a couple of cups of decaf as well? Thanks."

Ralph returned with two small plates and one piece of pie and set them down with a knife and two forks. "You can fight over that."

"We definitely will. How is the new truck running?"

"Can't complain. Things are good all over these days," he said, leaning over the counter and tapping his hands before pausing. "What are you really doing here?"

Tom let the first forkful of pie melt in his mouth. "This is very good. You know how it is. It's hard to sleep in a strange bed and all. I was curious about something, though."

Ralph's eyes narrowed a bit. "And what's that?"

"When McCready and Joline left on Friday night, you must have seen them heading down to the harbor walk. Is that right?"

He straightened, warily responding as he twisted the towel on his shoulder. "Yeah, sure."

"Makes sense. I've been behind the diner here at that time, and it's pretty hard to see anything down there. So you must have followed them down to the area where the boat hoist is, I would think."

He nodded, clenching his jaw.

"So, McCready never hit her or threatened her?"

"Yeah. He never hit her. I didn't say he never threatened her or that she never threatened him. What are you gettin' at?"

Tom took a sip of his coffee. "Nothing. It must have been pretty intense when the bikers rumbled down the path and had an altercation with them. Did it happen pretty quick?"

He squinted, confused. Ralph snapped, "Yeah, I guess so. They were taunting Joline, calling her a tease and stuff. She could be one, you know," he said with a smirk. "They started riding past them, probably to scare them a bit. Like I said, McCready tried to stop them but got a nice belt for his trouble. They both went down, and McCready helped Joline up and turned to stop them again, but she yelled for him to run."

Tom leaned forward. "That's pretty scary stuff, especially in the pitch dark."

"I'm used to the night, and my eyes get—what's that word—acclimated pretty quick."

"So, McCready takes off down toward the other end of the walk where his boat is docked?"

"Yup, he took off and turned to see if she was all right. He ran faster than I would have thought he could, and they took off after him. I thought there was no way he'd make it alive."

"Did all of the bikers take off after him? Did any stay behind to go after Joline?"

Ralph shook his head. "There were only three, and they all went after McCready, screaming something like, 'You're a dead man!'"

"Did you stay long enough to see what happened to Joline after that?"

He rubbed his hand across his lips and shook his head. "She took off. That's all I know."

"Wow. I guess Bill McCready owes you his life for testifying to his innocence, but it's a tragedy about Joline," said Tom with a deep sigh. "You must have seen Ray Jordy in the area."

Before Ralph could respond, the bell above the door rang, and J.C. came in, rolling his eyes as he spotted Tom and Angelo. "Do you two ever sleep?"

"We could ask you that same question," replied Tom as he slid the empty pie plate behind him. "We didn't expect you again tonight."

"Never mind. I'm not here to see you." J.C. lifted his gaze to Ralph behind the counter. "Cutter, I need to ask you a few questions." He turned to see if anyone else was in the diner. "If you're not too busy?"

"Shoot," replied Ralph with his arms crossed.

"Okay. We talked about what you saw on Friday night between Joline Chase, Bill McCready, and the Norsemen.

I'm tracking them down, by the way, but I need you to tell me what happened after that."

Ralph laughed.

J.C. pursed his lips. "And exactly what's so funny?"

Pointing to Tom and Angelo, Ralph said, "They were just asking the same question."

J.C. forced an insincere smile. "Oh, they were, huh? And what was your answer?"

"I didn't see anything else. McCready ran off. The three bikers took off after him, and Joline left. I came back here since I was the only one working."

J.C. put his hands on the counter and leaned toward Ralph, staring directly into his eyes. "Hmm. I timed it out with Ned Parker, who was sitting just where Father Tom is now, and it seems as if you were gone a whole lot longer than that. You came back sweaty and changed your apron. Do you usually do that during your shift?"

Ralph rubbed his arms as he kept them folded. "Sure. If it's dirty, I change it."

J.C. glanced down. "It looks pretty greasy right now."

"Look, Sheriff, someone took my other apron. That's all. What are all these questions about, anyway?"

"Wednesday is laundry pickup, right? You have two aprons with your initials sewn inside, and you toss your old apron into the laundry on Wednesday mornings and grab a new one that evening. Every week, the same routine, but this one Friday night, halfway through the shift, you want to be pretty for Ned, Mike, and whoever he's with that night, and you grab someone else's apron, too, which you never do. Doesn't that sound a bit strange to you?"

"Hey, look, I don't know what you're gettin' at. I got somethin' on the apron and changed it. No other reason."

J.C. stepped forward. "Why did McCready hand you papers for a forty-thousand dollar boat? And why did Jordy suddenly hand over his truck to you?"

Ralph shrugged, beads of sweat now dripping from his forehead. "There's no law against it that I know of."

"I don't know if you need to lock up the diner, but I've got to take you into the station."

"What? What's goin' on? I didn't do anything. You can't just arrest me because you don't like my answers. I didn't do anything."

We pulled your apron from Wednesday's laundry basket. You're right that it had something on it. Blood and that blood was Joline's. It was clearly wiped onto the apron by whoever was wearing it, and we found traces of that same blood on the knob of the back door here and the handle to the laundry bin. Now, how does that happen if Joline took off and you never touched her—a girl you were heard saying, what was that? 'Someone should teach that b— a good lesson someday'?"

Ralph turned, eyeing the door to the back room, but one of J.C.'s officers stepped in the doorway. Ralph blurted, "Yeah, but I didn't do it."

The officer approached Ralph. "Do we need cuffs, or are you gonna cooperate like a good boy?" He led Ralph out the door.

J.C. grabbed the diner's keys off the hook, shaking his head as Tom and Angelo slid off their stools.

Tom said, "That boy was ready to pop one day. He's got a bit of a hangup on being embarrassed, and Joline wasn't one to miss an opportunity when he tried to flirt with her. Maybe that mornin's incident with the coffee was the last straw or somethin'. Who knows?"

Outside the diner, J.C. locked the doors and turned to Angelo. "I appreciate the tip on the apron. We almost lost that bit of evidence in the wash." He smiled. "Now, you boys should feel free to head back to Boston anytime you're ready."

Tom patted J.C. on the shoulder. "We're heading out Sunday, and by Monday, you'll be missing us, *niddbc*. Did I say that right, my friend?"

J.C. smiled and headed toward the station as Tom and Angelo made their way back to the rectory, discussing the odds of the case being solved before they left. Was Ralph capable of murder? Was he still covering for McCready in return for the boat? Or did he witness something that night with Jordy that he then blackmailed him with?

Chapter 30

At breakfast, Tom and Angelo told Paul about their midnight trip to the diner and the evidence that led to Ralph Cutter's arrest.

"Thank goodness we may have some resolution on this case." Paul sipped the last of his coffee. "The truth always finds its way to the surface, don't you think? If you'll excuse me, I'm meeting with Laurie Chase this morning to discuss the funeral Mass for Joline. I don't know how this news will—well, we'll see how Laurie is doing."

After Paul stepped out of the kitchen, Angelo poured himself and Tom another cup of coffee. "So, if Ralph isn't guilty, how does he get that much of Joline's blood on his hands?"

Tom nodded. "I know. I'm not sure if he killed her, but my gut tells me he's guilty of something, even if it's only hedging on the truth. If he didn't do it, he's certainly been looking to cash in on the opportunity. He must have seen more than he's telling us. I hope the fear of being arrested shakes the rest of the story out of him."

"Yeah. Remember, there was blood on the side of McCready's boat and one of Joline's missing earrings. Maybe they were both guilty, but that wouldn't explain Jordy suddenly handing over his truck to Cutter or the way he's been acting. Colby Chase has been a difficult one to figure out, too. For a father of a slain daughter, he seems very anxious for us to stop looking into her death, and there is that incident you mentioned where Joline left her house with a bruise after the neighbors heard a loud argument. What was the falling out he had with Joline a few years back—and at the same time, Colby and Jordy's friendship went on the rocks?"

"All great questions, Angelo. I think there is more family history tied to all of this. You know, those painful hidden secrets that need to go through a gauntlet of emotions and hurt to come out and heal."

An hour later, Tom stood to bring his plate and cup to the kitchen sink. Through the window, he noticed Laurie chatting with Paul. He wiped his hands and stepped out the side door to greet her. He gazed empathetically into her eyes, silently waiting for her to tell him where she was emotionally.

"Father Tom."

"Morning, Laurie. I hope the plans for Joline are, um—"

"Yes, Father Paul and I had a good talk. I want the service to be as beautiful as she was." With that, the tears came streaming down her cheeks, and Tom reached into his pocket to retrieve a handkerchief. "Thank you." She wiped both cheeks. "Can I ask you a favor?"

"Sure. Anything," replied Tom.

"Could you walk me to the cemetery? I have to pick out the right place for Joline to rest, and I could use the company."

Tom smiled. "I'd be more than honored to."

They made the fifteen-minute trek to the cemetery in comfortable silence. It was a sacred time, even though preparing one's child for their burial seemed horribly wrong for a parent. There was an instant sense of peace when they entered the cemetery with its stone walls and the sunlight arrowing through a beautiful assortment of trees that had grown to shelter those resting on the grassy slope. They followed the path to a spot where Laurie stopped next to a large stone under a grand old tree with its crooked branches reaching out toward the harbor in the distance. A pair of playful squirrels chased each other up the thick, coarse trunk where "J²" had been carved into its bark years ago.

"I think Joline would feel at home in this spot. When she was little, we came here for picnics or to pick blueberries in that little patch." She turned and ran her fingers along the carving in the trunk. "One time, we carved this. Joline and Jenna. She's the only one who knew. Kind of our secret."

"Then, I think this is the perfect spot to honor her memory and give her rest."

"I hope so. I have no one to love anymore except for her memory."

Tom sat on the stone and gazed out at the hills rolling down the harbor where Joline's body had been found. "Laurie, I want you to know that Joline is still alive right now. We are made with immortal souls, and God never stops loving us and will never stop loving Joline, and I don't think you will, either."

"I want to believe that. I really do. Growing up, I never felt that love from anyone, but...um...I remember feeling something deep when I heard one line at church. Something from the Bible, I think."

Tom paused as he saw the carving of a lamb on one of the tombstones. "I think I've always been moved by one of the Psalms. *The LORD is my shepherd; I shall not want. In verdant pastures he gives me repose; beside restful waters he leads me, he refreshes my soul. He guides me in right paths for his name's sake. Even though I walk in the dark valley I fear no evil; for you are at my side—*"

"That's it! That's what I heard. That last line sent shivers through me but makes me feel loved and protected at the same time. I don't know why that is."

"Laurie, I think you've been to the dark valley in your life. And you know, all too well, what that place of cold darkness and loneliness can feel like. In that moment, any hope that you have can fear no evil because God is at your side—always with you. It's a moment of courage and hope for many who hear that verse."

Laurie pursed her lips and nodded, bringing Tom's handkerchief to the corner of her eye. "I think that's it, but I feel so ashamed, so unworthy. I don't deserve that love. I've never felt hope except for when Colby proposed, and I was expecting Jo." She lifted her head to peer out at the hillside drenched in sunshine. "I never remember the rest of that verse. I think that line always grabs me, so..."

"*With your rod and your staff that give me courage. You spread the table before me in the sight of my foes; You anoint my head with oil; my cup overflows. Only goodness and kindness follow me all the days of my life; And I shall dwell in the house of the Lord for years to come.*"

Laurie gave a nod. "I pray for only goodness and kindness to follow Joline. I do. She deserved so much better than me."

Tom gave a deep sigh. "Laurie, I have to confess something to you. I know I never met Joline, but I truly care about finding justice for her, and I care about you. Remember when we said that our children don't ask us to be perfect parents, only parents who care and love them? I think you truly cared and loved Joline with all your heart, and I'm guessing she knew that."

"I don't know. I might have believed that when she was little, but why did she seem to want nothing to do with me these past few years? Why did she act the way she did? The more I tried to get close to her, the more she pulled away."

"Teenage years, especially for girls, can be difficult. The closer they are to their moms, the more they seem to need to separate for a while."

Laurie moved uncomfortably. "Now we're separated forever, aren't we?"

"I don't believe that. I still have something to confess to you. When Angelo and I were at your house, we tried to see if there were clues in Joline's paintings that could shed light on who her killer might be. Angelo noticed a panel in the wall next to Joline's bed and a book inside."

Laurie furrowed her brow and shook her head. "What panel? What book? I'm confused."

"There was a journal hidden inside the panel. We assumed it was Joline's."

"Oh, my God," said Laurie as she stood and paced. "Where is it?"

"We didn't take it. It's still behind the panel, but we had thought it was hers because the entries were signed with a J, just like that illustration on her wall."

Laurie held her hand over her heart. "I'm so embarrassed. Did you read them? When could you have?"

"When I was talking to you in the hallway, Angelo took photos of the walls and only a few pages in the journal. I resisted reading them to honor her privacy. Still, when it became clear that she had been murdered and potentially involved with certain suspects, I needed to know if any clues could help identify the killer."

Laurie stood completely frozen, breathing deeply, almost gasping, squeezing her eyes tight. "If she read my diary, I can't imagine what she thought of me. Those were my deepest, darkest thoughts and emotions in that journal. I was pretty angry at times and wrote about some of the ugliest parts of my life. I thought I had it hidden away, and then it seemed to disappear. If she read that, she must have hated me." Tears flowed again as she squeezed her eyes tight.

Tom pulled a handkerchief from his pocket and offered it to her as he gave her a tender gaze. "Laurie, I don't think she could ever hate you. You loved art, and she emulated you. She may have actually tried to emulate you in more ways than you know."

"I'm the last person she should have emulated. I wanted so much for her. I wanted her not to be me. I hated myself. I felt worthless. I felt ugly. I felt ashamed. Why would she want to emulate me when I'm not a good person?"

"Laurie. I know those feelings are deep, and I know they are powerful. I know you believe them, but I can tell you without hesitation that none of them are true. You are beautifully made by a God who loves you no matter what. You have gifts, and nothing you've ever done or has been done to you is unforgivable. You are made with incredible worth, and you are a good person."

Laurie shook her head furiously and sobbed, crossing her arms as if to hold herself. "I can't go there. I can't believe that." Without lifting her chin, she started down the hill. "I'm sorry."

As Tom stood and watched her go, his heart ached, wishing she could be convinced she was good and worth loving.

Chapter 31

Tom made his way down the cemetery hill, thinking of all the people who lived and died over the centuries in this town. When he finally reached the harbor, the large boat hoist was in his sights, and he wondered if Colby was working.

As he approached, Colby had the control box strapped onto his shoulders and directed a large hoist. Just as the large hoist started to roll out of the berth, a little girl darted after her puppy in the path of the gigantic wheels. Without hesitation, Tom leaped forward and grabbed the girl and dog in one swoop just before the tires rolled over where she had just stood a second before.

A woman screamed.

Colby instantly stopped the forward progress of the lift and pulled off his cap to wipe his brow in relief before dropping to his knees.

Tom quickly approached. "It's okay, Mr. Chase."

Colby lifted his head, faced the glare of the sun overhead, and nodded. "Thank you. I don't know how I missed her. I always check a hundred times before moving that thing."

Tom reached out his hand and helped Colby to his feet. "You might want to think about taking a few days off. I imagine you have a lot on your mind—and heart."

Ray Jordy came running toward the scene. "What happened? Let me bring it in, Cole." He took the remote control box from Colby and peered up at Tom. "What are you doin' here?"

Tom walked Colby down the harbor walk and to the parking lot at the pier. "Mr. Chase, is there someplace we can talk?"

"Please, call me Colby," he said, staring into Tom's eyes. "I guess I owe you that." He pointed to his truck, and they drove a few miles to a spot in the woods overlooking Belfast. After sitting a few moments in silence, Colby turned and pulled two bottles of amber-colored beer from the cooler.

The bottles began to sweat as they hit the warm air, and Tom read the label to himself. *Lobster Ale.* "I won't ask if they taste like—never mind." He took the bottle Colby offered him and nodded. "Thank you. I hope you know how truly sorry I am for your loss."

Colby took a long swig from the bottle and wiped his lips, sighing deeply. "I guess I've been tryin' not to process it. I still don't believe it."

"I know. She was a beautiful young woman. I love the photo of you three on the mantle. Was she about six or seven in that photo?"

"Six." The beginnings of a smile disappeared quickly on Colby's face. "She was always so much fun and great to be with. It wasn't the two of us for very long, but we really loved her."

"Colby, I don't want to get personal—"

"Then don't." There was an awkward silence for almost a minute. "I'm sorry. I'm so used to keeping secrets in our house. Don't air your dirty laundry, as they say. It's hard when you can't talk some things out, even inside your own home."

"Laurie had a tough childhood, didn't she?"

Colby nodded. "We all did, but I think there's somethin' darker inside of her that she can't let go. We were so close, and she was so much fun before we got married, but then she distanced herself. The closer I tried to get, the more she pulled back, but then Joline came, and she was happier once she was born. Look, my old man wasn't at home for long. I was ashamed he abused my mom and embarrassed that he abandoned us. What had we done to deserve that? I felt so insecure in my home, and all I wanted was a home, a wife, and a family of my own. I wanted stability, and I figured

Laurie needed and wanted the same. She did, but she was afraid of it at the same time. Does that make any sense?"

"It does. Can I ask you why you've been so upset with me trying to help find out who did this to Joline?"

Colby shook his head. "Every time you spoke to or saw Laurie, she only got more upset. There's enough goin' on for her without stirring up the past. There's too much pain back there. Too much hurt."

"You really love her, don't you?"

Colby closed his eyes and then nodded.

"I can tell. And you loved Joline, didn't you?"

Colby turned. "Of course I did."

Father Tom sighed. "Laurie said that things had abruptly changed with Joline a few years ago or so. Does that sound right to you?"

He nodded silently.

"Do you have any idea what changed? Did anything happen to Joline?"

Colby peered up. "Everything seemed to change. She kept bringin' things up, pushing buttons, and gettin' a different attitude about everything. Almost like she didn't care how many risks she took."

"Did that cause more arguments at home?"

"Yeah, about everything and about nothin'. She would push until we lost it with her. I don't know where she came up with this stuff."

Tom turned. "Colby, I don't mean anything by this, but did she ever push you to the point that you hit her? I just heard from a neighbor that there was a loud fight, and she left the house appearing bruised and bloodied."

Colby stared at Tom, his eyes turning black with anger. "What kind of question is that?"

"Are you saying that Laurie hit her?"

Silence.

"What happened that Laurie would strike Joline?"

"She didn't! I did. I never hit her before or afterward. She just said somethin' that made me lose it that one time." He put down his empty bottle. "I think we should head back."

"Okay. I'm really sorry to have asked those questions. I think you and Laurie are both in a lot of pain, and that it extends beyond Joline's death. But I also think you two *do* love each other—and need each other."

Colby glanced over and then turned the key in the ignition. He drove to town, dropping Tom off at the rectory. When Tom got out of the vehicle and leaned over to say goodbye, Colby said, "Let's leave things be. Do you hear me, Father?"

Tom nodded, and Colby drove off.

Before Tom could step toward the rectory, J.C.'s jeep pulled alongside the curb, and Tom leaned over. "Don't you have a suspect to guard, Sheriff?"

Raising his eyebrows, J.C. replied, "Ralph is a slippery one in more ways than one. He's still holdin' to his story that he's innocent and doesn't know how any of that blood got on his apron or on the door at Traci's."

Tom leaned on the door. "So, what do you think?"

"He's got no alibi for the time of her murder and might have motive and opportunity. He was sleazy enough to keep McCready sweatin' until he paid up, and we have the blood. The problem is that it wasn't on him, and, so far, no one's come forward as a witness to him doin' it—killing Joline."

Tom sighed. "You also have blood and Joline's earring on McCready's boat and a witness with some questionable integrity and a motive to lie for him. Maybe he even helped McCready load her body onto the boat?"

"Hmm. That could be. But why would McCready want to kill Joline? What motive could he have had?"

Tom thought about his private conversation with McCready. "Yeah. What's weird is that Ralph didn't only blackmail Bill McCready, but it looks like Ray Jordy, as well. Have you had a chance to talk to Ray?"

J.C. gripped the steering wheel. "Are you saying that you think he might be the actual killer? He's known the Chases for a long time. I know he had an argument with her in the mornin', but—" He peered out the window at a child riding her bike down the street. "I'll have a talk with him." Turning back to Tom, he grinned. "Sunday, huh?"

Tom nodded. "Yeah. Angelo and I will be heading back on Sunday, and I know that it can't come too soon for you."

He put the jeep in gear and replied, "Well, I wouldn't put it that way, *niddbc*." Then he took off down the street.

Chapter 32

Entering the rectory, Tom yelled out, "Paul! Are you up for lunch—on me?"

Paul entered the kitchen and tilted his head, motioning toward the church. "It may be me who needs to take a rain check this time."

"What is it?"

"I think you have company in the church. Laurie Chase has been sitting there for some time. I asked if I could help her, and that's when she asked if you were around. I told her you were out, and she nodded and stayed. I think she's still there."

Tom headed to the church and slowly opened the front door to see if Laurie was still inside. In the narrow stream of sunlight, he spotted her kneeling and gently rocking in the front pew and closed the door. He made the Sign of the Cross and genuflected as he stood at the back pew. Inside the church, the high arches rose in the darkness with only the light of the stained-glass windows, the red vigil light, and a handful of prayer candles.

Finally, she turned her head.

He approached, and he could tell she had been crying. "I didn't want to disturb you if you need time."

She sat and shook her head, wiping her tears from both her cheeks. "I don't know what I'm doing."

Tom motioned to sit next to her, and she gave a gentle nod. "I think you're in the right place, then."

She sighed deeply. "I haven't prayed in so long. It never worked for me in the past. God didn't answer my prayers when I was crying out as a child, a teenager, or a mother, but I feel this need to pray for Joline."

"God answers prayers in ways we don't understand. He allows free will and allows circumstances to play out for a greater understanding of His will."

"At the house, you said that you thought Joline admired me and wanted to emulate me." Her chin trembled. "I'm so afraid that she did. I need to pray for her soul to be safe. I want her to be safe."

"Laurie, I've been praying for her, too. Praying for her is good, but why wouldn't you want her to emulate you?"

Lowering her head, she shook it back and forth. "I'm not a good person."

"Please believe me that you were made good and are good. We can all do things we regret and—"

"You don't understand. I'm not a good person! My mother never wanted me from the moment I was conceived. That's why I always wanted Joline to know how much she was wanted and loved."

Tom tilted his head. "That is a sign of a good mother, a good person."

"No! I did it out of selfishness, pain, and emptiness. I'm so afraid she found that journal when she was around fifteen and read it. I was not a good person to be like. I'm just so ashamed."

Her tissues were soaked, and Tom handed her his handkerchief. "Laurie, there is nothing you can do that God won't forgive. There's nothing you could do that would stop God from loving you."

Her face tightened as she shook her head. "If I ruined my daughter's soul, He can't forgive that. I was supposed to protect her." She paused. "I was nothing like what you'd want your daughter to be."

"There is nothing you could do that would be new to God."

She turned and stared directly at Tom, her eyes dark and full of fear. "I drank. I took drugs. I slept with more boys and men than I can count. I was unfaithful. I hated God. I hated my parents. I hated myself!"

Tom put his hand on her shoulder, and he could feel her body shaking as she sobbed uncontrollably. After a few moments, he said, "Laurie, I don't think it is you that you should be angry at. People do things, even the worst of things, for a reason—and most of the time, due to the pain they are trying to cope with."

She pulled herself back, furrowing her brow. "What do you mean?"

"Can I ask you a very personal question? I won't judge you, no matter what you say."

"What question?"

"Who is MC?"

Her face instantly drained to a ghostly white as she swallowed, and her mouth dropped open.

"I'm sorry if I'm asking something—"

She sighed.

"It's not your fault."

Her brows furrowed, and she shut her eyes tight again.

"Laurie, it wasn't your fault."

After several moments, she peered up into his eyes again, Tom hoping that she only saw compassion.

"I don't know. No one else is responsible for not being worth loving, for taking drugs, for being a sl—"

"Laurie, no matter what you've done, you're a good person. I've counseled many people, and I can usually tell when they've spent a lifetime blaming themselves for something that was done to them. Can I ask you if—"

"If what? If I was damaged goods?"

"Who was MC?"

She shook her head. "Why?"

Tom asked, "Did he ever do anything to you as a child that you would never want him doing to your daughter?"

The question caused Laurie to pull back as if Tom had struck her. "I don't know. It all seemed so—I don't know—gradual, so confusing."

"Do you mind talking about your childhood? What was your adoptive mother like?"

"She was there when my real mother wasn't, but she was not gentle or kind. She seemed cold and stoic, you know. If I skinned a knee, she would just clean it, bandage it, and tell me to be more careful. I don't remember her ever hugging me except when I ran to her. I didn't know if she could love me."

"What about your stepfather?"

Laurie's brow tightened, and she stared ahead of her. "Pops. He was older than her. He would pay attention to me. Help me with my homework. Sit next to me on the porch and read. He would give me long hugs and tell me I would be a great artist someday." She shook her head. "I don't know."

"So, he seemed to be the only person in your life who cared about you and showed you affection. Every child needs that, but I'm sensing some hesitation in you."

She closed her eyes and rubbed her mouth with her hand. "It's so confusing. I couldn't go to her, so he would come into my room and lay with me when I cried myself to sleep. Isn't that a good thing?"

Tom felt confused. "It can be. Laurie, who is MC?"

"Hmm. MC. Mamma used to call Pops, 'Mr. Clarke.'" There was an extended silence, and she shifted uncomfortably in the pew. Her face tightened again, appearing conflicted, shaking her head. "I didn't know what was right and what was wrong."

"Did Mr. Clarke ever touch you in ways that made you uncomfortable?"

Her eyes remained closed as she nodded.

"Laurie, was there more?"

She squeezed her eyes tight, but tears flowed as she nodded again. "I know I'm not a good person. I know it was my fault. I was wrong. I just wanted to be loved."

"Laurie, can you look at me?"

Her head shook as she lowered it. "I'm so ashamed."

"Laurie, I am so so sorry this happened to you. No child should ever be abused, especially sexually. You should never blame yourself for what an adult is responsible for."

Suddenly, she lifted her head. "But I—" She stopped short.

"I'm going to guess that you blame yourself because you felt closeness and pleasure, and it was confusing. You wanted to fight back, but you didn't. You felt as if you let it happen, and more than once?"

She gazed into his eyes as if he was the first person to see the world through hers, and then she closed them again, nodding, rubbing her forehead with the tips of her fingers. "How can I *not* be ashamed? How can it not be my fault if I let it happen? How can I be good if I've had sex with so many men and can't love my own husband? How can I not be responsible for Joline? Tell me!"

She abruptly stood to exit the pew, but Tom was in the way, and he put his hand up. "Can I ask you to sit here for a few minutes longer?"

"Why? Do you see what kind of person I am? Colby's not even Joline's father! How can you even look at me?"

Putting his hands on her shoulders, Tom replied, "Because you are a child of God. I understand how you feel because of what you believe to be true. I know you believe that because your mother couldn't keep you and your adoptive mother couldn't give you the affection and love you desperately needed, but what your adoptive father did to you was wrong and not your fault. An embrace is designed to feel good, and sex is designed to feel pleasurable, but they were intended for a mutually loving relationship. You have to believe me that your need was good, but it was his actions that were wrong. It was not your fault."

Her brows lifted, and her eyes widened. "But I didn't stop it. I didn't say anything. I went about as if it were normal and then spent my—" Tears streamed. "I've been running. I've been drunk or high more than I want to admit, and I've been, what's the word, promis—whatever. You would think I would never want to have sex again."

Tom took in a long breath, then let it out. "I've studied this for years and talked with so many people struggling with trauma and abuse. I want to tell you that it is not uncommon for a girl who has been abused to be promiscuous, to be with many men. The experience left them believing that they had to be sexually desirable to have self-worth. Many victims were left with depression, guilt, shame, anxiety, poor self-esteem, and relationship difficulties."

Laurie raised her hand, nodding to recognize the pattern that likely fit herself. "Mamma would always tell me to look my best so that the boys would like me. I'm so afraid I gave Joline that same message." She let out a deep sigh. "What did I do to her?"

"Laurie, a child needs things. You gave Joline love, affection, and care. I can tell by what you've told me that you care about her more than yourself. You can't blame yourself for the need to escape through drugs, alcohol, or even sex. They weren't healthy for you, but they can keep you emotionally numb to cope and, oddly enough, to feel as if you're taking control without risking abandonment. Even if sex is disassociated from your own body or the person you are with, it still impacts your body chemistry where levels of dopamine, serotonin, and endorphins are heightened."

Wringing her hands, she whispered, "It felt like an escape and like I was in charge, but it never lasted. I always felt ashamed afterward, like people looked down on me. Outside, I was the partier, but inside, I was becoming more withdrawn with more wounds than I could hide, but then—"

Tom half-smiled. "But then Colby came along."

"How did you know I was going to say that?"

"Just a feeling. He really loves you, you know."

She shook her head. "He can't. I've been an awful wife. We were married young, and neither one of us was a saint, but it was the first time I felt a sense of hope, like someone actually loved me. I kept starin' in the mirror and askin' myself, 'How could he?' but he's been like a rock to me. Someone I could depend on, but how did I repay that love?"

"Let me guess. The closer the relationship got, the more you needed to back off."

"Yes. I don't know how you know this," replied Laurie with a furrowed brow.

"Because you couldn't believe anyone could really love you. If he knew the real you, the one everyone had rejected or abused, he wouldn't; he couldn't love you. You couldn't let him get too close to see how ugly you felt inside, how unworthy you were, how bad a person you were. So, you drank and took drugs to numb yourself. You needed to flirt and have meaningless sex to feel in control and be attractive to men, but it never made anything better. It just made you feel more guilty, ashamed, and sure that you were the awful person you were afraid you were."

"How do you know this? I've been an awful wife, and he's known it, and—"

"And he's still here."

Nodding, her tears flowed. "And he's still here. God knows why."

"Yes, He does. Laurie, try to think about how a young person needs to process the world that is coming at them so fast it feels like it will overwhelm them. We create a perception of ourselves to be able to process it. If that perception is wrong or distorted like yours has been, it creates an unhealthy answer, but we still desperately cling to that perception of ourselves. We even search for ways to validate that distorted view to feel less anxious—even if for a very short while. Colby loves you. That is hard for you to process when you think you don't deserve it. Colby treats you right and won't abandon you, even if you give him every reason to, and that's downright confusing. You want his love, but you're afraid of losing it. You want to be close, but you're afraid he'll see the real you."

"Oh, my God, I think you're right, but it's just too late."

"Laurie, I believe there is nothing God cannot tackle and heal. Nothing. He still has a plan for you, and He will be your strength to move forward. He can forgive you, but you have to be willing to forgive yourself and, more importantly, realize that you've been a good person all along. No one is beyond redemption and healing."

She lifted her gaze to his, and Tom ensured that he showed no sign of judgment or condemnation.

He smiled gently. *"Even though I walk through the valley of the shadow of death, I fear no evil; for thou art with me."*

With that, she broke down and sobbed into his chest. She sniffed. "I think it's too late. It's too late for Joline, and it's too late for me and Colby." After several moments, she sat back up and wiped her nose. Her eyes were red-rimmed and puffy. "I need some time. I think I need to be alone."

Tom stood and gave her a hand to stand. "Absolutely. I understand. That was an awful lot I just threw at you. Please don't be afraid to call me anytime. I have nothing and no one more important to be available for."

She stepped out into the aisle, glancing up at Christ on the crucifix for a moment, and then made her way to the back of the church as Tom stood and watched, praying for her to believe there was hope.

Chapter 33

Tom exited the church, letting his eyes adjust to the sunlight as he approached the rectory to find Angelo and Paul sitting on the porch for a late lunch. "We would've saved something for you if we knew you were coming," said Paul with a laugh.

Tom smiled as he stepped onto the porch and grabbed a chip from Paul's plate. "I'm not feeling that hungry right now."

Angelo's head snapped up as if he'd never heard Tom say that before. "Sit, Father Tom. You can have half of my sandwich. How was Mrs. Chase? She seemed to scurry off."

Tom sat next to Angelo, glancing at Paul as if to tell him he knew who his true friends were. "She's faced a lot in her life and now has lost her only child. It's so much, but I have hope for her. I feel awful that we are leaving soon and are no closer to an answer than when we arrived."

Paul raised his head. "You don't think Ralph is responsible?"

"I don't know for sure, but some things don't make sense. If he was guilty, how could he blackmail both McCready and Jordy?" Tom leaned toward Angelo and whispered, "Laurie confirmed that the journal we found was hers. And we know those illustrations were hers, Jenna's, not Joline's."

Paul squinted. "What are you two murmuring about? Is this another time I should be getting lost to attend to my parish?"

Tom glanced at Angelo, and they nodded in unison. Paul sighed and took his plate and cup into the rectory.

"Wow. So, Laurie was the one who may have been sexually abused and was pregnant with Joline and wonders if the father is 'RJ?'"

"Something like that. I was so focused on Laurie when I talked with her; this is the first chance I've had to think of how it might relate to Joline's death. Was the paternity test from Ray Jordy about Joline, and is that what they were arguing about? Is that why there was a falling out with Colby about the same time Joline began acting out what she read in her mom's intimate journal entries?"

"Acting out?" asked Angelo.

"When girls are abused, they often believe they need to be sexually desired to have self-worth, so they can either withdraw or become promiscuous to gain a sense of control while remaining emotionally distant. If Joline started to test what it felt like by being more sexually aggressive—"

"You mean like seducing your history teacher at fifteen? Or your best friend's boyfriend halfway through a movie?"

Tom shot a glance at Angelo. He hadn't disclosed his conversation with Bill McCready, but he knew Angelo was as sharp as they came to figuring things out. "Let's just say that she started dressing more provocatively, taking risks in flirting with older men, bikers, and slimy waiters at late-night diners. She didn't back down from older men who didn't like being led on or teased. Usually, when girls journey down this path, nothing satisfies them, and they keep searching for the next challenge or thrill, but they keep finding out that for beautiful girls like her, men are too easy to seduce."

"Are you saying her death was her fault?"

"You know me better than that. She just may have pushed the envelope at times. More risk, more challenge. Maybe she felt confused when or if she read her mom's journal. Disappointed in the reality of her pain and methods of escape. Maybe her mom couldn't give her something she needed, and then she came to believe her father wasn't her real father."

Angelo finished off his lemonade. "I wouldn't know what it's like to have a father around, but I've seen the difference a good dad can make. I wonder if she confronted Colby or

Ray Jordy and how they responded. You don't think either of them would have killed her if she had, do you?"

Tom shook his head. "Not on purpose, but why was Ralph Cutter blackmailing Jordy? He did it to McCready over what he saw that night, and it's quite a coincidence that he suddenly ended up with Jordy's truck and some cash just after McCready was released."

Angelo glanced at Tom, and together they said, "And we don't believe in coincidences."

As Angelo stood up, Tom asked, "What are you up to?"

He shrugged. "I've got a few things to check out."

Tom stepped to the sidewalk as he watched Angelo disappear down the street and wondered what he should do next. Before he had a chance to think, a pickup truck zipped around the corner, over the curb, and abruptly stopped on the sidewalk. He jumped out of the way. The driver's door swung open, and Colby Chase jumped out and charged Tom, getting into his face. "Why? I told you to stay away from Laurie!" he shouted, grabbing Tom by his shirt.

Paul darted out of the rectory and pulled Colby off of Tom. "Colby, what are you doing?'

Colby stumbled back, breathing heavily, and yelled, "I just asked him to stop botherin' Laurie a few hours ago, and she comes home all upset again. I've never seen her this messed up." He pointed to Tom. "He keeps riling her up. She just lost a daughter!"

"Colby. Colby. Laurie came here asking for Father Tom. She needed to talk something out. He didn't go to her."

"I don't care. He's not from here, and things are tough enough without draggin' stuff up."

Tom tilted his head. "I do care, and you're right that I'm not from here. I think she's burying a lot of years of pain, and I'm guessing you know that. I'm also guessing you care more about her than anyone ever has."

Colby squeezed his eyes tightly as he stepped back and dropped to the stoop, shaking his head. "I don't know what to do."

Tom sat next to him and motioned for Paul to leave them alone. Paul hesitated but took Tom's lead. "Colby, if I told you there's a chance for Laurie and you to get to a better place and alleviate some of those years of pain, what would you do?"

He took a deep sigh. "I don't know. I want to say that I'd do anythin', but I'm feelin' like it's just too late. She can't love me anymore."

"But you still love her, right? I mean a lot."

He bit down on his lower lip, nodding. "Ever since I first saw her. I never had a real family; all I wanted was to have her."

Tom shifted his weight on the step. "I can imagine it was tough growing up that way and then to meet someone you could love—"

"She was the only girl I could ever love, but she could never love me the same way."

"Colby, what if I told you that she does love you the same way, but something was robbing her of showing it? What if there was a chance to get that something out of the way? What would you be willing to do?"

Colby lifted his head and squinted. "What somethin'? What are you talkin' about? I would do anythin' for her."

"I'm talking about doing something for the both of you. How much do you know about her childhood?"

Letting out a deep breath, Colby replied, "We both grew up in town. I know she felt hurt that her real mother didn't want her and that her adoptive mama wasn't that warm a person. I think she craved affection her mom couldn't give, but her adoptive father seemed to give her that. She never really talked much about him, though; he died before we married. Some sort of cancer that didn't waste its time. When I asked about him, she always changed the subject."

"Well, I think she needs to share something with you about him."

"What? What kind of somethin'?"

"Laurie needs to be the one to tell you, but it might explain a lot of the reasons she was conflicted in her closest relationships. My guess is that you were her rock, someone she could trust to protect her and Joline."

"Hmmm. But I didn't protect either one of them, did I? I failed, and she couldn't seem to ever really trust me. Funny thing is that I was the faithful one."

Tom stood up and peered into Colby's eyes. "If you could do something to truly help Laurie and have a chance at the marriage you want, would you be willing?"

"I don't know what it could be. I have nothing left to lose, but I'd do anything for her," he replied as he stood with Tom.

"Come on; let's go."

"Where?"

"Your house."

"Huh?"

Tom started walking, and Colby followed without a word. As they approached his home, Colby stopped and grabbed Tom's sleeve. "I don't know if this is a good idea. I don't think she's in any shape for this."

Tom turned toward Colby. "Sometimes, when people seem to be at their worst, that is exactly the right time to push through the pain. How long have you both been running from it? And where has it led you?"

Colby shook his head and followed Tom as he entered. "Laurie?"

They heard crying from the living room and found Laurie on the couch wiping her eyes.

"I can't seem to stop. I'm so tired of trying to hold myself together."

Tom quietly went over to Laurie and gently laid a hand on her shoulder. "Laurie, you have a wonderful gift of a man who loves you more than himself and would do anything for you. I think if you share all of yourself with him, you have a good chance to be much closer and find that love you've always longed for. It may take some work, but I can guarantee you will be so glad."

Colby sat next to her and held her hand. "No matter what you say, I won't run. I will never leave you, but we need to be all in, the good, the bad, and the ugly."

Her face contorted as the tears flowed again. "I'm so afraid. I've been awful to you. How can you keep loving me?"

"I made a promise more than nineteen years ago that I intend to keep until I die."

Laurie took a deep breath and a long exhale. "Oh, my gosh. Okay, but I don't know how to start."

"Tell me what happened with your father."

She shut her eyes, slowly shaking her head. "I tried for years to make believe it didn't happen, and then I started to blame myself. He never seemed like a bad person, and he was the only one to ever hold me, but—" She paused, squeezing her eyes tighter.

"Did he touch you?"

She nodded.

"Did he do more than that?"

She hesitated, glanced at Tom, and then nodded.

"That son of a bitch. Why didn't you tell me? I can't believe it. I'm so sorry, Laurie. That should never happen to anyone. Man, that bastard!"

"Father Tom said it's not uncommon for victims to blame themselves. I felt so ashamed and ugly. I believed it had to be my fault. Mamma kept telling me I had to be attractive if I ever wanted a boyfriend or husband someday. I started to believe that was all I was worth, and then—"

"And then what?"

"And then you came along. You were handsome, smart, strong, and you seemed to like me for me. No one had ever done that before. I couldn't believe you really loved me or would want to marry me, but I had this glimmer of hope, and then—"

"And then?"

"I got scared. I panicked that you would hate me once you really got to know the real me, what had happened. You would leave me. Inside, I was ugly, bad, unlovable." She grabbed another tissue to wipe her tears. "I still feel that way."

Colby squeezed her hand tighter. "Laurie, I would never leave you. I can't say I haven't been hurt and lonely, but I never want to give up on you or us."

She turned. "How can you feel that way? I've been cold with you like Mamma was with me. I've been—"

"Unfaithful?" asked Colby with a deep sigh.

Her nod was barely detectable.

Tom said, "If someone has been sexually abused, they can feel it was their fault. It may sound strange, but they might have sex with strangers to gain a feeling of being in control when the world feels out of control for them. There's no feeling of emotional closeness, just the feeling of being in control and a moment's sense of self-worth, and then it's gone, and the pain returns."

Laurie sobbed. "So much pain that I drank and took stuff to numb myself. I just wanted the pain to go away. I'm so sorry, Colby. You deserved so much more."

"I wanted more, but I never felt as if I deserved it. I kept hoping I could be enough someday. How many times?"

"How many times? Oh." She glanced at Tom, and her face flushed a deep red. "More than once. I don't even know because I was always too high to know what was happening. When I flirted and got someone's attention, it made me believe I was, maybe, worth something. I really want you to forgive me, but you have every right to leave."

Tom interrupted. "Colby, I'm going to say something that might sound strange, but this deep wound makes it harder to be close to the people we care most about. You back off out of fear of the pain of rejection. The person you want to be closest to is the one you are too afraid to be intimate with. In simple terms, I think Laurie loves you so much; she needed to put up a wall to protect herself from the intense fear of losing you because she believes she's not good enough for you. She's bad. She's ugly. She's shameful. She's—"

"Stop!" he shouted. "She's none of those things." He turned to her, lifted her chin, and gazed into her eyes. "You're not ugly; you're beautiful, inside and out. You're not shameful; you're forgiven. You're not bad; you are the best thing that has ever happened to me. I don't care what you've done. I only care about you getting whatever help you need to trust me and let down this damn stupid wall."

Tom smiled. "That sounds like the most sincere proposal I've ever heard."

Laurie started to shake. "What if I can't do it?"

Tom asked, "Laurie, do you think Colby's worth trying?"

She nodded and squeezed his hand. "But I don't know if you can forgive me for everything."

Colby turned toward her and sighed. "I don't think Father Tom is sayin' this will be easy for either of us, and I want to forgive, and I think I already know what you don't want me to know. Joline came to me about three years ago and started spoutin' off all this stuff about you. She told me that I wasn't her father, that you slept around and you did other things. I told her to stop, and she wouldn't. She said some nasty things, and our argument escalated—and that was the first and only time I ever hit her. I was so angry."

Laurie stared at Colby.

"Did you have sex with Ray Jordy? Is he the father?"

Tom asked, "Is that why you had a falling out with Ray at that same time? Did you confront him?"

"Yes, it's why we had a falling out, and, no, I never told him why." He turned to Laurie. "If we are goin' to be completely honest and try to work things out, this is one thing I need to know."

She glanced up at Tom and back at Colby, wide-eyed as she nodded and lowered her head. "I think so."

"You think so?"

"I don't know. I was so out of it. I don't know."

Colby stood up and paced the floor, rubbing his hands across the top of his head. "I don't know what kind of answer that is."

Tom got up and put his hand on Colby's shoulder. "Here's my professional opinion. I think you both have a lot of things to talk through, and some of it will hurt and take time to heal. The question will always be what you want going forward. Think about why you fell in love and why you wanted to be together. Sometimes, we fail because of traumas and pain from our past, and we need each other to let it out, get the weight off our shoulders, and support each other. Sometimes, we need to apologize and ask for forgiveness to heal. I sense that you've got something worth fighting for and holding onto. You just have to ask yourselves if you think it is worth it. Is she worth it? Is he worth it? I think you are. God thinks you are, and I think Joline still thinks you are. The best way to love her memory may be to be there for each other. I can help find someone for you to work with, and I think you will both be much happier and finally at peace in your heart."

Colby pursed his lips and nodded. "You're right. I'm willin' to do what it takes if Laurie wants me."

She glanced up in disbelief, jumped up, and embraced him.

Tom said, "I'm going to tend to a few things, and I'll be back if that's okay."

Chapter 34

Tom thought it was time to find out what the deal was with Ray Jordy. Was it his affair with Laurie where things began to break down between him and the Chases? What did he and Joline fight about that morning, and was he the real father? Was Ralph blackmailing him, and for what? As he trekked over to Ray Jordy's house, the questions circled in his head.

Ray wasn't home. Checking his watch, he thought it might be the end of Jordy's workday, so maybe he dropped by the Front Street Pub. As he left the front door of Jordy's house, he noticed a girl sitting on the stoop of the house next door that shared a driveway.

He called over, "Lizzie, is that you?" She peered over but didn't respond as Tom approached. "I haven't seen you for a bit. I've wondered how you were holding up."

She fidgeted with her hands. No makeup or finely brushed hair today. "Um. I don't know what else to do. Everything seems wrong."

"It's so hard to lose a best friend and not have a mom around to, you know, help you through it. Thank goodness you have your dad."

She shot him a glance that shouted out that he should know better.

"I didn't know you lived next door to Mr. Jordy."

Lizzie sat and twisted the ends of her hair. "Yep. They've known each other since school. Ray's mom was a single mom, and her sister owned the house next door, so he grew up there. When his aunt died and his mother took off with another guy, he was left with two houses, so he let us live here. Dad's never made a ton of money and drinks most of it, and Mom, well, she died when I was young. I only remember her as being sick and then gone."

"I'm so sorry about that. A girl really needs her mom around when she's growing up."

"Hmm. She seemed so bitter to me most of the time. I don't know if she could have been the mom I would have liked, and she was definitely angry at my dad. I don't know if it was because of his drinking or that's why he drinks. I know his father was one, so you'd think he never wanted to go down that same road. People are weird in how they deal with things."

Tom put his foot on the step. "You are an astute observer of human nature. Too often, we may repeat the things we hate or fear and ultimately harm ourselves."

"And everyone around us."

"So true. I understand the funeral for Joline will be on Saturday. I know that will be a tough day for you, so I will be praying for you."

"I don't know if you can pray enough. I'm—uh—I think I'm going to go in now if you don't mind. Thanks for talking."

"I understand. Don't be too hard on yourself, Lizzie."

Lizzie turned. "Do you have magic pills for that? Sorry, I need to go."

Tom thought about the questions he didn't ask Lizzie as he made his way down the road. Had Joline ever talked to Lizzie about Ray Jordy being her real father? Did she ever talk about him or have other interactions with him that were argumentative? Jordy had been more of the playboy out of the group, so maybe he had a hard time dealing with responsibility.

Tom sighed. He felt as lost for answers as when they brought Joline's body ashore five days earlier.

He tried to sort things out as he headed toward town, passing the local co-op supermarket, where he noticed Bill McCready coming out with two bags of groceries. He could tell that McCready spotted him, awkwardly keeping his head down as he loaded the bags into the passenger seat.

As Tom approached, Bill's shoulders slumped. "Father."

"Hi, Bill. I won't be around for too much longer, so there is some good news."

"Look. I'm sorry. It's just that people in town are talking. Some think I could still be guilty, and I'm probably feeling guilty. Do you know what I mean? Anne doesn't want to come into town, and Will's old enough to have friends who say things."

"I do understand. Hopefully, the truth will find its way to the surface. Do you mind if I ask a few questions?"

McCready glanced up. "No disrespect, but who can stop you?"

Tom's face warmed as he acknowledged the point. "It appears that Ralph Cutter witnessed you and Joline leaving Traci's that night and having a bit of an argument."

"I didn't kill her," McCready said, peering around to see if anyone in the parking lot was close by.

"I'm not going there. Did you see Ralph at all?"

"Not when we talked or when the bikers came at us."

"Hmm. It was brave of you to lead the Norsemen away from Joline. Trying to get to your boat before they could get you must have been pretty terrifying. Do you think any of them went back after Joline?"

McCready shook his head. "I didn't go out far and watched them head off. There were only three of them, and they stayed together up the hill. Route 1 passes over the river, and I could see them riding out of town, so I don't think they would have come back, based on the timing of her death."

"And you didn't see anyone else that night?"

"Not really. I think I saw that Jordy guy coming out of the Front Street Pub when Joline and I were talking, and then.." He paused, closing the truck door.

"And then?"

"I did see Cutter again when I brought the boat back in to get it on the trailer."

"You mean *his* boat?" Tom said with a hint of sarcasm. "Sorry, that wasn't nice. Did he make his way down to your boat?"

"Yeah. I only stayed out there for about twenty minutes or so, and when I docked the boat, there he was with that squirrelly smile of his."

"What did he want?"

"I didn't think anything at the time. He smirked and told me what a nice boat I had. I told him I was in a hurry, and he said, 'I'm sure you are,' and left."

"Hmmm. Did you notice any blood stains on him or his apron?"

McCready shook his head. "It was really dark. I could only see the moonlight on that bugger's face. I was only thinking of getting home to make sure my family was all right."

Tom replied thoughtfully, "Thanks, Bill. I hope everything clears up and you and your family can get back to normal."

McCready began to turn and then peered back, opened his mouth, and closed it again. Then he spoke, "And that other thing we discussed?"

"You came to me under the confidentiality of a confession. I agree that it was dead wrong, even if she wasn't legally a minor. I trust you've avoided those situations since and are truly sorry for what happened. I'll leave it with you and God. I would spend more time with Him, if you could, though."

McCready nodded and shook Tom's hand before getting into his truck and drove off.

Tom stood on the curb momentarily before Paul pulled up in his car. "Hey Tom, it looks like there was a bad accident late last night. You remember our waiter, Rick, from the restaurant?"

"Yes, I do. Is he okay?" Tom jumped into the front seat, and then Paul pulled away.

"I hope so. He actually asked if you could come along with me."

When they approached the hospital door, Tom could see that Rick was sitting up with bandages around his head and a cast on his arm.

Paul entered. "Rick. How are you doing?"

He grimaced as he adjusted his position in the bed. "I'm glad you give a hoot." Rick laughed. He quickly tightened his face. "That hurts. Tell me not to make myself laugh for a while."

Paul nodded. "Can I do anything for you?"

"Paul, don't be hurt, but could I talk with Father Tom for a bit?"

Paul turned toward Tom and nodded. "Sure, sure. I can ensure the staff takes extra good care of you while you chat."

As Paul left the room, Tom stepped forward, gazing empathetically at the patient.

Rick said, "You have kind eyes, Father Tom. I mean no disrespect. I kind of had a hard time with my father—or he had a hard time with me. I think that's when I started fantasizing what it would be like to be loved by a dad." A tear made its way to Rick's cheek. "I certainly longed for that. Oh, look at me. Blubbering with a stranger. I was hoping it would help to talk to someone who doesn't know me, but now I'm thinking that not many people really do know me. I enjoy putting on the show, but it gets tiring sometimes, and the sadness comes back when I am in for the evening—so I try to be out as much as possible. I remember sitting by the parlor window as a kid. There was a small field across the street, and all the boys were playing soccer or football. My heart ached to join them, but I knew I couldn't. I didn't fit in, so I found a persona that made me more interesting with the girls and other castaway boys." He glanced up. "You never had that problem, did you?"

Tom made eye contact. "Not so much when I was younger, but once I put on this collar, the reaction has been interesting at times, to say the least."

"Yeah, I guess you're right." He took a deep breath, and he winced. "Well, I've been thinking about things. You know—life and death. I do believe in some kind of God, but I don't know what he really wants from me. If I died tonight, what would happen to me? I act like I don't care, but I find myself caring very much."

Tom leaned closer. "Rick, that's a very good sign in my book."

"Hmm. But your book and your God don't really like me, who I am. I tried to talk with Paul one time, and he said that sex—it always comes down to that, doesn't it? He said, 'Sex should be a pathway to heaven and not a road to hell.' I got pretty angry and walked out on him, but now that I've gotten to know him, I can't imagine him trying to say anything to hurt me, so I'm confused. Does God hate who I am? How I live?"

Tom stared out the window at the puffy clouds and the blue sky. "One thing I know for sure is that God loves you. He loved you into existence for a reason. He made you for heaven. Sometimes, we try to piece together who we are based on things we feel, do, or like, but it really comes down to this: So, who *are* you? You, Rick, are an adopted son of a loving Father. He is the Father you've always longed for, the source of who you are, and He created you with meaning and purpose."

Rick squinted, appearing highly confused. "But He made me this way, and your Church tells me not to be this way, that I have no right to love who I love and how I love. I don't get what you're saying."

"My Church teaches that you are made with love, dignity, and purpose. You are made to love God and be loved by God. You are made to love others, to have deep and meaningful friendships, and to trust in His plan. Now, the Church does believe the biology and intent of sex have meaning and purpose, to bond a couple together as one and to create the miracle of a new life and a family. I'm a priest, so I'm not married and honor my vow to be celibate, but that doesn't compromise or make me less to God, my family, or any of my friends whom I love. I may not give you exactly the answer you want, but I would try to see God and the Church from a different perspective, loving you, respecting you, and wanting the best for you."

Rick exhaled a long breath. "Maybe this deserves a longer and deeper conversation, but I do get the feeling you don't hate me. Hate the sin and love the sinner, right? It's hard because I think of it as so much of who I am. Maybe I'm more than what the world wants to tell me I am."

Tom touched Rick's shoulder. "The world often wants to stick us in a much smaller box than we are. I see a very good man, and I hope you get good news from the doctors."

Rick nodded. "Earlier, I was thinking maybe dying wouldn't be so bad. I could stop the merry-go-round and the show, but now I think I'd like to be around for a bit longer."

"I'm glad to hear it, and I'm glad we met. Should I let you get some rest?"

"I am feeling tired. Hey, one thing before you go. I heard you've been interested in finding the person who killed the Chase girl, Joline."

"Well, I'd hope she can get some justice. Do you know something?"

"I don't know. I just thought what I heard seemed odd, knowing what happened to her. I was at Traci's early that Saturday morning for breakfast with a friend of mine. We like to sit at the counter where everything is going on, and I overheard that Ralph guy talking with someone."

"What did he say?"

"The diner was busy, so I only heard bits and pieces. The guy mentioned some girl who poured hot coffee on Ralph when he flirted with her, and Ralph shot him a crooked smile and said something that I didn't really think about until I've had this time to lie here and pass the time between shots of pain meds." Rick motioned Tom to lean in as he whispered into Tom's ear, "I don't know if it means anything, but I wanted to pass that on to you. I hope I get a chance to see you again."

Tom stood in the doorway. "Me, too, Rick. Take very good care, my friend."

On his way back to the rectory, Tom asked Paul to drop him at the police station. He hesitated a moment before going in, too. "Is the sheriff in?"

The officer motioned toward J.C.'s office, and Tom reached the open door to see him attending to some paperwork.

J.C. glanced up. "I guess this hiding spot isn't safe. What's on your mind?"

"I wish I could tell you. Did you know Laurie Chase growing up?"

"Not really. I'm too old to have been in school at the same time, and by then, I was on a few tours. I heard they were a little wild at times but harmless. Laurie, Colby, Ray, and Danny hung out. You know, teenage partyin', too much alcohol, drugs, skippin' school, and stuff. No robbin' banks or knockin' over old ladies. They've all had their troubles but haven't had any recently that I know of. Why do you ask?"

Tom rubbed his chin. "No reason. I did talk with McCready a few minutes ago. He told me that he hadn't seen Ralph during the altercation with the Norsemen, but Ralph did show up at his boat when he brought it back a half-hour later. He commented how nice a boat McCready had, so he may have been formulating his plan then."

"Or they were somehow in this together. Maybe, like you said, Cutter helped McCready load Joline onto his boat, and that's how the blood got on the boat and his apron? Maybe that's when her earring got loose? No one gives up a forty-thousand dollar boat unless there's a really good reason, and I don't trust that weasel, Cutter, as far as I could toss him."

"Has he said anything else?"

"He just said he didn't do anything, and we've got no witnesses."

"Huh. Maybe so, but he's got some explaining to do, and what did he have on Jordy? Hey, do you mind if I talk with him? I mean, he might want to see a priest," said Tom with playfully raised eyebrows.

J.C. stared down at his desk, rubbing the side of his hand across its surface. "Look, just don't buy any sob stories from him. I don't trust a word that comes out of that mealy mouth of his."

The officer led Tom to the holding cell, where Ralph was lying on the thin cot. He smirked as he glanced over at Tom with his black eyes. "Come to give me my last rites?"

"You don't seem too worried about that, Mr. Cutter."

Ralph swung his legs to the side and sat on the cot's edge as Tom held the bars, peering into the sparse cell. Ralph seemed like a different person out of his diner clothes, kind of lost, despite the confidence he was displaying on the surface.

"If I was guilty of killing that girl, I'd be worried, but I didn't, so I'm not. She certainly was pushing people's buttons to deserve a little pop." He snapped an elastic in his hand. "But not dying. She was too pretty for that."

"I'm glad you don't think she deserved to die. If you didn't do it, like you said, you could be the key to solving this case."

Ralph glanced up, eyes squinted.

"You'd be like the town hero or something. Besides seeing Joline, Bill McCready, and the three bikers, did you see anything else that night?"

"What? Are you playing detective now? I heard you've been asking questions all 'round town. Aren't you a priest?"

"Would you like to confess anything?"

Ralph shook his head. "Uh-uh. I don't need no priest or snoop. I'm all set."

"It seems as if someone saw you with McCready about a half-hour after the incident with the bikers. You were remarking on how nice his boat was, and now it's suddenly yours. If you said you didn't see anything else, and there is a witness who says you weren't telling the whole truth, things could look really bad for you in court."

Ralph shot another glance, tapping his fingers against his leg. "No. You're just playing with me. Why are you here? What's your game?"

"No games. I just don't want to see you going down for a crime you didn't commit just because the court doesn't believe anything you say. They might think you'd say anything to force people to give you expensive boats and trucks. If they find your word not to be credible, it wouldn't matter what you saw or what the truth was; they wouldn't buy it. I don't think you'd want that to happen. And if they ever found blood on your clothes or the diner—" Tom shook his head and whistled.

Ralph's eyes shifted back and forth as his expression froze. Suddenly, he laughed nervously. "You're just playing me. I didn't see anything or hurt that girl!"

"It seems as if not seeing anything turned out to be pretty lucrative. Don't you think? I'm just saying, if there is anything you saw and aren't including in your report, it could go against you."

Chapter 35

Tom stepped out of the holding cell area where J.C. stood staring at the whiteboard. "Did you break him?"

"Chinese water torture. It always works." Tom laughed. "I do think he knows much more than he's saying. Have you talked to Ray Jordy? Does he have an alibi?"

"As far as I can get out of anyone, he was at the Front Street Pub most of that night, but no one can say for sure he didn't step out. At different times, he was at the bar, in the back playin' pool, outside catchin' a smoke, and so on. No one was with him that whole time, but he showed up around four-thirty 'til about one."

Tom narrowed his eyes.

"What's that look for?"

"I was just thinking of the timeline. At least two people saw Jordy driving his yellow truck around town around five or so, following Joline. I guess it would be good to get confirmation that he wasn't gone from the pub for large chunks of time."

With a nod, J.C. replied in a mocking tone, "What a great idea. It almost sounds like police work."

"It does, doesn't it? Hey, I know you know your job, and..."

"And?"

"And that it's not my job. Listen, for being such a pain in the police blotter, how about me treating you to a beer or, even better, dinner?"

J.C. glanced at Tom and paused before replying, "Okay. That sounds good." He gave the other officers instructions and accompanied Tom down Main Street. The harbor was busy, and halfway down the street, they stopped in front of Rollie's Tavern.

"Fine with me," said Tom. He entered with J.C. and was greeted by the owner. "It's Rick, no, no, Ryan, right?"

Ryan smiled. "I've been called worse."

"And probably today," said J.C., patting his shoulder.

They approached the long wooden bar and grabbed two stools. Tom leaned over. "Do you like Guinness?"

"How about supporting a local brewery?" J.C. raised two fingers and called out to the bartender, "Two Mountain Man Double IPAs." As Tom took a sip, J.C. asked, "Well, does it beat your Irish stout?"

"To be fair, that's not actually possible, but when in Belfast—" He took a long sip. "It is good, though." He glanced down the length of the bar. "That looks like Danny Haskell down there with the two that brought Joline's body in."

J.C. leaned back. "Yeah. McMahon and Lowe."

"I don't think I could make a habit of pounding down a bunch of these and then heading out to sea early in the morning."

J.C. laughed. "It didn't sound as if you needed any help gettin' seasick out there."

Tom shrugged. "I have to admire them for it. So, I did talk to Ralph, and—"

"And he gave you nothin'. Do I have that right? He's in no hurry."

His brows furrowed, Tom asked, "Why's that? Who wants to hang around in jail with everyone believing he may have committed murder?"

"Suddenly, Cutter's someone in town. I don't think he minds that, plus he always has some angle he's workin'. He isn't in the cell more than ten minutes after you talked to him, and in swoops my favorite lawyer—check that, I don't have any favorite lawyers."

"I guess if I was charged with murder, I'd be thinking of a lawyer, too."

"He doesn't seem too worried about the murder rap. The lawyer's name is William DeVeau, and don't ask if it's the actor, Willem Dafoe. If there's a buck to be had, DeVeau is on it like sausage gravy on biscuits."

"Isn't that down South?"

"Aren't you from down South?"

"Boston?"

"Like I said," replied J.C. with a smirk. "Let's just say that DeVeau's nickname is 'Dollar-Bill DeVille' for a reason. He's fixin' to sue the town for wrongful arrest and defamation of character. I don't think that last one would be worth too much. I'm guessin' his blackmail schemes might fall apart if he tells us everythin' he saw, so he's lookin' to make a triple play on a young girl's death. Like I said, how could you possibly defame the character of someone like that?"

"I wonder what would happen if Ralph applied all that effort to something worthwhile. So, you don't believe he did it?"

Staring ahead, J.C. replied, "I don't know what to think. I know he's lyin' about somethin', but it could be to save his own hide. Joline's blood didn't come from nowhere, and you found out that he was lyin' about talkin' to McCready later that night. He's just a sleazy sack of you-know-what, and I don't have the time or the patience for it."

"I can imagine. I know I've only been in town for a handful of days, but you start to see people's lives a little closer when something like this happens. I'm a little worried about Danny down there. Solly said he's been less dependable lately, and Lizzie indicated he'd been here at the bar more than usual. She needs someone around, too, since she lost her best friend." He paused as he glanced down to see Danny staring into his mug while Jay and Rich were talking. "Sorry, I didn't mean to get off track. I don't know if I helped, but I tried to make Ralph think about losing credibility with a jury if he was holding back or twisting anything."

"Does he have any?" J.C. replied with a half-smile. "I'm not takin' my eye off the two main suspects, but I've got to start castin' a broader net, thinkin' about other possibilities."

"We got that timeline narrowed down so close to when she died and then the time to remove her body. I'm having a hard time with Ralph's story that he only saw McCready take off with the bikers and Joline walk off alive and well. He must have seen something to be trekking down the harbor walk to catch up with McCready and possibly threaten him with blackmail. McCready seemed to indicate that he was afraid of the Norsemen and what they might do to him or his family, and that's why he was in such a rush to get out of Belfast. It's possible, but it doesn't add up."

"You've got that right, Padre. I did follow up with Ray Jordy. He swears Ralph didn't blackmail him and that he was at Front Street the entire night. He also says that his argument with Joline that mornin' was about nothin'. He doesn't even remember what they talked about. I'm not sure if I buy that, but I can't think of any reason he would have to kill her unless there's somethin' I don't know about yet." He tilted his head. "Is there somethin' I don't know about?"

Tom scratched his head and shifted in his seat. He couldn't say anything about the paternity test envelope Angelo found in his house or Laurie's journal entries.

J.C. shook his head. "You know, it's one thing to be a pain in the rump, but being a useless pain in the rump is worse. Please don't hold out any information, Father. I have a feelin' you've got pieces of the puzzle that I can't see, and this picture is too full of holes as it is." He stared at Tom, waiting for him to crack, and then finished off his beer when it was apparent no information would be forthcoming. "Let me ask you a question. Do you give your boss as hard a time as you give me?"

Tom's eyebrows furrowed. "My boss? The bishop?"

J.C. shook his head.

"Oh, you mean the Big Boss. I'm sure I do give God a very hard time at times."

J.C. laughed. "So, why did—"

"Why did I become a priest?"

"How did you know I was goin' to ask that?"

"Eventually, everyone does. Well, I really love what I do. My parish. The people I've been blessed to meet, but the real reason is that I fell in love with the Boss and His call to become a disciple of Christ—" He paused and smirked. "And a pain in the butt to my local sheriff."

"Well, you are doin' an awesome job on that last one, Padre."

"Thanks. I do try my best. Hey, speaking of sheriffing... do you know Rick, who waits tables at Meanwhile in Belfast?"

"Yeah. I'm heading over there later to see how he's doin'."

"Well, he told me something that he overheard Ralph say in the diner on Saturday morning before you showed up, and before we knew Joline had died."

J.C. leaned in. "What's that?"

"Well, he said that Ralph was talking with some guy who was kidding him about some girl who poured hot coffee on Ralph when he tried to flirt with her. Supposedly, Ralph said something like, 'Well, that won't be happening again.' He didn't hear Joline's name but thought it was odd. We know that Joline was seen pouring hot coffee on Ralph's hand the day before, so—"

J.C. slid off of his stool. "Okay, Sherlock. That is very interestin', but I still think you should focus on that call from your Boss, don't ya think?"

Downing the last of his beer, Tom watched J.C. disappear through the front door. Danny Haskell was sitting alone at the other end of the bar. He moved down through the crowd, not sure of what he would say, but, by then, Danny was gone.

As Tom turned around, he noticed Danny heading out the front door and caught up with him outside, lighting a cigarette in front of the pub. "How are we doing tonight, Mr. Haskell?"

Danny took a long drag and let the smoke seep out his nostrils and mouth before even acknowledging Tom's presence. "That's a good question, isn't it?" He peered down the street to the harbor. "I, uh—" He stopped, pressing his lips together.

"Danny, it's not been an easy road in your life, has it?"

He glanced over at Tom and then closed his eyes before taking another drag on his cigarette as his hands shook.

Tom cleared his throat. "I would imagine Lizzie has brought some joy."

He nodded. "She was always a good kid. I really love her and enjoy her. I think it made her mother a little jealous, but what's new?"

"I know your wife had a tough battle with cancer, which had to have been so tough on you having to raise Lizzie on your own and still work as hard as you do. I've been saying prayers for Kristie."

"Don't waste your time. She's not prayin' for me, that's for sure." Danny stopped to light another cigarette.

"I'm sorry to hear that."

"Hey, things were good when we met and got married, but she soured. I guess I can't blame her to some extent, but she got so bitter. What's the word? Vindictive." He took a long drag and stood from the post he was half-sitting on. "Hey, look. I've got to go. Thanks for talkin'. Um, I assume you're headin' back to Boston soon?"

Tom laughed. "Everyone in town seems happy that I'm leaving soon. Yes, leaving on Sunday. I'll be at Joline's funeral on Saturday if you are attending."

Danny's head lifted, and with a furrowed brow, he snapped, "Why wouldn't I be?"

"No reason. I didn't know the timing of your fishing obligations, that's all."

"Sorry. Things are just very messed up for me right now." He turned, murmuring, "Have a good evening, Father."

Chapter 36

Tom meandered back to the rectory, thinking of his exchanges with the town's people. He knew it took time to really know people, to develop friendships and trusting relationships, and here he was, only six days in town and poking his nose into sensitive areas for folks who had difficult paths in life. Opening old wounds could be dangerous when there was no plan to be around for the healing process. He'd be gone in a few days and would never know if he had done more harm than good despite his intentions. "Everyone keeps trying to tell me, but do I listen?" he whispered to himself.

Suddenly, an arm came from behind and grabbed him. "Who told you that you could go around just talking to yourself in this town!"

It took a second for Tom to recognize Paul's voice and reach back to grab his head, but Paul wouldn't let go.

The sight of two priests wrestling each other on the sidewalk may have seemed like fun to them, but an older woman passing by reached out her cane and gave Tom a good whop on the leg. "You two should be ashamed of yourselves. What kind of example are you setting?"

Tom and Paul quickly stood at attention. "My apologies, Mrs. Whitcomb," said Paul, his face flushed with embarrassment. "You are absolutely correct. We were just fighting over who would lead the Rosary on Friday. That's the way they do it in Boston."

"Well, this isn't Boston, is it?"

Tom held in the laugh welling up inside of him. "Mrs. Whitcomb, you are absolutely right. When in Belfast, right?"

"I can't imagine what else is going on in Boston, but this isn't a good sign," she said, thumping her cane on the ground. "Good day, gentlemen."

As she ambled off, Tom whacked Paul on the arm, and he returned the friendly smack.

Paul huffed. "There's probably going to be a town vote to kick me out, too, by the end of the week."

"It will be good to have you back in Boston." Tom laughed as he put his arm around Paul's shoulder. "I think I needed that."

"I think you did, Tom. I think you did," said Paul. "Now, how about I cook us up a nice dinner?"

"How about having Angelo cook us up a great dinner?"

"Okay," Paul retorted.

When they reached the rectory, they didn't even have to ask. Angelo had already cooked an Italian-style roasted lamb with potatoes and had a large salad full of fresh vegetables.

Paul leaned over the stove, breathing in the rich aroma. "Ahh, I can smell the garlic and rosemary. What is that called, Angelo?"

"*Abbacchio al Forno con Patate.* It's a nice evening; let's eat *al fresco.*"

"Sounds great!" said Paul as he got out the plates and silverware, and Tom mixed some fresh iced tea.

They sat on the porch as the early evening summer sun drenched the porch, and a light breeze kept them comfortable.

"Angelo, I'm going to up my offer for you to trade teams. Just name your price," said Paul with a laugh.

Angelo sipped his cold drink. "I've heard rumors of sidewalk wrestling, even between priests, in this town. I think I'll have to stay with the city where it's safer."

Paul said, "Speaking of safer, I guess people must be feeling less anxious with the suspect for Joline's murder behind bars. Do you think he's guilty?"

Tom leaned back. "Well, there's certainly some motive and definitely opportunity. There is evidence of her blood on his apron and the back door of the diner. He's not exactly the noblest of characters in town, and he was overheard saying something that indicated he knew Joline had died before those boys brought her body in on the boat."

"Do you think he's the one who bopped you in the dark the other night?"

"I don't know. It was right behind the diner where he tends to take a lot of his smoke breaks, and he seemed uncomfortable whenever I asked questions," replied Tom.

Paul turned to Angelo. "Are you convinced?"

Angelo shrugged. "Lots of questions still unanswered, to be sure."

They played chess for a few hours, and Angelo turned in early for the night, so Tom and Paul took advantage of the time to catch up a bit more before finally heading to bed. Unfortunately for Tom, the questions about his doing more harm than good with his time in Belfast crept back into his mind, which brought back the nightmares involving the death of his college girlfriend, Corlie, and unstoppable ruminating about what he could have and should have done differently. Could he have been less selfish and more loving to her? Had he learned his lesson as he engaged with those mourning now for Joline in Belfast?

He started drifting off around three o'clock until he thought he heard a sound at the front door. He got up but saw nothing inside or outside and returned for another attempt to drift off. The next day was Friday. Saturday was the funeral, and Sunday, he would be on his way back to Boston, having neglected his old friend, Paul, for most of his visit. He opened his eyes to the dark of the room; staring at the ceiling, he said, "Lord, please show me the way."

Tom started to drift off again around six o'clock, just about the time Paul hit the floor singing Wham's "Wake Me Up Before You Go-Go," but the problem was that Paul couldn't sing. Tom attempted to muffle the sound with a pillow over his head, but to no avail, and he gave up and shuffled into the kitchen, where Paul was dressed and making toast.

"Hey, hello, sleepyhead. I hope you slept as well as I did last night."

Tom raised his eyebrows and glanced over at Paul. "How often do you get serenaded to sleep?"

"But I didn't sing anything until this morning?"

"It's a long story. What's for breakfast?"

"We have toast. Toast and jam. Toast and peanut butter or toast with butter. Lots of good choices. It seems as if Angelo went out before I got up, so, sadly, we are without our chef—or your chef."

Tom grabbed his cup of coffee from Paul. "And don't forget that. At least I know you'll invite me back next year *if* I bring Angelo along. So, what's on your agenda today?"

"Hmm. I need to see the Chases today and spend some time on the homily. I'm not expecting Laurie or Colby to speak at the funeral service. Do you agree?"

"I think it would be so hard, especially knowing the person responsible could be sitting in the church. I hadn't even thought of that."

"Oh, boy. You're right unless Ralph Cutter is guilty. Most of the people I've talked with think he is."

Tom placed his two slices into the toaster. "I don't know if there will be any peace until there is the certainty of the evidence or a confession."

Chapter 37

After sharing their simple breakfast, Paul excused himself to work on the eulogy before Laurie and Colby arrived. Tom felt a bit at sixes and sevens over what to do with his time, but the answer was always pretty simple, and he proceeded to the church to sit and pray. As the door cracked open, he could hear a creaking sound from one of the wooden pews. Stepping in, he spotted Laurie Chase's familiar silhouette and hesitated.

"I know those footsteps," said Laurie without turning.

Tom stepped down the aisle to the pew where she sat. "I didn't—"

"Want to bother me. I think we have our routine down now, don't we? I'm not sure why, but I've been coming here each morning. I almost feel as if it's the only place I can be with Joline. Is that weird to say?" She motioned for Tom to sit.

"Not at all. It's quite beautiful, and I'm glad you feel you can be with Joline."

A tear rolled down her cheek, and Tom handed her his handkerchief to wipe it before another fell. "You'd think I'd be all cried out by now."

Tom sat with Laurie in the silence of the moment. After a while, both simultaneously began to say, "You know—" and shared a quiet laugh.

"What were you going to say?" asked Laurie as she turned to Tom.

"You should go first."

"No. I want to know."

"Well, I had this sudden feeling deep down that you are going to be okay. I know Joline is being well taken care of, and while I sense a lot of hurt in Colby, he really loves you unconditionally, but just now, I felt a strength in you that I hadn't sensed before."

Laurie lowered her head and cracked a grin. "Funny. You talked with Colby and me, and we kind of retreated into our corners. I know he needs something from me that I haven't had to give, but I think I've just been afraid to give it to him. I'm so scared about getting close and trusting anyone, but I think something has changed."

"What do you think it is?"

"You've made me stop and think about a lot of things I've been running from. I think I'm getting awfully tired of running and hiding. I kept thinking it was protecting me, but what evidence do I have that it's done anything but harm to Colby, Joline, and me?"

Tom didn't respond.

Tears streamed again. "You—" Her lower lip quivered as she wiped her tears. "You know all the ugly things about me, and, um, I feel no judgment. I almost feel like it's more okay to share things with you when before I would run. I've been thinking about all my years with Colby. You're right. He knows a lot of my sins, my faults, and my cheating him out of the love he deserved, and he's still there. Right next to me. There are things he didn't know about, too. It makes sense now that Joline must have confronted him with what she read in my journal about him not being her father. It makes sense that everything changed for her when she found out all my—well, all the things I did to shame her. I think she was too ashamed to be close to me but tried to be like me, repeating my mistakes. I don't know if I can ever forgive myself for that."

Tom touched her shoulder. "I think you can, and I think it will be important that you do. Once you know in your heart that what happened to you as a child was not your fault, you will not judge yourself so harshly for the negative effects it has had since."

"I think I know that in my head, but not down here yet," she replied as she held her hand over her chest. "I talked to

Colby last night, and he looked into my eyes like he wanted to try. It gave me a lot of hope, but then we ended up with the question he's been asking himself for the last three years. Is Joline Ray's daughter and not his? Did I sleep with his best friend?"

Tom wanted to ask what she told him, but he bit his tongue, and she didn't answer.

Laurie sighed. "I want to try. I want to stop avoiding and protecting. I want the help I need to heal and move forward. What I don't know is if I can give Colby the answer he wants."

She sat in silence a moment more, then thanked Tom and said she wanted to take a walk and think.

Tom sat and prayed for Laurie and her family for some time, then made his way back to the rectory to read but felt restless and decided to take his own walk into town. The air was fresh and warm, and everything was in bloom. He felt a temporary joyfulness as he watched a puppy running ahead of his owner and then turning to taunt him. Tom approached Main Street and crossed to the sunny side, and ran into Sue, Megan, and Lizzie trudging up the steep hill.

"Hello, Father," said Megan with a smile. "I think there are some of those orange-molasses cookies at the bookstore if you have a craving."

"I'll keep that in mind. How are you ladies doing on this nice summer day?"

Sue said, "We're okay. Still missing Jo and all."

Lizzie nodded but didn't add anything to Sue's comments.

Tom pursed his lips. "I can certainly understand. She'll always be a part of you, so it's a good way to remember her." They stood there awkwardly for several moments, and Tom said, "Well, have a good day, and I'm guessing I'll be seeing you all tomorrow."

He continued down the sidewalk, shifting from side to side as he came upon older residents ambling along or congregating in conversation, some lifting their heads and saying hello. By the time he reached the harbor, he could see

Solly's lobster boat slowly making its way to the docks. He spotted Solly behind the wheel, but it didn't look as if Danny Haskell was standing on the deck with him. Tom stepped forward and finally recognized Angelo holding the end of the rope, ready to tie it to the dock when Solly pulled alongside.

Tom grabbed the second line from Angelo and tied that line. "Solly, have I lost my first mate to the sea?"

Solly peered up, scratching his white beard. "Best partner I've had in a long time, and he works for free!"

"Ah, the same salary I pay him." Tom laughed.

"If we hadn't already dropped our catch at the co-op, you would have been helping us unload about sixty keepers," joked Angelo as he handed Tom a bag.

"What's this?"

"My pay. Solly forced me to take three lobsters for our dinner tonight, and I didn't fight him too hard on it."

Solly chuckled. "All I know is that the missus is a happy woman, knowing I wasn't out there alone. Angelo was great company and a big help. He catches on pretty quick."

Tom smiled. "Just like me."

Solly raised his eyebrows and stared at Tom without a word.

Tom helped Angelo onto the dock, and once Solly was set, they sauntered down the walkway. "So that is where you disappeared to early this morning or late last night. I thought I heard the door around three. Why the secret excursion? You usually have a reason for what you do."

Angelo scanned the area before responding. "I was doing some snooping earlier last night. What I found out was that Ralph wasn't blackmailing Ray because Ray doesn't own the yellow truck."

"Who does, then?"

Angelo peered around once more. "Danny Haskell."

"What?"

"Ray and Danny live side by side in town. Ray lets Danny and Lizzie live in the house, and Danny lets Ray drive his truck. Danny's had a few DUIs, so he's really not supposed to be driving anyway."

"Wow. What does that have to do with you trying out for a new profession on the high seas?"

Angelo sat on the nearby bench and waved Tom over. "It got me thinking about what Ralph would have on Danny to blackmail him into giving up his truck so quickly, so I came down here yesterday to talk with Solly. You know that Danny has been drinking even more and missing day after day with Solly. Solly was desperate for help, and I thought I might pick up some insights on his partner."

"Captain Angelo. So?"

"I didn't get much from Solly other than him saying Danny has been acting strange lately. He did say that Danny would talk about Joline from time to time, maybe because she came over to his house to see Lizzie. I'm not sure. But I did find something very interesting while we were hauling in the traps."

Tom scratched his head. "Something was in one of the traps?"

"No. No. When Solly was winding the pot hauler to bring up a trap, I noticed a tiny piece of something blue in the pulley assembly. It's like the pulley wheel on an old clothesline."

Tom leaned in. "And? What was it?"

"I couldn't tell at first, but when Solly was busy fixing the netting on the trap he hauled in, I luckily had a lockpick on me that I could use to pry it out. Guess what it was?"

"I can't. That's why I'm asking you."

"What was Joline wearing when we saw those autopsy photos?"

Tom shook his head. "Let's see. Don't tell me. Something blue. Wait. It was a blue plaid blouse. Is that the blue you saw?"

Angelo pulled out a piece of wet cloth that definitely appeared to be a match for Joline's blouse. "Remember that her blouse had a piece torn off?"

"Oh my gosh. Angelo, are you thinking that Danny took her out to sea that night and came back in before we arrived to go out that Saturday morning?"

"I don't know, but Danny was awfully quiet that morning. I just figured it was his nature, but Solly mentioned that he seemed oddly quiet and jumpy."

Tom pointed down to the docks where the *Emily Lauren* was pulling in. "What were their names again? Ray and Rick?"

"Jay and Rich," replied Angelo.

"See, I haven't lost it yet. I have seen them spending a lot of time with Danny at the bar lately. I don't know if that's unusual, but we can find out."

Tom and Angelo headed to the dock and grabbed the ropes to help tie down the red lobster boat.

Tom smiled. "How are you doing, Jay? Rich?"

The boys appeared tired and ready for a hot shower. Jay said, "We had a good haul today, so it will help pay some of the bills. I guess we're doing all right."

"Great. It's hard to believe it's been almost a week since you had the task of bringing Joline's body in. I think of how hard that must have been."

Jay glanced quickly at Rich. "Yeah. Not something I would want to do again."

"You boys go out pretty early, right? Pitch-black out and all. Fr. Paul and I went out on the *Miss Lizzie* that morning with Solly and Danny around three-thirty, and you boys were already gone. That's a long day."

"Yup," grumbled Rich. "Well, we've got to take care of things here. It's been good talking with you. I heard you're heading back home soon."

Tom smiled. "Everyone in town seems excited about that. Hey, quick question." Neither Jay nor Rich glanced up as they started grabbing gear on the deck. "When you were heading out that morning, did you see anything unusual?"

Rich shook his head as he remained busy.

"Was the *Miss Lizzie* here when you pulled out?"

Both men stopped but kept their gazes down. Rich grumbled, "I don't know. It was dark."

"Okay. So if someone was motoring in, they would have had their lights on, and you would have noticed them?"

"Of course."

"So, no lights either?"

Rich lifted his head, the soiled, brimmed Red Sox hat covering it. "Like I said, we didn't see anything unusual. I don't mean to be rude, but we've still got a lot of work to do here."

Tom lifted his hand. "Totally understand. I hope you get a chance to relax a bit before you have to take the boat out again."

As they walked away, Tom glanced at Angelo and recognized his expression. Why did it feel as if Jay and Rich weren't telling them everything? What did they have to hide?

Chapter 38

Tom and Angelo stood at the bottom of the hill. Tom said, "We've got to see the sheriff."

Before they made it to the station, J.C. pulled alongside them halfway up Main Street. "Just a few more days, boys," he shouted.

Tom and Angelo stepped to the open window, and Tom said, "I don't know if you're going to like this or not, but we've got some interesting information for you on Joline's case."

J.C. rolled his eyes. "If it has to do with firmin' up the case against Cutter, I'm all ears. If it's another rabbit hole, please do me a favor and save it."

Tom glanced at Angelo and then down toward the harbor in silence. Before he could answer, he spotted the yellow truck down by the docks and someone talking with Jay and Rich beside their boat. The man jumped back into the truck and sped up the street as Tom turned back to J.C. and opened the door. "We can talk while you're chasing the yellow truck!"

Tom and Angelo jumped in as J.C. exclaimed, "What's goin' on here?"

"Trust me, Sheriff. I think that might be Danny Haskell speeding away in his yellow truck."

J.C. pulled out and spotted the yellow truck turning the corner and passing the movie theater. "Can you boys please tell me what we're doin' here? What would Danny Haskell be doin' drivin' Ray Jordy's or Ralph Cutter's truck for? He's not even supposed to be drivin', period."

The truck pulled out onto Route 1, and J.C. followed.

Tom kept his eye on the truck. "J.C., Angelo found out that Danny Haskell is the real owner of the truck, so it must have been him that Ralph Cutter was blackmailing for something. Angelo spent the morning on Solly's boat to see if Solly might provide some clues, and on the boat, he found, well, Angelo, you tell him."

Angelo pulled out the piece of blue plaid cloth and held it out for J.C. to see.

From the expression on J.C.'s face, he seemed to recognize the material immediately and began to speed up. "Are you two sure this is Danny we're chasing?" as he turned on the lights and the blaring siren.

Tom joked, "Unless Ralph escaped from your cell. I don't know what the deal is, but Danny's been more in a funk than usual, drinking more, missing work on the boat, and spending a lot of time with Jay McMahon and Rich Lowe these days. We just tried to ask Jay and Rich if they saw anything unusual when they went out that Saturday morning and if the *Miss Lizzie* was docked when they left."

The yellow truck finally pulled to the shoulder, and as J.C. slowed down behind the truck, he turned to Tom. "And what did they say?"

Angelo piped in, "They got very quiet and uncomfortable, basically telling us they had to get going. Solly said that Danny's been very different over this past week, taking Joline's death very hard."

Tom and Angelo stayed in the vehicle while J.C. stepped out and approached the driver's side window of the yellow truck. Angelo murmured, "We couldn't leave without stirring things up a little more for our friend."

"I think this will accomplish that. I'm just wondering how this will hit Laurie and Colby. It sounds as if Danny, Ray, Colby, and Laurie were a very tight group growing up in this town, and Lizzie and Joline were like sisters."

J.C. called for a deputy to pick up the yellow truck and let Tom and Angelo walk back while he brought Danny into the station for questioning. By the time Tom and Angelo made it to the station, J.C. had already interrogated Danny and locked him up.

They peered up from the bench when J.C. reappeared, scratching his head. "He confessed." They followed J.C. into his office. "At first, he played ignorant, but as I started asking more questions, he stopped me and confessed, claimin' it was an accident and that he took her body out to sea on the *Miss Lizzie* early that mornin'."

Tom asked, "So, what do you think?"

J.C. shuffled his notes from the interview. "It makes sense, but what I don't know is if Ralph was an accomplice. He had blood on his apron and the door of the diner. He could have left the bloodstains and her earring on McCready's boat to divert the blame. I don't know. I'm guessin' he saw what happened, helped Haskell carry her body to the boat, and then trekked down to the McCready's boat to plant the evidence."

"Sad. Did he say what happened or why?"

"Nope. Once he confessed, he clammed up. He must have panicked and has been feelin' guilty ever since. That could explain the increased drinkin' and missin' work and all."

"Hmm. I wonder if it was Danny in the yellow truck that was seen following Joline to the high school that Friday evening by Ben Hatch's farm and then leaving the high school?" queried Tom.

"And was it Danny who attacked you behind the diner the other night and drove off in the yellow truck? Maybe he thought you were poking around too much into the case?" added Angelo.

J.C. stood up. "Well, you two can play detective on your own time. I've got to nail down the case and protect a town." Tom and Angelo got the hint and stood up to leave, then J.C. added, "And thanks. I do appreciate all the help. Now it's time to get in our own lanes."

Standing outside the station, Tom patted Angelo on the back. "You are so good. You have such an instinct for sniffing things out and focusing on the right thing."

Angelo laughed. "I haven't told you about all the dead ends I was tracking down." Lifting his chin, he added, "I think news travels fast around Belfast."

Tom turned to see Colby and Laurie heading to the station from one direction and Ray Jordy coming from another. He took a deep sigh. "Oh, boy. I can't blame them, but they look pretty wound up."

Colby stormed past them and into the station as Laurie paused, "We heard some news. Is it true? I can't believe it is."

Tom tilted his head. "We know very little, but it looks as if Danny just confessed. He said it was an accident. He may have panicked and then taken Joline's body out to sea. Angelo found the torn piece of her blouse jammed into the pot hauler pulley, and it sounded as if Ralph had been blackmailing Danny for his truck in exchange for his silence. Those are just guesses, so we should find out for sure."

Ray had entered the station, and Laurie followed along with Tom and Angelo just behind. They could hear shouts from the cell area as they dashed to see what the ruckus was. J.C. and one of his officers tried to pry Colby and Danny apart. Each had their hands around the other's throat, their faces as red as a cock's comb and just as angry.

"I'm going to kill you!" screamed Colby.

"You're no better!" yelled Danny, gritting his teeth as he held his grip.

"You killed my baby girl!"

"Why do you think she was your girl?"

Ray jumped into the fray, trying to pull them apart, but Colby elbowed him with his other arm. "Stay out of this, Ray. You started this!"

Laurie screamed from the doorway. "STOP! STOP! STOP!" She held her hands up as tears ran down her face.

With that, J.C. separated the three men and took a deep breath. "I don't care who you are. If I have to pull anyone apart again, I will put you all in jail. You got it?"

Colby's eyes burned with fire as he pulled his shirt back over his shoulder. Pointing through the bars at Danny, he seethed. "He killed Joline!"

Danny peered over at Laurie and squeezed his eyes tight. "It was an accident. I didn't do it on purpose."

"You take the life out of her and dump her body into the ocean and—"

"I loved her," said Danny.

"What kind of love is that? You're half-drunk most of the time and can't even take care of your own daughter," chided Colby.

"She *was* my daughter. I could tell from the time she was born."

Colby shot a glare at Laurie. "What the hell is he talkin' about?"

She shook her head, and her mouth fell open. "I don't know. I thought—"

Staring at the floor, Ray Jordy mumbled, "She thought she was mine."

Colby grabbed his shirt. "Why would she think that?"

J.C. pulled Colby's hand off Ray, who replied, "I don't know. All I know is that you stopped talking to me three years back. We were best friends, and you never gave me any reason, and then Joline comes to me several months back saying that she thinks I'm her real dad."

Colby gritted his teeth. "Why would she think that? Why do *you* think I stopped talkin' to you?"

"I don't know who told her that, but she really pushed it with me. I finally paid for one of those paternity tests and showed it to her outside of Traci's last Friday morning. She was upset that I denied it, and when I showed her the results of the test, she stormed off."

Colby stared at Laurie, whose eyes were squeezed tight as she shook her head. "Laurie, who would have told Joline a thing like that?" He turned back to Ray. "She kept tellin' me I wasn't her dad and that you were— agh, I don't know what to think."

Crying, Laurie peered up at Colby. "She read it in my journal. I didn't know what I was doing back then. I was so messed up, happy that we were married, but scared as hell about really loving someone and them loving me back. The four of us had so much fun together. We had an unspoken bond, but we still escaped the pain with too much drinking and drugging." She glanced over at J.C. "It was that summer night at the park. We were so out of it, and I think I was hanging onto Ray to make you jealous, and you got angry and took off. You just left me, and I think something happened. I know something happened, but I was so confused, waking up on the grass and seeing RJ lying a few feet away, I didn't know what to think. A few weeks later, I took a pregnancy test, and it was positive, and I knew we'd have a row."

Colby's back scraped along the cement wall as he slipped to the ground, covering his face with his hands.

Ray peered down. "Cole, I loved Laurie, but I would never cheat on you. Never. You were my best friend, and best friends don't do that."

Everyone turned back to Danny, who was looking on in silence. "I've always loved Laurie. I was always jealous of Colby—strong, handsome, and with the girl that I wanted to be with. I was so high that night that I didn't know what I was doin'. I was the odd one out. The small ugly ducklin' of the group of misfits, and here was the girl I dreamed of kissin' me, and things just went too far."

Laurie shook her head in disbelief. "No. Danny. No. I've never had any of those feelings for you."

"I know."

"Joline?" asked Laurie.

Danny nodded and shot a glare back at Colby. "I felt so guilty for so many years, but Kristie made sure she left me with her vindication. I confided to Kristie about what happened, and she became angry and bitter. On her deathbed, she forced a smile and whispered to me, 'I got back at you. Lizzie was never yours. Now you have nothing.' She told me Lizzie was your daughter."

Ray lifted Colby to his feet, and he approached the cell with J.C. holding him back. He shook his head. "That never happened. I never cheated on Laurie. I took a vow. Lizzie isn't mine."

Danny's eyebrows furrowed in disbelief. "What?"

J.C. whispered something in his officer's ear, and the officer left, returning with a folder. J.C. said, "Can we all hold for a second?" He flipped through the pages of reports in the folder. "I thought I had seen this. We took DNA samples of everyone durin' the investigation." He held out a blue sheet of paper. "This report confirms that Joline's parents are Colby and Laurie Chase. I don't know what other things happened, but she's no one else's daughter."

Danny dropped himself to the cot in his cell, and Laurie put her arm around Colby, who began to cry more than Tom had witnessed him cry since Joline's body was found. Ray placed his arm around Colby's shoulder, and they led him out of the cell area.

Laurie exchanged glances with Tom at the door and nodded as they exited to make their way home.

J.C. now stood by Tom and Angelo. "I've never seen anythin' like that before."

"There's a long road ahead for all of them. I'm hoping it leads to a better place."

On their way back to the rectory, Tom said to Angelo, "I'm feeling sad for Danny."

"Why's that?"

"Well, you know how devastating the impact of a tough childhood can have on you. All four of them had that, but Danny's seemed to have haunted him in a different way. He's repeating his father's escape in liquor, and he's never found anyone to fill that hole."

"I guess having a bitter wife who despises you, a daughter who you believe isn't yours, then seeing your friend with the girl you love and raising the daughter you've thought was yours all these years couldn't be easy."

Tom nodded. "Absolutely. I wonder what happened that night that would end up with Danny strangling Joline? Why was he following her around that night? Was he just being protective or waiting for an opportunity to talk to her? Maybe he told her she was his daughter, and she rejected him?"

"Well, Joline had found out earlier that morning that Jordy wasn't her father, which she believed was the case for three years. That could have put her on an emotional rollercoaster."

"You could be right, Angelo. Graduating can be a scary proposition on its own. It may sound like a contradiction, but sometimes, people retreat to risky behavior when the world becomes uncertain. She's pouring coffee on Ralph, taunting the bikers without fear, pushing McCready into another encounter, and then seducing her best friend's boyfriend in the middle of a movie with her friends. Who knows what state of mind she might have been in when Danny confronted her at that time of night."

Angelo stopped. "Makes sense. Kind of an explosive encounter for both of them, but it sounds as if Ralph must have witnessed something to be able to blackmail him. He might have even helped him carry Joline's body onto the boat."

"That's what J.C. is wondering as well. Hmm."

"What's with the 'hmm'?"

"Did I say that? I thought the pieces would all fit together if we could put together the whole timeline for Joline that night, and there'd be justice for a poor girl's death."

When they reached the rectory, Angelo held the door for Tom. "I'm sure the sheriff will try to squeeze out the whole story between Cutter and Haskell."

"I hope so."

Chapter 39

Tom was obviously more in his head than in the conversation with Paul and Angelo at lunch. At one point, Paul waved his hand in front of his eyes. "Ground control to Father Tom," he sang, giving his best David Bowie impression.

Tom laughed and shook his head. "Sorry about that, Ground Control. My mind is still spinning."

Paul got up. While pouring another cup of coffee, he said, "I'd have thought a solved case would bring you back to earth for your last days Down East."

"You're right. I promise to be all yours from now until Sunday when we sadly have to head back to Boston."

Angelo quipped, emphasizing a Boston accent, "I'm not leaving until I get one of those lobstah rolls I've been hearing about since I got here."

Paul's phone buzzed, and he jumped up to answer it, carrying it to another room. Then he returned. "That was Laurie Chase. She told me more about her version of what happened this morning at the station."

Tom nodded. "It was pretty intense, but I think it may have cleared the air on a lot of harmful assumptions that had divided those four friends for so many years."

"And giving Colby Chase his daughter back to mourn," added Angelo.

"Good point," said Tom. "I know Lizzie Haskell is eighteen now, but I'm worried about her being alone in this with her dad behind bars."

Paul nodded. "Me too, but Laurie said they invited her to stay at their house until she knows what's going to happen to her dad."

"That's good," said Tom. "She's had a tough week, too. It seems as if Danny didn't even believe she was his daughter all these years he's been raising her alone. Despite his dependency on the drink to avoid dealing with things, he did stick by her. She must be devastated."

"I would think so," replied Paul. "Laurie said Lizzie thanked her but wanted to stay at home, and Ray Jordy said he would look in on her since she was just next door."

"That's good of him. Well, I know I've been a terrible guest, and I'm going to try to make up for it these last few days."

Paul tilted his head. "Then you can help me with my homily and get things set up for Joline's funeral tomorrow."

Tom worked with Paul that afternoon on writing the words he would say, and then they worked with the cantor on the songs and arrangements for the 10:00 Mass.

That evening, they shared the lobsters Angelo had caught with Solly and sat on the porch to reminisce about their days in the seminary and early days as priests. Paul told Angelo a few stories that Tom wished he hadn't shared.

"Sometimes, I'm surprised we didn't get kicked out," said Paul with a laugh.

"Don't give that look as if it was all me," quipped Tom. "Angelo, Saint Paul here once changed the words for the songs we would sing at evening prayers."

Angelo grinned. "How bad could it be?"

Tom started to answer just as Paul stood up, shaking his head. Tom turned to Angelo with a mischievous smile, "Maybe another time."

They sat until the evening sky turned dark, the stars began to take their places, and Tom's and Angelo's lack of sleep caught up with them. They all turned in early.

Laurie Chase did not come to the church or stroll by, which Tom thought was a good sign that meant she was with her husband, Colby, now mourning together and supporting each other. J.C. never passed by in his vehicle, hopefully home with his family, knowing the key suspects were in custody and the streets were safe. Danny wouldn't be drowning his pain and doubts in his selected sedative. He still had a daughter who needed him, especially now that he knew she was his.

Tom prepared for bed, saying his nightly prayers to thank God for the day and the gifts he reminded himself to appreciate. He prayed for his brother, Luke, who was working in Peru and who he missed daily. He prayed for his deceased parents and family members, Sister Helen at St. Francis, and a long list of others. Then he thought of those he met during the recent days, praying to see them with the dignity that God did. How did the events, relationships, and traumas experienced along the way impact who they were and who they weren't today? Laurie, Colby, Ray, and Danny, the tight band of four that had found solace in each other's company but had too easily let it unravel with the inability to trust, tainting their relationships and the next generation. There was probably a lesson for McCready and even one for Ralph Cutter that would help him appreciate what shaped their protective public selves. He prayed for grace and strength for all of them and guidance on what his role should be. Before he could pray for himself, he had drifted off and slept until the morning sun brightened his room and the delicious aroma of something Angelo was cooking wafted up from the kitchen to his room.

He quickly dressed and followed the tantalizing scent. Tom grabbed his cup of coffee from Angelo and joined Paul at the kitchen table. "Good morning, men. How are you feeling this morning, Paul—nervous?"

Paul glanced up from his typed eulogy. "I am. Emotions at funerals are always so unpredictable, but when a young person is buried, it hits everyone so much harder."

"Including you."

Paul chuckled. "Including me."

Angelo brought over hot plates of poached eggs, bacon, pan-roasted mushrooms, spinach, and peppers. "This should give everyone energy for the day."

Before they knew it, the townspeople were beginning to file into the church full of morning sunlight and beautiful arrangements of flowers. Paul and Tom greeted folks as they entered and gave their condolences. There wasn't a seat remaining, and a hush came over the crowded church when Joline's casket and her parents arrived at the back. Laurie gave Tom a long hug, her tears soaking his vestments. Colby never let go of Laurie as he shook Tom's hand with a silent nod. Tom was happy to see Ray Jordy standing next to Colby and ready to help carry his daughter's coffin to the front of the altar.

Paul said a blessing over the coffin, and a profound heart-wrenching silence filled the church as Paul, Tom, Laurie, and Colby led the coffin, now draped with the blessed pall, down the center aisle. The pall, a white sheet of hope, was all that was needed to remind everyone of Joline's baptismal garments that welcomed her into this fellowship of believers, coming full circle from a new life celebrated by baptism to her new life experienced through physical death and won by Christ's Resurrection. The cantor began singing "Amazing Grace," and her powerful voice, in this poignant moment, clearly invoked deep emotions from everyone, including Tom.

When they reached the front of the altar, Colby let Laurie into the first-row pew next to Joline's closest friends, Lizzie, Sue, and Megan, all wearing dresses and their eyes reddened from crying. Laurie reached over to clutch each of the girl's hands as Paul and Tom approached the altar, and Paul gave a blessing to the congregation to begin the celebration of the Mass.

Lizzie rose and read from the Old Testament Book of Wisdom for her life-long best friend.

"A Reading from the Book of Wisdom.
The souls of the righteous are in the hand of God,
and no torment shall touch them.

They seemed, in the view of the foolish, to be dead;
and their passing away was thought an affliction
and their going forth from us, utter destruction.
But they are in peace."

As she read the rest of the verse, Tom gazed around the packed congregation, listening intently. J.C. Coombs sat a few rows behind Laurie and Colby with his family. Traci was to the left, next to Michael and Theresa from the theater. He was surprised to see Bill McCready with Captain Mike in the back corner. Even Ned Parker took the time to attend, as did Ginny Anderson, the lady with the Jack Russell dog, Solly, his wife, and, of course, many students from the high school. Tom's gaze moved back to Lizzie as she finished the reading and made her way into the pew to sit with Sue and Megan. Tom peered down toward the three young women, ready to begin their own lives. He froze for a second but then reminded himself that he was reading the twenty-third Psalm of David next.

Tom stood at the lectern, clearing his throat as a lump formed before he could begin.

He gazed down directly at Laurie, and tears began to roll down her cheeks as she bit down on her lip.

When he reached the line, *"Even though I walk through the valley of the shadow of death, I fear no evil; for thou art with me,"* he could barely get out that last phrase, and he prayed that he would help the congregation understand that God was, indeed, with them all. When he was finished, he noticed J.C. wiping a tear from his face.

After readings from St. Paul and the Gospel of John, Paul stood at the lectern to give his homily and a reflection on Joline's life. Tom could tell that Paul was having a hard time beginning as he paused in the silence of the congregation for several moments.

"As many of you know, my very good friend, Father Tom, has been visiting this week, and it's made me realize how much I love this town, my home, because of all of you sitting here to support the Chases, united together to mourn the death of a very special young woman, Joline.

"Laurie and Colby and all of us are confronted with the reality of death and all its pain." He paused for a moment. "But it is our faith that unites us. It is our faith that consoles us and gives meaning to Joline's life and death, even in the midst of all of our questions about why this would happen to such a young and beautiful daughter of Belfast when she was just beginning her life. Well, as I said one week ago, I don't believe Joline was just starting her life; I believe she lived it each and every day, trying to find herself and her purpose. We ask why God would take her life, but I see God only giving life, our precious life here on earth, and an even more profoundly wonderful life in His loving arms in heaven. We pray as a community for Joline's soul and God's loving mercy for her life that has changed and not ended.

"I mentioned my dear friend, Father Tom. We try to remind each other that we will never be perfect priests, but we work to live out our vocations with honest passion and compassion. Today, we in this church know we are never perfect, but trust that God can give us the grace to learn, love, and grow. Sometimes, we blame ourselves, refuse to forgive ourselves, and seek to protect ourselves. But we are called to love ourselves and lean on each other. Joline asked me before her confirmation if we have to be perfect to get into heaven. I told her that only God could be perfect. She did live her life with passion, joy, and confidence."

There was a bit of laughter.

"She tapped into God through her creative art, joy for life, friendships, curiosity, and desire to be true to herself. She was lucky to have parents who loved her deeply and friends who made her life so much more. She was blessed to be born and raised in a community like ours that will support those she leaves behind. We may lay her body to rest today, but not her soul, not her good deeds, not her love, and not her memory. When she was young, she told me she didn't know if she wanted to go to heaven because resting in peace sounded boring. When we discussed that it was anything but boring, rather joyful, and amazingly vibrant, like one of her paintings had come to life that she could jump into, she smiled and said that was where she wanted to go. May her soul and spirit be with God in the light and joy of heaven, and may each of us keep her spirit alive in our loving memories of her in our hearts. God bless you, Joline. Amen."

Although he had helped him earlier, Tom hadn't seen Paul's final homily and was moved by Paul's words. He could see the grateful expressions in Laurie and Colby's eyes for honoring her memory so beautifully. After sharing the Lord's Supper and final blessings, the family and the town proceeded out of the church, following Joline's coffin to the spot on the cemetery hill, where Tom had sat with Laurie beside the tree she and Joline had marked as their special place.

Tom's heart swelled at the sight of so many people from the town gathered around Joline's sun-filled resting spot as a community of loving support. The casket lay above the open grave, covered in all the flowers found in the portrait of Ophelia above Joline's bed. She would have loved how beautiful it was and how this moment felt as Paul gave the final blessings, and Laurie dropped to her knees to say goodbye to the daughter she loved so much, a love she had never experienced from her family or herself. As people slowly departed to head back to the church hall for lunch, only Laurie, Colby, Ray, and Tom remained.

As the sun gently touched their faces, Laurie turned to Tom. "I don't know if I can leave her. So much of her life was in front of her. So much of me still wants her, needs her with me."

Tom nodded. "I know. I hope you know that she is still with you always. One of her gifts might be to remind all those who knew her that life here is not all there is and to remember what is really important. Our relationships with God and each other become so much more important than what we get caught up in here on earth. Maybe she is giving that gift to more people than you realize. You will always miss her, but she is always with you, in your heart and in her soul that will never die."

Tears rolled down her cheek as she wiped them, holding up her handkerchief. "I brought my own today," she said with a half-smile.

Colby put his hand on her shoulder. "I think we should get down to the hall when you are ready. We'll come back."

Laurie nodded and glanced at Tom. "You are coming?"

Tom replied, "I am. I need to make one stop on the way, but I will be there."

"Thank you," she said and then gazed into his eyes, pausing for a moment. "Thank you for everything."

Chapter 40

Tom walked down the hillside cemetery into town, where he passed the Colonial Theater, trying to visualize the scene from that night. Just up the street stood the police station, where he wasn't a stranger any longer. That morning, the officer on duty was Jeff Hardy—young, with reddish hair and a uniform he needed to grow into in more ways than one.

"What is it, Father? I would think you'd be at the funeral."

"I was. I just wanted to stop by and make a request."

"Shoot. The sheriff is at the funeral with just about everyone else in town, except for me and the prisoner, Mr. Haskell," he replied with a motion of his head toward the cells in the back.

"You are right about that. I think everyone came, and it was a beautiful service. Do you think it would be all right for me to talk with Mr. Haskell for a minute?"

Officer Hardy scratched his head and pursed his lips. "Well, the sheriff did leave me in charge, so I guess I can make the call on this. Is this one of those confession things or something like that?"

Tom shook his head. "I just wanted to talk, in private if possible. I know Ralph Cutter is right next to him."

"Oh, Ralph is out on bail, and his charges moved to accomplice and witholdin' evidence or somethin' like that. Um, shoot, I guess it can't do any harm if you just talk. I think you'll have to sit outside the cell, though. I don't want to take any chances with a murderer and all."

Hardy set down a chair several feet from the cell and raised his voice to wake Danny from his slumber. "Danny, you've got company!"

Danny fought to open his eyes and then closed them again when he caught sight of Tom standing by the bars of the cell door. Hardy stepped out, closing the door enough but leaving a crack in case he had to respond to any problems.

"I didn't mean to interrupt, and I hope it's okay that I dropped by."

Danny slowly swung his legs from the bed and sat on the cot that squeaked as he straightened up. "I've got plenty of time and nowhere to go. Why are you here?"

Tom moved his chair next to the cell door and sat close enough to talk softly. "Danny, you love your daughter, right?"

His brow furrowed at the question. "Of course I do. Why would you ask something like that?"

"I just think people don't know how good a person you are and how much you love your family. I think you got a bum steer as a kid. I know a lot of people who share a sense of abandonment that wasn't their fault, and they didn't deserve it. One thing I know is that, in the pain, they tend to either avoid relationships as an adult or really want a family to love and to love them back."

"What's this all about?"

"I wanted to see how you were doing. Joline's funeral was very beautiful. I know you cared about her. I'm guessing all those years of caring don't disappear just because you found out she wasn't your daughter. I can imagine that there was a moment of quiet on the boat when you held her and grieved losing her. It may have been the first time you could tell her she was yours and that you loved her."

Danny dropped his head, and tears fell to the hard floor. "Why do you think I cared for her? No one else thinks I did. They think I killed her on purpose. I'll hang, and no one will even remember what happened in a few years."

"Well, Lizzie will."

Danny nodded. "Hmmm. Yeah. She's a good kid."

"I saw a photo of you staring at Joline at the graduation and remembered people seeing this yellow truck following her around that night; maybe you worried about her getting too cocky with those bikers? Maybe Lizzie mentioned that?"

"Okay, so?"

"Well, like I said, the funeral Mass was very nice. In the sanctuary with Father Paul, I noticed the girls sitting in the front row next to the Chases. It was beautiful to see Joline's friends there to support her parents at this time. You know, I noticed Megan first and then Sue and finally Lizzie, all in dresses, all crying, but one thing stood out that was different. Do you know what that was?"

Danny shook his head. "I haven't a clue. Why are you talkin' in riddles?"

"Megan had one of those brightly-colored bands the kids wear around their wrists. Hers was green and had the letter 'M' on it. Nothing else."

"So? Girls wear bracelets and bands all the time."

"I agree. I noticed that Sue had a yellow band with the letter 'S' on it. The odd thing was that Lizzie was the only one without a colored band."

Danny uncomfortably adjusted his body, making the cot squeak. He sighed deeply. "Father, I haven't got a clue what you want me to say. So, Lizzie doesn't wear a colored band."

Tom pulled out his phone. "You know, that was what I thought, but it seemed odd, so I studied some pictures from graduation, and here's one with the four girls all wearing colored bands. Megan has green, Sue yellow, Joline red, and here's Lizzie with a blue band." Tom turned the phone toward Danny to see clearly in the photo that Lizzie was wearing a blue band.

Danny remained silent.

"It's not clear enough to see if there is an 'L' on hers, but I remembered a painting Joline had in her bedroom. I didn't know what it was about. It was a flag with four colors: green, yellow, blue, and red, and you can see here that she painted connected rings across each color with the letters 'M,' 'S,' 'L,' and 'J' in each color band. I think it must have been something to bond this band of four close friends, and you can see that Lizzie is next to Joline as her closest friend."

Danny rubbed his folded hands back and forth across his mouth. "So?"

"Please don't tell anyone, but I somehow got Joline's autopsy photo." He tilted the screen to show him the photo of the lifeless Joline, her eyes closed, her face blue, and her hands folded on her chest. "I'm sorry to show you this because I know it's hard to face, but what stood out was that she was wearing a colored band on each wrist. Like Megan and Sue, a red one on her left wrist and this blue band on her right wrist. If you look closely, there is a 'J' on the red one and an 'L' on the blue one."

Danny shook his head. "What is this all about? Why are you tellin' me all this? I feel like you're playin' a game with me."

Tom leaned in. "I don't want to do that, Danny. I think you're actually a good person who has been dealt a tough hand of cards. You may have been infatuated with Laurie but loved your wife and your daughter, Lizzie. I think you loved them a lot. Solly said you were a good worker and laid off the booze for many years, but—"

"But what?" snapped Danny.

"But your wife grew bitter about something you told her. Fear of abandonment and losing the love of your wife set in. Even though you hated your father's drinking, you started drinking because it helped kill the fear and pain of this change in her. Now, you're not sure if Lizzie is even yours. I figure that is why you said what you said to me the other night."

Danny tightened his brow. "What was that?"

"It was when I called you 'Captain Haskell,' and you said something like, 'I have no boat to be captain of and no one to carry on my name.'"

"Hmm. I still don't know what's goin' on here."

"When did she call you that night?"

Danny shot up from the cot. "What call?"

"When did Lizzie call you about Joline that Friday night?"

Danny paced and shook his head. "I don't know what you're talkin' about. This is crazy talk."

"You love your daughter, don't you?"

"You already asked me that. Of course, I do."

"And you would do anything for her?"

"Sure," said Danny, looking Tom directly in the eye. "She's the only one in my life who never gave up on me, who still loves me. I've cheated her and haven't given her what she deserved, but I would do anythin' for her, sure."

"Would you—"

They could hear the sudden opening of the front door to the small station and Officer Hardy jumping up. "What's goin' on, chief? Is she here to visit again?"

Tom poked his head out the door, panicking as his heart raced when he saw J.C.

"What in the blue blazes is he doin' here, Hardy? What is he doin' with the prisoner?" bellowed J.C.

"I-I, he just—I just thought—"

"I don't pay you to think. I pay you to keep priests out of the jail cells."

Tom stepped out into the station room and gave a fake grin to J.C.

J.C. rubbed his forehead and peered over at Lizzie. "Tell them what you told me."

Her eyes squeezed tight, and she began to cry. "I can't do this. I can't let my father do this."

Tom reached over and handed his handkerchief to Lizzie, who wiped her cheeks as more tears flowed. "I didn't mean for any of this to happen, but my father isn't to blame."

J.C. pulled out a chair. "Tell me exactly what happened that night. Just go slow and start early on."

She took several deep breaths, and her face tightened with fear. "I just can't go on lying about this. We were to meet at the movies at seven, but Joline was late so we walked around until the nine o'clock showing. My boyfriend or my ex-boyfriend, Nick, got us tickets, and we went to the show.

Halfway through, Joline said she wanted to leave but for us to stay. It turns out she flirted with Nick, and the two of them ended up in Nick's car doin'—I don't even want to think about it. She could have any boy in town, and she went after Nick just because she could."

J.C. wrote in a notepad. "And how do you know what they were doin'?"

There was a sudden yell from the cell area. "Lizzie! What's goin' on?"

J.C. motioned to Hardy to close the door and nodded to Lizzie to continue.

She raised her head to hold back the tears. "Rudy Jenkins. I wanted to talk to Nick after Joline left, and they were both gone. I darted out the front doors of the theater to see which direction they headed, and Rudy was passing by. I told him that I was feeling worried about what they were up to, and he said he would go look for them."

"And he found them."

"He sure did, in the act. He said he confronted both of them, yelling, and then he clocked Nick with a punch and warned him to stay away from his girl. Yeah, like she stayed away from my guy."

"Stick to the story of what happened," implored J.C.

"Um, Rudy came back to the theater and told me what happened. I was devastated. After the show was out, I told the girls I was going home and started looking for both of them. I didn't know what I was going to do with Nick, but I wanted to throttle Joline. We'd been best friends since forever, but she'd changed. She started acting so weird and had an edge to her, doing things just to get a reaction from people. It got to be almost midnight, and I couldn't find them, so I went home pretty angry."

"Was that it?"

"Well, I didn't want to run into those bikers who were harassing us earlier that night. Joline pissed them off; sorry for that, and they were around town, but I was too restless to sleep, so I snuck out to look for her again."

"And you found her?" asked J.C.

Lizzie lowered her head and nodded.

"What happened?"

"Lizzie!" was the muffled sound from her father through the door of the prison cells.

"What happened?" J.C. asked again in a soft but stern voice.

"We argued. She seemed totally unashamed of what had happened. She didn't seem to care, and I got angry. We started screaming at each other."

"Where was this?"

Lizzie stopped. "By the big machine thing that picks up the boats. I don't know what it's called. When she started laughing about it, I just grabbed her, and she held my arms to keep me from hitting her and started smiling like it was a joke. I'd never seen her like that."

"What happened next?"

"I—I—I don't know." Lizzie began sobbing, and her body shook as she squeezed her leg with her hands. She shook her head back and forth. "I, uh, I just lost it! I reached out to grab her. She fought me, and my hands got to her neck, and I just started squeezing. I was so angry, and then—" Lizzie just stopped, and there was complete silence in the room.

"And what?"

Lizzie squeezed her eyes tight as her face contorted.

"Lizzie!" yelled Danny.

The tears flowed. "And she just dropped to the ground. It was so dark, but I knew she wasn't moving. She just laid there, completely still. I just went into a panic. I'd killed her. I killed my best friend with my bare hands. My dad didn't do anything; he's innocent. I didn't mean to do it. I really didn't mean for this to happen."

J.C. asked, "How close were you to the boat hoist?"

"Um, it was maybe fifteen feet away from us."

J.C. shot Tom a glare.

Tom asked, "Is that when you called your father?"

Lizzie froze and didn't respond.

"How did Joline's body end up a quarter-mile out in the ocean?"

She shook her head. "I'm the guilty one, not my dad. He shouldn't be in prison."

Lizzie fell silent. The blood drained from her face. Her eyes widened for a moment before she stared at the floor.

J.C. turned to Officer Hardy. "Let's put her in the open cell for now."

Hardy hesitated. "She's only a girl."

"She's eighteen and just confessed to a murder."

Chapter 41

J.C. sat in his office, tapping the wooden desk with his fingers and appearing more unsettled than Tom had ever seen before.

"What are you thinking?" asked Tom.

Elbows on the desk, he leaned on his hands and shook his head. "I don't know. I thought we had this."

"Why would she lie and confess? To save her dad? He loves her too much to let her do that."

Opening the folder on his desk, J.C. flipped through the large stack of photos and reports. He stopped at a page in the report that had a diagram of a human body with notations on it. It may have been the final autopsy report. He put his finger on one of the notations. "I don't think she killed Joline."

Tom propped up in his chair, happy to hear the possibility. "Why is that, Sheriff?"

He paused for several moments. "I haven't told anyone this because I didn't want to tip off the person responsible. The autopsy clearly says that she didn't die from strangulation. She died from head trauma caused by a hard blow with a blunt object. Blood filled her brain cavity. She may have been alive for some time after the blow and then collapsed while fightin' with Lizzie or whomever. Lizzie may think she killed Joline, but the strangulation marks aren't deep enough, and it doesn't match the coroner's assessment."

"Huh. So that is why you asked her how close she was to the boat hoist where Joline may have struck her head earlier?"

J.C. nodded.

"So, do you think Danny was responsible?"

He shook his head. "Ray Jordy claims to have headed home around 12:45 a.m. and saw Danny takin' off in the yellow truck closer to one. Another neighbor saw movement in his house between midnight, and about that time, so I think he was home believin' Lizzie was home in bed."

"But you've been holding Danny for her murder."

"I've been tryin' to get to the truth." J.C. scratched his head. "He certainly will be charged for dumpin' her body and witholdin' evidence in a murder investigation."

"Hmm. I figured Danny was covering for Lizzie. All the girls had colored bands on their left wrist with their initials on them, but Lizzie no longer had her band on, and I noticed Joline was wearing two bands, one with a 'J' and a blue one with an 'L' that Lizzie was seen wearing at the graduation earlier that day. I thought it may have gotten torn off in the scuffle between Lizzie and Joline. Danny noticed it when he came to remove Joline and any evidence from the murder scene. He may have put it on Joline's wrist before loading her body onto the *Miss Lizzie* to bring her out to sea."

J.C. smirked. "Very clever, but how did you know that Joline was wearin' two bands, and they had initials on them?"

"Oh, it was on the autop—"

"Just what I thought. Maybe we can file some charges against you and your friend, the thief, but right now, I just need to figure out what really happened that night."

Eyebrows raised, Tom said, "You're not going to like this, but I think the only one that may have seen the whole thing would be—"

"Ralph Cutter." J.C. stood up and turned to Tom. "Do you want to take a short ride?"

"Don't you want to tell Lizzie and Danny that they didn't kill Joline?"

"Not until I find out the whole story, first."

A few minutes later, they were pulling up in front of one of the subsidized rent apartments across from the high school football field, and J.C. rapped on the door that had tape covering a cracked windowpane. There was no reply.

"Maybe he's not home," said Tom, peering around.

"I'm sure that's what he wants us to think. I saw the shade lift slightly when we drove up." J.C. banged harder. "Ralph, I know you're in there. Open up."

The door stuck a bit as Ralph cracked it open, giving a crooked half-smile. "My lawyer said I didn't need to talk to you or be harassed anymore."

J.C. pushed open the door and scanned the small, messy apartment. "I love what you've done with the place, Ralph. I just need to ask you a few questions."

Ralph was unshaven and still wearing his grease-stained tee shirt from his last shift at the diner.

The blackness of his eyes always caught Tom's attention.

"I don't have anything to say."

Motioning over to the kitchen table, Ralph lowered his wiry body down on an old, rickety chair, and J.C. and Tom sat.

Ralph eyed Tom. "What's he doing here?"

J.C. sat back. "Just in case you don't tell me exactly what you saw last Friday night, and we need to administer Last Rites when I get through with you. Now, tell me."

Ralph rubbed his right hand across his mouth, then stared down at the table and nervously drew circles with his index finger. "What do I get? How do I know you aren't going to trick me?"

"Tell me," J.C. said with a serious glare in his eyes.

Ralph glanced at Tom and back to J.C. "Okay. It was a quiet night, and I was bored. Joline was with that McCready guy in a back booth of the diner. They were arguing about something, and then they went out the side door, so I took my butt break to see what was happening. They went down the hill toward the boatyard, and I followed them. McCready tried to get away, and Joline threatened to tell on him something about them having sex when she was in school and all." Ralph smirked.

"Keep goin'."

"Well, then the three Norsemen bikers came roaring down the walkway and stopped when they saw Joline and McCready. They were calling her all kinds of names, but she didn't seem afraid, talking back as she always does. I could see why they wanted to give her a little pop," he said as he snapped the rubber elastic on his wrist and narrowed his eyes.

"And?"

Ralph shook his head. "Ah, they started revving their engines and making passes like they would run them over. One of them clipped McCready pretty good with an uppercut, and his face was all red from the blood. Another one, I think the guy with the flag bandana, knocked Joline against the boat hoist. She must have hit her head pretty good. McCready swung a pipe at them to ward them off. I didn't think McCready had it in him, but he helped Joline to her feet and kept swinging that thing and trying to move them away from her. She told him to run, and they just chased him down the path. I guess he got away okay."

J.C. wrote in his notebook. "So, this is when you went down to see if Joline was okay?"

"Nope. She acted fine, wandering off."

Tilting his head, J.C. said, "Ralph, I know there's more. We have Joline's blood on you and the diner doors."

Ralph drummed his fingers on the table as if weighing his response. "Okay. I started back up the hill behind the diner to have my smoke and heard shouting, so I turned back down and saw it."

"Saw what?"

Ralph rocked as his two hands rubbed against the surface of the table. "I don't know. That Haskell girl and Joline started arguing and calling each other names, and then it turned into a real catfight, grabbing each other, pulling hair, and stuff. When she grabbed her neck and started choking her, Joline just dropped to the ground like a rag doll. I could tell the Haskell girl was in a panic, trying to revive her and stuff, and then she got on the phone with someone while she ran off."

"Keep goin'."

He shrugged and shook his head. "I don't know. I went down to see if she was okay, and she was dead. I lifted her head, and there was blood all over her, all over me. She was definitely dead."

"And how far was her body from the boat hoist?"

Ralph pursed his lips and squinted. "I don't know, maybe twelve or fifteen feet. I panicked and tried to get out of there. I started heading down the walkway toward the bridge to figure things out and walked to the end, where I saw McCready slowly bringing his boat in."

"And you just happened to have one of Joline's earrings with you and decided to pop it onto McCready's boat with some of that blood to help point the finger at him instead of you."

Ralph shook his head. "What? See, this is the trick to frame me. I didn't kill that girl. I didn't get rid of her body. I had nothing to do with it. This is why my lawyer told me not to talk to you."

J.C. closed his notebook. "I know. You didn't plant false evidence and blackmail McCready. You didn't blackmail Danny Haskell by telling him that you saw his daughter fighting with and killing Joline Chase or seeing him load Joline's body onto his boat."

Ralph stood up. "I never saw that. Her body was just gone when I made my way back. I panicked and scrambled back to work at the diner."

Tom nodded. "Sweaty, washing the blood from your hands and changing your blood-soaked apron, ready to work out your plans to capitalize on a family's grief and a dead girl's body. Nice."

J.C. stood, and Ralph tried to pull back as the sheriff clapped the handcuffs around his wrists.

"What is this for? I told you the truth."

Nodding with pressed lips, J.C. replied, "Sure. You told us about withholding evidence in a murder investigation and blackmailing two families and bein' an all-around low-life."

Back at the station, J.C. brought Lizzie and Danny into his office as he locked up Ralph and whispered to Hardy, "Let's let him sweat in there for a bit before you book him. And see if you can bring in those three Norsemen bikers who have been harassin' everyone in town lately."

Tom stood by the doorway as J.C. motioned for Lizzie and Danny to sit. J.C. paused as he leaned on his elbows and tented his fingers to his mouth. "This is important, so listen. You should have come to me as soon as this happened. No coverin' up, no burials at sea, no givin' into blackmailin' scumbags. You should've come in."

Tom caught Danny's eye and gave him a slight nod.

"There will be no charges for murder against Miss Haskell because she didn't kill Joline Chase."

"But—"

J.C. raised his hand. "Joline Chase didn't die of strangulation. She had a head wound that was bleedin' out before Lizzie got there. She was dying, and that's why she collapsed in your arms. I'm not happy about you fightin' with her, but it didn't cause her death. Withholdin' evidence, not tellin' the truth in a murder investigation, and disposin' of a dead body are all serious issues we need to deal with, but I'm not holdin' you here. Just don't go anywhere."

Danny stood and gave Lizzie a long embrace. He finally backed off and gazed into Lizzie's eyes with tears flowing from his own. "I'm goin' to take better care of you."

Lizzie's eyes were red, her mascara running down her cheeks. "If you're going to love me, you've got to promise to love yourself."

He nodded, shook J.C.'s hand, and then turned to Tom. "I always thought Lizzie was the only one in my life who believed in me. I think you might be the second, and that means a lot. Thank you for caring enough to push for the truth."

Tom gripped his hand, shook it, and whispered into Danny's ear, "You owe me the honor of dinner at your house when I come back to visit—for that bump on my head I think you gave me."

Danny lowered his head a bit. "Sorry. I was trying to protect my girl, and you were gettin' too close. I really didn't mean to hurt you. Now I have a year to learn how to cook."

Lizzie smiled. "Don't worry; I'll do the cooking." Outside the door to J.C.'s office, she paused to hug Tom. "Thank you for caring. I still feel guilty."

He lowered his gaze to peer directly into Lizzie's eyes. "Don't forget the gift of all the years of a deep bond and friendship you shared. Don't forget that you were a sister to her. Having a fight or needing to work through a tough time doesn't erase that. It's really important to forgive yourself and forgive her for your life and her memory. You can see the impact on lives when people don't address their issues. God bless you, Lizzie, and I'll be looking forward to that dinner—now that I know you'll be cooking," said Tom with a broad smile.

After Danny and Lizzie left, Tom glanced up at J.C. "Don't worry, I'm on my way. I'm glad you could bring all the pieces together for Joline, her family, and the town."

J.C. tipped his imaginary hat, and Tom headed out the door.

Ginny Anderson lumbered up the walk with her Jack Russell, who jumped up on Tom's legs.

"How are we doing, boy?" Tom peered at the woman. "And how are you doing, Mrs. Anderson?"

"You remembered. That was a beautiful service today."

"Very beautiful. I'm heading to the hall to see how Laurie and Colby are doing. Good talking to you."

As Tom approached the church, he could see people beginning to leave the hall, and he hoped he hadn't missed the Chases. When he entered, groups of people remained, offering their condolences. Laurie glanced up, lowered her head and gave Tom a friendly scowl as he approached, and she met him halfway.

"One quick thing, huh?" quipped Laurie with a touch of sarcasm in her voice.

"I am so sorry, Laurie. She was well-loved. So many people came to be here for Joline and both of you."

She gave him a long embrace. "I can't tell you how much it meant to have you to talk with during all of this. You didn't judge me, and you helped to give me hope. I will miss Jo so much, but you made me feel as if she's still here with me, and I think you've given Cole and me another chance. I want to stop cheating on him and myself. I know there is a long road of work for us to get there, but we talked about it and want to try."

Tom smiled. "I am so glad to hear that. More than you know. I do have an update for you."

Laurie stepped back as Tom waved Colby over. "I was at the station to see Danny Haskell."

Colby cocked his head with a wary expression.

"He isn't responsible for Joline's death. He thought he was covering for Lizzie, who had a fight with Joline, who collapsed during their tussle."

Colby shook his head. "What are you sayin'? Are you saying that Lizzie killed Joline, and Danny was coverin' for her?"

"That's what they thought, but Joline died from a blow to the back of her head she received earlier and not from Lizzie squeezing her neck. Those bikers who had been riding around town were harassing Joline and Bill McCready down by the boat hoist. Bill tried to protect her, but one of them drove his bike past her and knocked her head into the boat hoist. It may be manslaughter, but neither Danny nor Lizzie are responsible for her death."

Laurie asked, "How do you know this?"

"Ralph Cutter witnessed the whole set of events that night, and his story, while a little late, makes sense. He was using his information to blackmail McCready and Danny."

Colby wrapped his arms around Laurie. "Is Coombs going after the bikers?"

"Yes," replied Tom.

"I don't know what to think."

Tom leaned in. "I think you had a band of friends who supported each other growing up and can still be great friends. I think Joline was lucky to have her own band of friends and both of you as parents. We all have places of pain and hurt to work through, but you still have each other to work through them. If you love each other, there is an opportunity to do more of that, and you can keep loving Joline, too."

Ray Jordy approached. "What's going on over here?"

Colby turned to Ray. "It looks like Danny isn't responsible for Joline's death, and Father Tom is tellin' us that our misfit group can stick together again as good friends."

"Sounds okay to me," said Ray, patting Colby on the shoulder.

"Hey, don't we have to be at the house for the people coming over?"

"We do," replied Laurie. "I just want to get something. Hold on."

Colby turned to Tom and shook his hand. "I know I didn't give you much of a chance durin' the week, but I want to thank you. I guess you were right that diggin' all the stuff up for Laurie might have caused some hurt and bad feelin's, but she needed to do that to move on, so I appreciate your not listening to me and that you stuck with her."

Tom watched Laurie as she thanked Paul for carrying a package in brown wrapping paper. As she approached, she took the package from Paul and gave it to Tom. "I think you liked this, and I want you to have it."

Tom opened one side, and chills ran up his neck as he recognized Joline's small painting of the little girl on the cliff. "Oh, my gosh. This is too special. I can't take this."

"I think Joline would be happy for it to be with someone who let her fly and would appreciate it," replied Laurie with glistening eyes.

She hugged him again and left with Colby and Ray on each side.

Paul and Angelo approached Tom, standing on either side of him as he watched the door close. Angelo asked, "I feel as if I missed something."

"I'll tell you at dinner tonight."

Chapter 42

Tom, Paul, and Angelo sat together on the rectory porch for their last summer dinner together. There were too many leftovers from the catered lunch to waste, and it made for an easy meal after a long day. Tom caught them all up on the latest twist in the sad case of Joline's death, but at least the whole truth had finally come out.

The phone rang, and Paul got up to answer it.

Angelo said, "I knew something was up when you called about those photos and didn't show up at the luncheon for Joline."

Paul returned from the call. "That was J.C. Coombs. He wanted us to know that the Norseman biker with the red-white-and-blue bandana, a.k.a. Mr. Willard Platz, has been taken into custody. He tried to punch out J.C. during the arrest, and I guess the sheriff clocked him one pretty good because they had to carry him into the station."

Tom smiled. "Don't mess with a Penobscot Indian Sheriff, I always say."

Paul chuckled. "Speaking of Penobscot, J.C. told me you boys can't leave town until after you come and share lunch with his family at J.C.'s place tomorrow."

"Well, we can't miss that." Tom turned to Angelo. "And you thought he was anxious for us to leave town!"

Angelo laughed. "I thought everyone was anxious for us to leave town. There might be a parade tomorrow in celebration."

Paul said, "Now, boys, this is a nice and welcoming town. It just takes a little time to warm up to folks who break into police stations, people's homes, and commit other felonies."

With that, they clinked their glasses of wine and enjoyed the sounds and feel of a beautiful summer night, along with a few rounds of viciously competitive chess, before heading to bed.

After Sunday morning Mass, Tom, Paul, and Angelo headed out to the homestead of J.C. Coombs and his family. When they reached the dirt road on the other side of the Passy, Tom slowed down to enjoy the wooded surroundings until they reached the wood cabin next to a stream.

J.C.'s son came running out to the car, waving them in.

Tom leaned his head out the window. "Hey, Joseph, your leg seems to have healed well."

Joseph beamed. "It hurts, but I can still run fast."

Tom parked and got out of the car. "No wolves are going to catch you!"

J.C. approached as Mrs. Coombs waved from the doorway. "Father Tom, Father Paul, Angelo, welcome to our humble home." He shook Tom's hand and accompanied them to the porch.

"You have quite a beautiful home here, Sheriff," commented Angelo.

Joseph grabbed Angelo's hand and started pulling him. "Come and see my wigwam and stuff I made."

J.C. shook his head. "Joseph, leave Mr. Salvato alone."

Angelo grinned at the boy's exuberance. "I would love to see your special spot."

As Angelo followed Joseph, Tom and Paul stepped onto the porch with J.C. and greeted his wife, who was holding their baby daughter.

J.C. tilted his head. "Is she sleeping?"

She nodded.

Paul lowered his voice. "Beth, good to see you again, and thank you for coming to the service yesterday."

"It was beautiful. I loved what you said and was so glad we attended. Father Tom, so good to see you. I'm glad you had time to share a meal before heading back to Boston. Do I have that right?"

Tom smiled. "You do. I'm honored that you asked. Most of the folks in town couldn't wait for our departure, but I don't mind staying a bit longer. Is there anything I can help with?"

"No. No. You sit on the porch with Mr. Grumpy here. I've just got a few things to get ready. I think I'm going to have to put this one down."

"Mr. Grumpy?" said Paul.

Beth patted her husband's hand. "Oh, I think this case has been difficult, but I'm sure we'll have the old J.C. back soon."

J.C. motioned toward the door. "She has to get a few things ready."

They sat on the porch and listened to the sound of the stream as they watched two chipmunks chase each other up and down a tree in the yard.

"Sheriff, I have to commend you for doing an awesome job solving this case. I think everyone will feel safer knowing the person responsible will be behind bars, and justice will be served," said Paul.

J.C. rubbed his forehead and gazed out at the woods. "Well, that's one reason that Beth and I wanted to invite you three out here. I know I was sometimes a bit unfriendly toward Angelo and you, Father Tom. I apologize, and I truly appreciate all the help you gave me. We may not have ever solved this crime without it."

A voice came from inside the kitchen. "I'm glad you finally said it."

Tom leaned from his spot on the bench toward the screen door and added, "I recorded it on my phone!"

"Very funny," said J.C., handing Tom a Guinness from the cooler on the porch. "Seriously, I want to thank you and Angelo, and I'm glad to have had a chance to get to know you both."

Paul tapped J.C. on the shoulder. "I told you, didn't I? I told you he could be helpful."

J.C. held back the Guinness from Paul for a second and chuckled. "Yes, you did, Padre. Yes, you did."

Tom enjoyed the moment of peace amidst the birch trees and evergreens. "As long as we're showering each other with compliments, I have found a very good man in the town's sheriff. Belfast is fortunate to have a strong leader who cares about the community and his family. I am blessed to know you, and I'm even going to toast you," said Tom as he raised his bottle.

Beth cracked the screen door. "Well, if you boys are finished slobbering over each other with compliments, the food is ready."

They laughed as Joseph rounded the corner with Angelo behind him carrying a carved staff.

Beth said, "He has as good a nose for food as his dad."

When they entered the house, an authentic native Penobscot feast awaited them and was more than worth the delay in heading home. At the table, J.C. stood and said, "*Kinikinik Volcanda Kottliwi Kwahliwi Tapsiwi*, that means, 'Great Creator, bless us and smile upon us.'"

They all raised their glasses and then began to dig into all the local native dishes. The conversation was fun and lively, but Joseph definitely supplied the most enthusiastic entertainment, no doubt happy his father was able to be around more than he had over the past week. Tom always appreciated one of his favorite perks of being a priest: getting to know so many wonderful people and their families in their joys and struggles. Moments like this were what he loved.

After dessert, they all stood on the porch to say their goodbyes. Tom hugged Beth and thanked her for sharing their home, her dedicated husband, and a wonderful meal to carry them home. He gave J.C. an extended handshake and smile that seemed to need no special words as they had come to respect and appreciate each other. J.C. said he would give Paul a ride back to the rectory so that Tom and Angelo could get a head start on their four-hour ride back to Boston.

In front of Tom's old Honda Accord, Tom hugged Paul. "Next year, I promise golf and fishing all the time."

"Sure, sure. And that would mean you'd stop being you, which is never what I want. It was good to see you, and I'll be down in Boston next month, so you'll have to feed me," replied Paul.

"Let me know what kind of toast you want," said Tom with a laugh as he settled into the driver's seat, and Angelo rode shotgun. They waved to the Coombs, and Tom made the Sign of the Cross. He turned the key, and the old car tried to turn over, only sputtering and groaning. He smiled and tried again as the tired engine caught and started up. "Purrs like a kitten."

Tom and Angelo talked about their trip and the Chases on the way home, but by the time they pulled in front of St. Francis rectory on Sunday night, Angelo was sound asleep. Tom gazed up at the beautiful church with its steeple reaching into the sky and thought about the parish neighborhood he was blessed to be pastor of over all these years. When he spotted Sister Helen coming out to welcome them, her broad smile and gray habit ruffling in the light breeze, he was glad to be home.

The End

About the Author

Award-winning author Jim Sano grew up in an Irish/Italian family in Massachusetts. Jim is a husband, father, lifelong Catholic, and has worked as a teacher, consultant, and businessman. He has degrees from Boston College and Bentley University and is currently attending Franciscan University for a master's degree in Catechetics and Evangelization. He has also attended certificate programs at The Theological Institute for the New Evangelization at St. John's Seminary and the Apologetics Academy. Jim is a member of the Catholic Writers Guild and has enjoyed growing in his faith and now sharing it through writing novels. *Joline* is his eighth novel.

Jim resides in Medfield, Massachusetts, with his wife, Joanne, and has two daughters, Emily and Megan, and a granddaughter, Harper Elizabeth.

Published by
Full Quiver Publishing
PO Box 244
Pakenham, ON K0A2X0
Canada
www.fullquiverpublishing.com